CUT & RUN

The Misadventures of Alex Perez

ALBERTO ARCIA

Arte Público Press
Houston, Texas

In Memory of Joyce Elliott—A most remarkable mother-in-law.

Dedicated to those who shared in the adventures, especially Bear.

Special thanks to my dear wife, Betsy, for funding my writing efforts and to Roger for his sense of humor.

Cut & Run: The Misadventures of Alex Perez is made possible through grants from the City of Houston through the Houston Arts Alliance and the Exemplar Program, a program of Americans for the Arts in collaboration with the LarsonAllen Public Services Group, funded by the Ford Foundation.

Recovering the past, creating the future

Arte Público Press
University of Houston
452 Cullen Performance Hall
Houston, Texas 77204-2004

Photography by Jair Mora
Cover design by Mora Des!gn

Arcia, Alberto, 1946-
    Cut & Run : The Misadventures of Alex Perez / by Alberto Arcia.
        p. cm.
    ISBN 978-1-55885-438-3 (alk. paper)
    1. Authors—Fiction. 2. Fiancées—Fiction. 3. Central America—Fiction. 4. Domestic fiction. I. Title. II. Title: Cut and Run.
PS3601.R39C87 2009
813'.6—dc22
                                                      2009036689
                                                      CIP

♾ The paper used in this publication meets the requirements of the American National Standard for Information Sciences—Permanence of Paper for Printed Library Materials, ANSI Z39.48-1984.

9 0 1 2 3 4 5 6 7 8   10 9 8 7 6 5 4 3 2 1

Chapter 1

Marriage Trap—Houston—1975

I opened my eyes, peeked out of the blanket, and saw frost on the windows. Damn, it's cold again. Another northern . . . third one this month. How is that possible? This is Houston, for heaven's sake! Other than annoying rain, our winters are supposed to be mild. I lowered the blanket, exposed my head to the elements, and saw my breath. I hate cold weather. The house I lived in was old and drafty, and during cold snaps you could hang meat inside.

Ramona's body was wrapped around mine; she was a good source of heat, but she had a snore going that was rattling the windows. To get her to stop, I would have to wake her up, and then she'd get amorous. I was not in the mood. Last night's lovemaking session had drained me, frankly. What I needed was a cup of hot tea, yet abandoning my warm bed did not seem appealing in the least.

I slipped a foot out from under the blanket and further explored the climate. I knew immediately that bravery was needed for this feat. I had been foolish after our tryst and allowed Ramona to talk me out of putting my pajamas back on. I took a deep breath, jumped out of bed, slipped on the slippers, reached for my robe, put it on, and went into the living room to stoke the fire in the iron stove.

The central heating unit had stopped working late last winter. All we had for heat now was an old wood stove we purchased at a neighbor's garage sale; it was suitable. There is something about the smell of burning wood that makes a person feel good about life —especially if it's mesquite. The aroma was stimulating; it gave the old place a sort of rustic ambiance. The bookshelf that constituted my library stood in the corner of the living room. The piano no one ever played (but was a good place for family photos) took center stage. The entertainment center with my record player, LP albums, and eight-tracks added a harmonious touch to the décor. I loved living here.

The stove started to put out heat. I went into the kitchen, put the kettle on, grabbed a few teabags, and proceeded to make our morning drink. As I passed by the kitchen window I noticed Charlene's car pulling into the driveway. Oh no, the bitch from hell is here. I left the kitchen and scrambled to the bedroom but found the bed empty. I cruised to the bathroom and opened the door.

"Hurry up and get out of the shower. Attila the Honey is knocking at the door."

A wet middle finger extended out from behind the shower curtain followed by a harsh, "Be nice to my mother. She pays the bills."

I had to agree, for Charlene was funding Ramona's existence, and I was riding on her daughter's coattails . . . a matter that galled the old woman. She often said (to me) that I was nothing more than a bump on a log, an immigrant trying to live the "Life of Riley."

This was a wrong assumption, of course. It was true that I was temporarily out of mainstream work, but I was presently engaged in pursuing a literary career. Charlene had a myopic view of things, which was why she considered me to be a freeloader. To be frank, her opinion bothered me because the old goat assumed I had no value. But, hell, I made love to her daughter an inordinate amount of times, and I also mowed the lawn. Most importantly, I provided

Ramona with suitable companionship. The last boyfriend her daughter had wore leather and straddled a motor.

Ramona was a very pretty Caucasian woman with long, slender legs, straight dark hair, and sensuous brown eyes. She also had large mammary glands, and honestly, I loved those big tits. (Who wouldn't?) Ramona not only fed me, she also washed my clothes, ironed my shirts, and gave me nice and useful gifts. Except for dealing with her insatiable desire for physical attention, I had it easy. She demanded very little of me. I loved my life, such as it was.

A few months back, finding myself in need of more than rum and cigarette money and not wanting to ask my girlfriend for an increase in my "allowance," I was forced to sell my purple Fiat 128 Sedan. Needing to replace my wheels, I purchased a brand-new English bicycle—a sleek Raleigh ten-speed. The store manager gave me a good deal on a red one. She was a beauty to look at and a pleasure to pedal. Ramona owned a German-made VW Beetle, so whenever I needed to wander far from the area, I garaged the bicycle and borrowed her car.

We were fortunate to live in the Montrose area of Houston, a place filled with head shops, restaurants, record stores, boutiques, and sidewalk cafés. Montrose had a thriving artists' community, which suited my sense of belonging.

I enjoyed riding my bike to La Dolce Vita, the corner Italian café where I could always find a number of friends to discuss or debate anything. These discussions over espresso or cappuccino were fun and provided me with a good way to pass the time. Being of sound mind and body, I observed a strict set of rules with my circle of friends: Politics and religion were off limits. I preferred to keep my arguments and criticism focused on literary matters—a deep enough pool considering that someone in the crowd was always willing to have their novel critiqued.

After hearing several heavy-handed knocks on the front door, I reluctantly opened it. Biting my lip, I prepared to greet this most aggressive woman.

"Hello, Charlene. What brings you here so early in the morning?"

"Not your sorry ass, Alex, that's for sure. Most men are at work by now. Where's my baby?"

"Ramona's going on twenty-five. She hasn't been a baby for at least six years now. Presently she is in the bathroom. May I offer you a cup of tea?"

"You know I don't drink that sissy stuff. Don't you have any coffee in the house? You know, the stuff grown-ups drink in the morning?"

I gritted my teeth. The woman grated on my nerves. I was about to curse her when I remembered that Charlene was funding my life. I took a deep, calming breath and tried to think of pleasant things. No need to start a ruckus this early.

"I have a can of Café Francois, but it's instant."

"All you have is that French crap? Don't you have any *real* coffee around?"

I was getting ready to show Charlene the door when Ramona walked into the living room. Her stance implied she was in a combative mood. I needed to tread on rice paper if I wanted to enjoy the morning. Like her mother, the woman loved to argue.

"Quit being an ass, Alex. Go make Mother some coffee. Use the chicory blend we brought from Louisiana last weekend. The can is in the back of the cupboard, left side, third shelf."

I willingly left the living room. Charlene's abrasive personality drove me crazy, and Ramona changed sides so often I suspected she was part inhuman. I found the coffee, started a pot, and then tried to sneak across the dining room toward the safety of our bedroom. Halfway there, Charlene beckoned. By the tone of her voice, I knew I was going to experience another one of her dissertations concerning my purpose in her daughter's life.

I had always suspected these personal attacks were tacitly supported by Ramona. Call it male intuition or a sixth sense, no matter, but the glimmer in their eyes told me I was about to become the victim of a double-pronged offensive. I braced for trouble.

In an uncharacteristically soft voice, Freddy Krueger started her advance. "Alex, do you love Ramona?"

"Yes," I said, without thinking that statement through.

"She loves you too, and to be truthful, I can't imagine why. You're not what I consider a catch."

"Mother, please. You promised to keep it friendly."

"Okay. You're right, I did . . . sorry." She apologized to Ramona without giving me so much as a glance.

She smiled and fiddled with her curls for a second. Recognizing the move, I took a deep breath and prepared to withstand another assault.

"Let me get straight to the point, Alex. I want to know if there's any reason why you two should not get married."

She looked into my eyes, and my knees quivered. If the first attack was designed to soften my defenses, it worked. I was pale as a ghost. She followed the brutal frontal charge with a brilliant flanking maneuver. She looked at Ramona and uttered words that cut me to the quick.

"Do you want to marry him, sweetie?" she said with a loving smile.

I was in big trouble. This situation had the feel of a well-planned and orchestrated campaign aimed at robbing me of my bachelorhood. Ramona complemented Charlene's battle strategy by launching a surprise attack of her own.

"Yes, Mama, I love him. I want to marry him."

Her declaration caught me with my pants down. This marriage stuff between us was old news. We had discussed it a number of times and had agreed to keep the relationship only sexual and friendly. I was about to speak when Genghis Khanine swarmed all over me.

"Is there any reason why you do not want to marry my daughter, Alex?"

All of a sudden, my brain became void of blood. With my bachelorhood lying on the line, my wits failed me, and I uttered a statement that doomed me, "Why should I bring the cow home when I'm getting the milk for free?"

Charlene bristled at my insolence. Ramona burst into tears and fled the living room. Gathering my thoughts, I foolishly believed that what I had said actually worked to my advantage. Without Ramona there to cut off my escape route, I felt safe.

I was wrong, of course. Godzilla was not done attacking me. Charlene smiled, fiddled with her curls again, and took a different approach.

"Listen, Alex, I'm going to lay it out clearly for you. You either marry Ramona or I will pull the plug on her finances. As much as I love her, I will not stand by and see her be used by someone I suspect is nothing more than a Latin American gigolo. It is obvious to me that she loves you, but I'll be damned if I am going to pay for both of you to play 'Hide the Salami.'"

She paused for a moment, making sure I was taking it all in. I was. Then she glued her beady eyes on me and continued to hammer away at my resolve.

"Maybe your salami has magical properties, the proof being the constant smile on my baby's face. I can accept that, and her happiness is important to me. Still, smiley face aside, I am not paying for my daughter to get laid, period. You either marry her, or I won't put out another dime."

She let me roll that statement over in my mind, and then, just as my eyes showed a glimmer of panic . . . she came in for the kill.

"As your banker, I require security for my investment. A marriage certificate would do fine for a start. What do you say, Alex? Will you marry Ramona, or would you like to hang your hat elsewhere?"

All I could think was, Oh God, please help me! I'm about to be eaten alive by this female praying mantis. I was doomed, and I knew it. I could not allow her to cut off the money flow as poor Ramona needed one more year to graduate from the University of Houston. Besides, the thought of leaving Ramona's home scared me to death. It wasn't that I couldn't take care of myself but that I did not *want* to take care of myself. Not only was she good in bed, but she gave me money and was an excellent cook. Feeling corralled, I mustered up my reserves and went on the offensive.

"In my country, it's customary to give the groom a dowry. If you want me to marry Ramona, I want that white 190 SL Mercedes Benz convertible you keep in the garage and drive only on Sundays. I also want an all-expense-paid vacation to Panama. I will marry her in the presence of my own dear, sweet mother. And furthermore," I said, getting all puffed up, "you must promise to pay all the bills while we are gone, as I plan to drive there, and I have every intention to take my damn sweet time."

Charlene bristled some more. Her eyebrows narrowed, her beady eyes came together, and her right cheek began to twitch. For a fleeting moment, I thought I had won the battle. What a babe-in-the-woods I was, not even aware that victory was never even remotely possible. I was being attacked by a woman who wanted her daughter married. I was completely overmatched.

Charlene's beady eyes caught fire, and she glued them to me. I swallowed hard. When I noticed her lips begin to develop a slight upward curve on the corners, I panicked. I knew she was fixing to put the lid on the jar.

"It's a deal," she said, "and since I'm the one giving the dowry, there are some stipulations I must insist upon."

"And they are?" I asked defiantly.

"The Mercedes Benz will be placed in Ramona's garage *after* you two are married. The title will be signed over to you when you celebrate your first wedding anniversary—my present to you. I will pay all the bills until Ramona graduates; I planned to do that anyway. I'm fine with the trip to Panama. If we're going to be related, it would be nice to meet your mother. However, since I didn't fall off the turnip truck yesterday, I will go with both of you to Panama. I must be sure an official marriage ceremony takes place. You can't blame me for being mistrusting, Alex, because you know as well as I do how much of a scoundrel you are. We can take my brand-new Mercury Marquise station wagon. It's sturdy enough to make the long trek through Central America, and it will provide us with cold air and comfort."

I glared at her, but my knees were shaking. Sensing my vulnerability, the abominable snow-woman leaned my way and growled, "The stipulations that I have put before you are non-negotiable."

I swallowed hard again. I was in pain. The woman had a dead-grip on my balls. There was nothing for me to do but let out a sigh. What the hell, I knew this free ride wouldn't last forever. I had been feeling the sharpness of Charlene's claws for a while now. Unable to find a way out of my predicament, I looked into my future mother-in-law's eyes and said, "Okay, Charlene, we have a deal."

"Good. I love a man that understands when he has been bested."

Dumbfounded, I walked away. I couldn't believe I had just bargained my status as a single man for a car. Needing to think things out, I grabbed the road atlas and entered the bathroom. Despondent, I sat on the throne and began to study it. After calculating the distance between Texas, Mexico, Belize, Guatemala, Honduras, El Salvador, and Costa Rica, a huge grin came upon me. If I throw into the equation some out-of-the-way places to visit, it could take us at the very least three weeks to get to Panama. Surely that was enough time for me to find a way out of my marriage contract. I rubbed my hands together with devilish delight and began to work on a plan of escape. Surely, for a guy with my take on life, avoiding a priest should be nothing short of a cakewalk.

Chapter 2

We left Houston in late January, hoping to get in and out of Panama before the seasonal rains arrived. The plan was to dilly-dally in Mexico for a spell, visit as many Mayan archaeological sites as possible, find the Pan-American Highway, and then cruise it all the way to Panama. We were armed with maps, tourist books, and an ample supply of junk purchased at Wally World. We brought a large ice chest full of American beer, along with Perrier water and diet and regular Coke. It was our intention to find the Indian women who gathered at these sites and barter cheap plastic toys for their carved and woven stuff. To my chagrin, Charlene insisted on bringing an assortment of emergency rations. We had Vienna sausages, canned tuna, crackers, peanut butter, peach jam, Bacardi rum, and plenty of American cigarettes. You would have thought we were going to the far side of the world instead of my homeland.

It took us seven hours to get to McAllen, which was close to the border. Not knowing what type of accommodations would be available to us on our journey to Panama, we booked a room at the Sheraton Hotel. We had a fine steak dinner, and I had a good bedroom romp with Ramona.

The following morning, we crossed into the Republic of Mexico and began to understand the folly of driving a car loaded with goods. A customs officer came our way and pulled us out of the line. He told us the person responsible for checking our bags and writing a report was not on duty at the moment. He was gracious in explaining our options: We could pay him a flat fee and go on our merry way, or we could wait until the inspector on duty arrived. Being of sound mind, I knew the bribe would increase if any more officers became involved. We paid ten bucks to cross. Hell, it was cheap at twice the price.

We were also taking a few electrical appliances for my mother. Upon hearing that I was coming home, she loaded me with requests for General Electric gizmos. I was bringing her an AM/FM clock radio, an electric carving knife and a beautiful state-of-the-art four-slice toaster. Aunt Margo wanted a blender, oscillating fan, and a mixer.

The plan was to drive all day, get to Tampico, and find lodging before darkness. We had been warned by friends and travel magazines that the best way to avoid bandits was to stay off the roads at night. We had taken a vow to adhere to sound advice. On the way to Tampico, we broke the first rule having to do with good sense . . . we picked up a couple of passengers.

"Look at the line," I said, moaning. "I can't believe it stretches this far. There must be a hundred cars ahead of us. I hope they don't load them all on the ferry. Are you women sure you want to take the ferry? I read a story in the Houston newspaper the day before yesterday that had to do with an overloaded African ferry. It capsized when someone noticed several crocodiles. The article said that everyone on board went to see them, and the ferry flipped over. Those that weren't eaten by the crocs drowned."

"Cut the crap, Alex. There's no need to scare Ramona."

"Listen, Charlene, she's not a child. Besides, the story is true. In certain parts of the world, everyone with a ticket rides, and they don't worry about capacity limits or croc sightings."

"I don't want to get on the ferry," said Ramona.

"See? Look what you've done. Now we're going to have to double back and take the long way toward Tampico. You're an absolute jerk, Alex."

I gave Ramona a dirty look, turned the car around, left the ferry line (with a hidden sense of accomplishment), and drove until we found a PEMEX station. I stopped and told the attendant to fill the car up with super. Being the only one in the group that spoke Spanish, I left the vehicle and entered a food market that was next to the gas station. While standing in line to pay, a young boy approached me.

"Hola, mister. How are you today?"

"Hello. How are you?"

"I asked you first," he said.

I rolled my eyes and looked at the kid. He seemed to be around twelve. His eyes told me to hang on to my wallet.

"What do you want?" I asked.

"I want a ride. Can you take me and my little brother with you?"

The man behind the counter gave me a look of disapproval. I paid for the bread, goat cheese, half a dozen Coronas, and four pineapple sodas. Loaded with fresh food, I walked out with the boy following me.

"Mister, can you take me and my little brother with you?"

"I don't think so, son. There's not enough room in my car. Here, take this five-dollar bill. You and your brother can have dinner on me. What do you say to that?"

He waited until I handed the bill over, and then looked at me with pleading eyes. "Mister, you're driving a big car with only two women. You have plenty of room. You can take two skinny kids with you. How about it? Can you give us a ride? I'll pay . . . I have five dollars. ¿Por favor?"

I felt stung. The scruffy kid was offering me my own money back. "Listen to me, son. I can't take you or I would, believe me."

"I am not your son, mister. My father is Jaime Buffet, the famous American singer."

"You mean Jimmy Buffet," I said with a laugh.

"Jimmy to you. He's my father, so I call him Jaime. He comes to Tampico a lot to visit us and my mother."

I was beginning to understand the reason for the grocer's expression. This kid was a hustler. I contemplated the situation. Maybe there was a story here. I decided to explore the situation further. It had possibilities.

"What's your name?" I said.

"My name is Jaime Buffet. You can call me Junior."

"Oh, brother," I mumbled.

"Alex, get your sorry ass over here!" Charlene yelled. We both looked at her. "*Esa señora tiene mucho filo, ¿eh?*" said the boy.

"Yes, Junior, that woman has sharp edges. Where's your brother?"

"His name's Raúl. Wait here. I'll go get him."

Before I had a chance to answer, he was off. He returned with a kid that looked to be around seven years old.

"Listen, Junior, I didn't say you could ride with us."

"Alex!" Charlene yelled again. "Get your ass in the car. We're hot, and it's getting late. We need to find a room for the night."

I looked at her, then at the two street urchins and grinned. "You know what? There are too many women in the car, Junior. You and Raúl can climb in the back seat with Frankenstein's mother."

I approached the women and explained the situation. To my surprise, Ramona loved the idea. Charlene, other than marking her territory, didn't say much. I introduced the kids, found that Raúl did not, or as Junior put it, would not speak. I also found that Raúl liked to ride in the front seat. He jumped from the back, and any efforts to remove him proved fruitless. The ragamuffin sat between Ramona and me. He smiled and touched all the buttons on the dashboard. Soon, we were listening to a Mexican radio station that played Ranchera music. Ramona kept snapping her fingers while the kids tapped a beat with their hands.

During a lull, Junior felt the need to tell us that Raúl had some weird ways because he had no mother.

"I thought you told me he was your brother?" I said.

"Yes, he is, but we don't have the same blood."

"What happened to his mother?" Ramona wanted to know.

"She died," he said.

"How did she die?" Ramona asked.

"She got run over by a train."

"Oh, brother," I mumbled.

"Where's his father?" Charlene said.

"In prison. He killed the driver of the train."

"Oh, give me a break," I said. Charlene shushed me, and Ramona shot me an annoyed look.

"Who takes care of him?" asked my naïve girlfriend.

"I do," said Junior.

"Are you family?" Charlene wanted to know.

"No, not by blood. I found him begging on the streets of Nuevo Laredo one day. I liked him and took him in. I'm his big brother now."

"Does he have any family?" Ramona asked.

"He has an uncle. I'm trying to find him."

When Raulito, as the women were now calling him, grabbed hold of Ramona's hand and kissed it, I checked my wallet. These kids were good. "I know where you can get a good room for cheap," Junior said.

"The old woman prefers the fancy hotels. I don't think a cheap room is her style," I said.

"Screw off, Alex. I'm made of sterner stuff than that." Then she turned toward the boy. "Where is this place, and how do you know of it?"

"It's called El Pelicano Loco, and it belongs to one of my uncles. He can use the business."

"Is that where you two are going?" Charlene said.

All of a sudden, I realized I hadn't asked them where they were going. I picked up on Charlene's question and repeated it. "Where are you and Raúl going?"

"Where are *you* going?" Junior said.

"I asked *you* first," I said with a devilish smile.

Junior thought about it for a moment. "I told you I'm trying to . . . find Raúl's uncle."

"Do you know where he is?" Ramona said.

"No, I don't. He's somewhere in Mexico, maybe in Mérida."

I gave him a look through the rearview mirror that said "I'm on to you." I knew quite well he picked Mérida from the pamphlets Charlene carried on her lap.

"Where is this El Pelicano Loco Hotel? Is it far?" Ramona said.

"No, Señora, it's not too far, and it's not a hotel. It's *cabañas* by the sea. You'll like them."

"Do they have hot water?" Charlene said.

"*Sí*, Señora. They have plenty of hot water."

Two hours later, we arrived at a small coastal town on the other side of Tampico. To Charlene's dismay and to my enjoyment, we found the El Pelicano Loco. Cabañas by the sea? It was nothing more than a rundown group of stucco cabins with thatched roofs. I looked at Charlene's face, and she was not happy. Enjoying this, and not wanting to allow her an escape route, I nailed the coffin shut.

"If you are really cut from a tough cloth, and if Ramona is indeed a-chip-off-the-old-block, then this should be a walk in the park. What do you say, can I book them?"

She glared at me. Ramona was all for it, so Charlene gave me the green light. Junior and I left the car, went inside one of the cabins that had "Oficina" written on the door, and spoke to a man who turned out not to be related to him. It didn't surprise me. We paid ten American dollars for a dilapidated cabin that was supposed to house four. After checking it out, we decided that it probably could house four midgets, as long as none of them are overweight.

A loud roar came from the bathroom. My future mother-in-law had discovered that the toilet had no seat. That roar was followed by another as she noticed that the lavatory and shower cubicle had one spigot each, and it didn't put out hot water.

Charlene was not amused at being lured into this place by Junior, but Ramona insisted we put a good face on the situation. She was an old Girl Scout, very adept at fixing a nice camp.

"This is sure turning into a nice adventure, don't you think?" I said cheerfully.

Charlene shot me the bird. Ramona chastised her and agreed with me. We were on a journey, and in order to enjoy it, a good attitude was needed by all.

She prepared the cabin by putting her sleeping bag on the rickety bamboo bed frame that was supposed to pass for a double bed. She made a cozy spot for her mother on what amounted to nothing more than a cot. She took my bag and made a place for the kids on the floor. Since there wasn't any room in Ramona's bed for me, I decided to sleep on the hammock that hung outside the cabin. I advised both women to sleep with one eye open. They gave me dirty looks, but nevertheless placed their purses inside the sleeping bags.

Sometime during the night, the sea breeze abated, and the pesky sand fleas swarmed. I abandoned the hammock, opened the car, searched for the bottle of Bacardi, and took several swigs. I made myself as comfortable as possible in the back seat, smoked a cigarette, and tried to think things out. Traveling with these two street urchins was bad business. Somehow, somewhere these kids were going to steal something from us. I was sure of it.

Acting on my hunch, I took my passport out of my bag, removed my MasterCard from my wallet, and placed both of them in the zippered pocket of my pouch. I secured the cash snugly in my money belt. Not being comfortable with the women's sense of awareness, I made a mental note to keep an eye on their passports as well. I also resigned myself to follow the adventure. Surely there was a story here. I began to pen notes.

It didn't take long for the car to become too warm; I could not get comfortable enough to sleep. Pissed, I rummaged through the gear and found my mosquito net, rigged it, and climbed back into the hammock.

I woke up soaked by the humidity. I entered the cabin and showered with cold water. When I finished, I opened the curtain and stepped out to an unexpected sight. Junior was squatting on the toilet taking a dump.

"*Buenos días,* Señor Alex. How are you feeling today?"

"Hola, Junior. Why are you standing on the toilet?"

"You don't expect me to put my ass where everybody's asses have been, do you?"

So hygiene, not thievery, is the reason there are no toilet seats on Mexican public restrooms. I felt enlightened.

"How much money did you get for bringing us to this dump? That man was not your uncle."

"He gave me twenty pesos. I have to make my own way, and I have to take care of Raúl. Sorry about the lie."

"What else are you lying about?"

He was about to speak when a strained look appeared on his face. Knowing what was about to come out, I vacated the bathroom quickly.

"The lavatory is open," I said to Charlene. The old battleax went in and screamed.

After Charlene yelled at me, we started out looking for a place to eat. We found a small restaurant and ate a good breakfast. Satisfied, we drove toward the city of Veracruz. With the air conditioning on high, we had a good time singing while moving about the countryside. To my surprise, Junior knew some songs by Jimmy Buffet.

"Yuck! Who farted?" Junior asked.

"Probably Ramona's mother," I said. "It smells old."

"Screw off, Alex."

"Yuck!" Junior said again. "*La vieja está podrida.*"

"What did he say?" Charlene wanted to know.

"He said you are rotten inside . . . gastronomically speaking, of course."

Ramona broke into a laugh. When Raúl pinched his nose with his fingers and grimaced, Charlene lost her temper.

"To hell with the lot of you," growled the beast. "You can't expect me to eat beans and eggs for breakfast and not pass gas."

Chapter 3

Bandits at Nine O'clock

We spent the next night at a roadside park camp on the outskirts of Veracruz. We arrived late and were tired of driving. Searching for a hotel with a secured parking lot in that big city didn't appeal to us, so the roadside camp would have to suffice.

The lighted area of the campground was packed, so we drove to the section without lights. It didn't take us long to find a suitable spot. We parked and unloaded our gear. Ramona was a tent putter-upper extraordinaire. She used the lights of the car to set up our evening shelter. When she finished, she turned her attention to the provisions we had packed and fed all of us. Dinner for the adults consisted of sweet bread stuffed with goat cheese and beers to drink. Ramona fixed the boys tuna fish on crackers, which they washed down with two of my pineapple sodas. After dinner, we crawled into the tent and found our beds. I slipped into Ramona's sleeping bag since mine was being occupied by the boys. Before we turned the battery-powered light off, Charlene reminded me about the two young boys sleeping within.

"If you heat her up, I'm dousing the fire with a bucket of water. Please have some class and refrain from playing 'Slap and Tickle' tonight."

What a bitch Charlene was. What nerve! The woman galled me. Disgusted with the insinuation, I removed my hand from Ramona's thigh and moved my ear away from her wet frantic tongue. Ramona's amorous ways were flattering and delightful. I couldn't say the same for her mother. From the very beginning of our courtship, she has behaved like a woman starved for sex. I felt like I had hit the proverbial "mother load." A horny woman is every man's dream.

There were many things about this woman that I liked. Not only was Ramona a physical delight, her sexual appetite had an unusual twist. She had this thing about performing ritualistic sex. This worked for me because it allowed me to get into character. I'm into blindfolds and ropes. She loved to get me naked outside the bedroom, arouse me, and then pull me by my manhood to a bed that had the feel of a sacrificial altar of love.

The nest had the aroma of either jasmine or sandalwood, and the room was always full of lit candles. Making love to her with Jethro Tull's "Passion Play" playing on the turntable brought the feeling of religious ecstasy into my heart.

The trick to making love with that LP album was getting the first orgasms out of the way before the inane piece about "The Hare that Lost Its Spectacles" came into play. That was a mood killer, for sure. Still, it did afford us a sort of intermission. She always headed for the bathroom so she could ready herself for a second go-round, and I lit up a smoke and contemplated life.

Whenever we had achieved a particularly good roll in the hay, she would reward my performance the following evening by having a present neatly placed on my side of the bed. Sometimes she hid it under the pillow. She treated me like I was an object of desire. Hell, I felt like a Mayan warrior who was being given one last gift before the priestess sacrificed him.

Most of my friends were constantly complaining about their girlfriends and wives; how they hardly ever got any love action, and if they did, it was always the same way. I laughed at them. Ramona made me proud.

Fighting the urge to kiss her wanton lips, I rolled to one side, took a deep breath, cursed, and closed my eyes. Two killer farts later, all of us were out of the tent. Ramona made a cozy spot in the car. With Raúl snuggled in her arms, we fell asleep.

The following morning, I woke up suffering severe neck and back pain. I made a promise to myself to get off the road in time to find proper lodging. Ramona made coffee and fixed us a nice breakfast. Charlene passed up the morning meal and opened a beer. I gave her a look of disapproval—a thing I loved to do whenever I had the chance.

After breakfast, we discussed the day's route and decided that instead of driving to Chiapas (as we had originally planned) and seeing the Mayan Pyramids of Palenque, we could take a detour and cut across the state of Tabasco. The women wanted to visit the ruins of Cobah and Tulum, which were located in Quintana Roo. Their reasoning? After Tulum we could make a swing across the Yucatan and catch the Mayan archaeological sites of Chichen-Itza and Uxmal. Then, we could spend a night or two in Mérida, drop off the boys, do a little shopping, and enjoy the trappings of a good hotel. Later, we would drive to Chiapas and see Palenque, after which we'd trek across the country until we hooked up with the Pan-American Highway.

The plan seemed sound. We knew of the danger involved in driving at night, especially on stretches through desolate country. The map showed that the road we were going to take would be long with few villages along the way. To stay safe, we had to reach our destination before dark. With that in mind, we set forth.

Half an hour later, Charlene decided she needed to use the toilet. The obstinate woman knew before we broke camp that she had to take a dump but had refused to use the one in the campground. Now, the need to dump her load became pressing, and our noses were being violated, so we killed precious time finding her a proper bathroom. There wasn't a decent public toilet in any of the many roadside restaurants or gas stations we came to. Reluctantly we drove into Veracruz and found her a hotel bathroom. When we finally hit the road, we were already behind schedule.

Evening caught us 150 kilometers from our destination. Deciding to be prudent, we joined a convoy of cars that were led by two sixteen-wheelers. We felt safe in the group. We figured these big trucks were transporting goods from Veracruz to Chetumal. Feeling secure traveling in the middle of this convoy, I drove while everyone slept. Around nine, I lost contact with the last car. Like the others, it drove into a roadside village. A few minutes later, one of the big trucks found a clearing and stopped. Feeling the hand of fate resting upon my shoulders, I prepared for the worst and prayed as I followed the last truck. I was hoping the driver had a woman waiting for him in Chetumal, but no such luck. A half hour later, the driver turned into a dirt road and disappeared. Now, we were traveling alone on a deserted highway. We had been warned by friends and all the travel publications not to do what we were presently doing, yet here we were. I knew it was foolish and dangerous.

I drove out of the state of Tabasco without any problems and crossed into Quintana Roo. Almost immediately, the asphalt pavement gave way to gravel. I slowed the car, waking Junior.

"¿*Qué pasa*, Mister Alex?"

"Nothing's wrong, Junior. We just entered a gravel road."

The road was so rough I had to keep the speed down. I opened the windows halfway, and needing to bond with the boy, I offered him a cigarette. Why not? He was a street kid.

We were smoking and making small talk when we noticed a large wooden sign about thirty yards away.

"*Aduana*," mumbled Junior. "Are you going to stop?"

"I'm not sure," I said, as I applied the brakes, bringing the speed down to twenty.

The customs house was nothing more than a small wooden frame building with one lone lightbulb in the front. I didn't see any cars parked anywhere on the premises. Neither the sign nor the building looked official, so I became suspicious. My keen sense of awareness told me to beware of bandits. Instead of stopping, I kept on going, as there was no need to take any unnecessary risk.

Before long there was a car behind me. The headlights were closing in fast. When the vehicle started to pass us, Junior yelled, "Look, Mister Alex, *bandidos!*"

Sure enough, there were a couple of guys in white T-shirts inside the car, and one of them had his arm out pointing a pistol at me.

"Ramona!" I yelled, "Bandits at nine o'clock."

"What?" she said, as she rubbed her eyes.

Junior shook her and yelled, "*¡Bandidos!*"

When Ramona caught sight of the man with the pistol, she freaked and screamed. The commotion woke Charlene and Raulito. The bandit with the pistol yelled at me to stop the car. There was no way I was going to let them steal my mother's four-slice toaster, so I stepped on the gas, and the Mercury roared ahead.

Charlene opened the ice chest and started to pass out beer and sodas. On command, the group started flinging them out the window. The bandits were driving an old, but nice-looking Lincoln Continental. They dropped back, trying to keep the car a safe distance from the projectiles. Soon a gunshot rang out, and Ramona screamed again. I floored the gas pedal. Seconds later, another shot rang out.

"Stop the car!" Ramona said. "No amount of money is worth dying for."

"She's right," Charlene said. "I'll stash my American Express card in my underwear. They can have the money. Please stop the car, Alex."

"I'm not letting these assholes steal my mother's toaster. To hell with both of you . . . I'm not surrendering without a fight."

I was hauling ass. The Argentine racecar driver Juan Manuel Fangio had nothing on me. To my chagrin, a sharp curve appeared out of nowhere. There was no way I could make that turn. I was going too fast! In a matter of seconds, I made the decision to grip the wheel and go straight. We missed a tree by inches, drove through the brush, and went airborne. We all screamed. After spending what felt like an eternity in the air, the car landed on the side of a ravine. When the world stopped shaking we were still right-side-up and heading down a steep grade.

I finally managed to stop the Mercury's downward surge. We got out and quickly checked for injuries. Finding none, I grabbed the toaster and followed the group as we ran for cover. Fortunately for us, the area was thick with vegetation. We remained hidden and prayed the bandits would be content with the loot in the car and leave us alone.

We crouched and listened for the sound of men walking through brush. No one appeared. Feeling safe, we came out to inspect the damage to the car. The traveling box we had mounted on the luggage rack and had secured with a chain had broken loose and gouged a hole on the driver's side windshield. Except for some scratches and small dents, the vehicle seemed fine.

Much to my discomfort, Charlene didn't think the damage was slight. She hit me with her purse and cursed me for destroying her new station wagon.

"If you hadn't been so picky about where you took a dump, we would have been in Chetumal before nightfall," I said with righteous indignation. "This whole mess is your fault."

"Quiet," Junior said. "Stop fighting and listen! Someone's coming."

"Oh, no," I moaned. "Here we go again."

We barely had the adrenaline rush under control when we heard the bandits coming down the ravine on foot. I threw the toaster inside the car, told everyone to jump back in, and we drove deeper into the woods. The Mercury Marquis plowed through the dense brush like a John Deere tractor. I was impressed.

We found a good spot and stopped. We cursed the full moon, grabbed the machete and flashlight plus several bottles of water, and hid in the bush. When we felt safe, Junior and I sneaked out to check and see whether the bandits were still on our trail—and there they were with pistols drawn.

"What are you going to do now, Mister Alex? Are you going to fight them, or are you going to let them take your mother's toaster?"

"I'm assessing the situation, Junior. I can't believe I left the toaster behind. Why didn't you remind me?"

"I am responsible for my brother, but you're not my brother," said the boy, suddenly sounding very grown up and responsible. "What are you going to do now?"

"What do you think I should do?"

"They've got guns, and you only have a machete. I don't think you should fight them. Maybe you can give them something other than your mother's toaster."

"Like what?"

"How about the old woman . . . why don't you give her to the bandits? She's rich. They'll take her and go away."

"I don't think giving them Charlene will help us."

"Why not? She's rich."

"Listen to me, Junior . . . I know she's rich, but these bandits will not be satisfied with just her. They'll probably keep looking for the rest of us."

"Then give them your wife. Ramona has big *chi chis*. They can take both women and leave us alone."

"Ramona's not my wife, at least not yet. I'm driving to Panama to marry her, and those big *chi chis* are mine. I don't want to share them."

"You want to marry a woman with a mother like Charlene? Are you loco, Mister Alex?"

I admired the ragamuffin's wisdom. He was wise beyond his years.

"I don't want to marry her," I mumbled. "I *have* to marry her."

"It's the same thing. I don't care if those big *chi chis* give out chocolate milk. Her mother is a big problem."

"We have a bigger problem at the moment, Junior. The bandits are coming our way with guns. What do you suppose we can do about this situation, son?"

"I'm not your son. My father is Jaime Buffet."

I was about to reply when the bandits started to argue and push each other around. Before long, they were heading back to wherever they came from. I was surprised but also relieved because I was seriously considering Junior's advice. Here was a prime opportunity to get out of my marriage dilemma.

"Look, Mister Alex, the *bandidos* are leaving," said the boy. "Charlene's going to think you're a hero. She'll give you a big hug."

"Charlene's not a huggable woman," I said.

"What's her problem? She's not a happy person?"

"Charlene's been married and divorced three times, Junior. The woman can't seem to hang on to a man, married or otherwise. Her husbands have all run off with younger women, and the boyfriends take their girlfriends along when they go on vacation with her. She has a bad opinion of men. She thinks we're all hustlers and can't be depended on to do the right thing. What do you think about that?" I asked, hoping to rattle his lying soul.

"I'm good with it," he said. "She's going to be your mother-in-law, not mine."

We returned from our scouting mission expecting to be hailed as heroes, but it was not to be. Instead, I was promptly chastised for my role in endangering their lives with my "crazy driving." Disappointment set in, and I felt unappreciated. I wanted to be hugged.

A plan of action was discussed and adopted. We decided it would be prudent to stay put until daybreak. Of course, this meant that we were going to have to spend the night in the bush. Junior said there were pumas in the region, which unnerved Ramona almost as much as the croc story from the ferry. We slept in the car with the windows rolled up until a bodacious fart from Charlene forced us out. We left her in the car. Risking our lives fighting pumas was better than dying from poisonous gas. We found suitable trees and hung the hammocks we had packed. Raúl slept with Ramona.

I was up at daybreak, lit the propane stove, and brewed a pot of coffee. The aroma filtered through the woods, and soon everybody was up. Charlene came out of the car, grabbed the pot, and poured the coffee on the ground.

"What in the hell is wrong with you?" I said.

"You're a dumb-ass, Alex. The smell of coffee will bring the enemy to our camp. I can't believe Ramona's in love with such an imbecile. I die a thousand times when I think you'll be the father of my grandchildren."

I was about to defend myself when I heard a "Pssst." I turned and saw Raúl. He waved me over, grabbed my hand, and led me to Junior who was sitting on a log. The ragamuffin asked me to sit by him. Then, with a sheepish smile, he asked for a cigarette. I refused to give him one.

"You're too young to be smoking," I said. "Just because I gave you one earlier doesn't give you the right to hit for more. You need to buy your own."

"Mister Alex, if you'll give me a cigarette, I'll tell you how you can keep the chocolate milk *chi chis* without having to get married." So I gave him a smoke.

As soon as he lit it, Raúl moved next to him and shared the cigarette. My look of disapproval caught Junior's eyes. Again, he felt the need to explain the boy's eccentricities.

"Raúl has a taste for the finer things in life, Mister Alex. He loves chocolate milk and only smokes American Marlboros."

I lit another one and passed it to Raúl. What the hell . . . I was in Mexico. The rules of propriety here were certainly different. Caucasian Americans are tight asses; we Latin Americans have a certain *savoir faire* that is enviable. We puffed away. When I noticed a look of contentment painted on Junior's face, I said, "Well? I'm all ears."

Before I could learn what the clever little scoundrel had in mind, Charlene showed up and immediately began to curse me for giving the kids a cigarette. Soon, Ramona joined the tirade. I was severely chastised for corrupting two innocent kids.

"Listen to me, Alex," said Ramona. "When we are married, I want to have children, but I'm worried that you don't have a clue about how to raise them. The adult—you—in this case, shows by example what is right and what is wrong. You can't be the kid."

"All I did was burn a fag with these two street urchins. Give me a break."

She glared at me with those big dark eyes. When she placed both hands on her hips, I looked for a place to sit. Having been down this road before, I knew the speech was going to insult my sense of fatherhood. I stared blankly into her face.

"I'll grant you that Junior may be older than his years," she said. "But Raulito is still unspoiled. He needs to be nurtured. He needs love and attention. I am certainly not going to allow bad behavior around him. Please, no more smoking with the kids. Is that understood?"

"Listen to me, Ramona. You need to be a bit more in tune with our young traveling companions. These kids are hustlers. We will be touched before we leave Mexico, I'm sure of it," Alex said.

"You're such a fool. Mother's right . . . I don't know what I see in you. Your lovemaking cannot be the glue in our relationship. I need more than physical prowess."

"Listen to me, Ramona. If you intend to become my wife, you cannot be a chip off the old block. I will not stand for it. One set of fangs imbedded on my buttocks is enough. The road to the altar is a long one, so you better watch your mouth if you expect me to stand there with you."

"What are you going to do without me, Alex. Work for a living? I treat you better than you deserve. Marrying me will guarantee your lifestyle. Maybe one day you'll make it as a writer, or then again maybe not. But this much you can count on . . . I will always love you, and I will always give you a suitable allowance. You need me to protect you from the harsh elements, so pay attention to your behavior. I want to give birth to a child, not to marry one."

What a bitch. I can't believe she thinks I can't take care of myself. She must think she's the only woman in the world. The last thing I need in my life is a control freak. These two women will be the death of me. Disgusted, I walked away.

Junior and I were given the job of finding a way out of where we were. We scouted the area and found a way to drive the car up the ravine and onto the gravel road. We gave each other high-fives, loaded everyone in the car, and drove off.

Several miles down the road, we came across a detachment of federal police; we stopped at the road block and were immediately surrounded by the *federales*. They ordered us out of the car at gunpoint and said we were under arrest. A soldier told us to follow him while others searched the Mercury. I was hoping they wouldn't steal my mother's toaster.

We were led to an officer who introduced himself as Capitán García. He seemed to be an amiable fellow. He asked us why we didn't stop at the customs checkpoint. He also wanted to know why we ran away from the police.

"What police?" I asked. Then, to my horror, I saw the two men that chased us the night before, except today they were wearing uniforms instead of T-shirts. Oh shit, I'm in big trouble now.

It was a good thing I spoke Spanish because Capitán García did not speak a word of English. Understanding the predicament, I dug into my bag of tricks. The best defense has always been a good offense, so I verbally attacked him. I waved my hands and complained loudly about the dimly lit and deserted-looking customs building. I berated him about the unmarked police vehicle chasing me. I complained about the two men wearing T-shirts instead of uniforms. I was outraged that they pointed pistols without identifying themselves and then shot twice at us. I emphasized that we thought we were being attacked by bandits. I demanded that he arrest the two men who chased us, because I felt they were doing some bandit work on the side.

Junior came forward and told Capitán García that we were good people, not smugglers. He said we were giving them a ride to their family's home in Chetumal. Raulito started to whimper and grabbed Ramona's leg. These boys were god-sent. I made a mental note to give each one a pack of smokes.

The Mexican officer believed the story. He chastised the two men who had given us such a fright, apologized, and allowed us to go on our way. Counting our blessings, we left the *federales* behind and drove until the car ran out of gas.

"Oh, damn," I said. "The fucking *federales* siphoned our gasoline while we were being questioned. I'm sure we had a half tank before we were stopped."

"Watch your filthy mouth, Alex," Charlene said. "There are children in the car. You probably neglected to fill the tank all the way up in Veracruz. Accusing the police of siphoning gas is absurd. You are such an ass."

I looked for a clearing, and we coasted to a stop. Ramona, being the queen of the outdoors that she was, set camp, and prepared lunch. Junior and Raúl loved the Vienna sausages and peanut butter and jelly crackers. Unfortunately, all we had left to drink was one diet Coke, one water bottle, and two Coronas that Charlene refused to share.

"I can't believe we threw all the beer and pineapple soda out the window last night and saved the diet Coke. Who was in charge of the bombardment?" I queried.

"What a moron you are," said Charlene. "The Cokes were cans, but the beer, Perrier, and pineapple sodas were in glass containers. We needed to puncture the bandit's tires or smash their windshield. I was in charge of the artillery, which is why we didn't get caught."

"Yeah, right," I said with a smirk. "That's also the reason you still have something to drink other than water or diet soda. Greed is not a virtue, Charlene. You could share one of the Coronas with me."

"Not on your life," she said with a smile. She ate more cheese and opened one of the beers. I was hoping that at some point all the cheese she'd been eating would plug up her bowels. Maybe that would cut down on the deadly farts.

"This is not safe, Alex," said Ramona. "What are you going to do about our situation? We can't stay here."

"Yeah, Alex . . . what are you going to do about the mess we're in?" said Lizzy Borden's mother.

Feeling the hand of fate resting upon my shoulder again, I shuddered. The unsavory situation we had just experienced was still imbedded in my mind. I certainly wanted no more police or bandit trouble.

I tried to think of a way out of our mess, but all of a sudden the need to piss hit me! I left to find a tree. A person can't think with a pressing bladder.

Chapter 4

Don Pedro's Cow

We looked at the map and realized that the only place to get gas was in Chetumal. Junior and I volunteered to hitchhike with the empty five-gallon container. Ramona objected; she was nervous about being left alone on the side of the road with a car loaded with merchandise. I told Junior he needed to stay with them. That didn't sit well with him. He wanted to go with me.

"Getting gas is a man's job," Junior said.

"I know. That's precisely why I'm going. You need to stay here and protect the women."

"What can I do? I'm just a kid."

We were discussing who would stay behind when an old man with two kids in tow approached us.

"*Buenos días*," he said, tipping his sombrero. "I'm Pedro Ávila, and these handsome boys are my grandsons, Antonio and Armando." The boys grinned and removed their hats.

"You cannot stay here for very long. This is dangerous for you. There are too many bad people on the road. You need to come with me. I will offer you my home until you can fix the problem with your car."

Having had enough excitement to last us a lifetime, we conferred and accepted his offer. Charlene asked him if there was any way we could tow the car to a safer place. He told her not to worry. He knew where there was an ox that could be harnessed to pull the car. Charlene asked if we could borrow it. The old man smiled and told her with an apologetic tone that it could not be borrowed, but it could be rented.

Soon, we found ourselves in a small, but neat and clean cinderblock house. It wasn't far from where we were stranded, and that pleased us. Raúl made friends with Antonio and Armando. Junior stayed by my side.

It didn't take us long to notice that the food pantry at Mr. Ávila's home was empty. How to accept Pedro's hospitality, without becoming a burden, became a source of concern. Charlene wanted to offer the old man money for our room and board. I didn't want to offend him by offering to pay for what he had offered for free. Still, we needed to find a way to put money in his pocket so food could be purchased. Looking around the place, I noticed they had a cow tied in the backyard. I told Pedro that we were grateful for the offer to spend the night, but first we needed to take care of the vehicle.

"Yes, you are right," said the old man. "Let me get my sombrero, and I will take you to the man who owns the ox."

"Listen, Don Pedro . . . instead of doing business with the owner of the ox, I'd rather do business with you. It's getting late, and unless you have a problem with the idea, I want to rent your cow. She seems sturdy enough to help us pull the car. Charlene wants us to do it now. What do you say? Can we rent the cow in the backyard?" Don Pedro scowled at the suggestion.

Wanting to cut off any escape route the old man might come up with, I mentioned that in view of the fact that there was no woman in the house, my wife was honor bound by our Texas culture to cook for all of us. I asked him if there was a store nearby because the women wanted to buy some special ingredients.

"Ramona wants to cook a Texas-style meal for you and your boys," I said. "You are in for a treat, because she is an excellent cook." His stomach growled. Seizing the moment, I mentioned she could turn out a meal fit for a king. His stomach growled again, and then he begrudgingly accepted the offer to let us rent his cow. The old man told us with a sigh that it had been a while since a woman cooked in his kitchen. I asked him if he was a widower. He closed his eyes and bowed his head.

"*Sí*, my beloved Rosa died many years ago."

"Do you have children, Don Pedro?"

"*Sí*, I have two boys and a girl. Both my sons are in Texas. My daughter's husband died on the way there. He paid a *coyote* to take him to San Antonio, but he was locked in a hot railcar with other unfortunate souls. They were abandoned to die. Soon after his death my daughter María brought her boys to live with me. When they were settled, she left for Chicago to meet with a cousin that had a job in a restaurant. She made it without any problems, thanks to God almighty. María has a good job now and sends money from time to time, as do my sons. Life here is good for an old man, but it lacks opportunities for the young—especially those with ambition."

He mentioned there was a small store close by where supplies could be purchased and explained with some concern that the cow in the backyard was their only means of daily support.

"We get milk from the cow twice a day, then we trade it for things we need. I am not convinced Lucinda can pull your big car, but since you're my guests, I'll go along with your suggestion."

That being decided, the old man fetched his sombrero. Ramona headed to the store with the three boys. Charlene, Pedro, Junior, and I walked with the cow. I was hoping Lucinda wouldn't die pulling Charlene's heavy car.

We found the Mercury where we left it, placed a loose rope with a knot around the cow's neck, and tied the other end to the frame of the station wagon. Charlene walked alongside the driver's door. She had the window down and was pushing and steering at the same time. Junior and I pushed from behind. Pedro encouraged the unhappy cow with a stick. Halfway there, I was beginning to think this affair looked like another one of my harebrained ideas.

The cow was straining so much she was leaking milk. I could tell the old man was worried, and I felt bad.

We finally made it to the house, and none to soon either, because the cow looked exhausted. I was relieved and thanked God for this kindness. Pedro grabbed a bucket and filled it with water from a cistern and washed Lucinda's udders, then poured the rest of the water on the hot cow.

Ramona and the boys returned from the store with an extra kid and a man leading a burro. Pedro went outside and greeted the donkey driver. The beast of burden had two deep wicker baskets attached to a homemade wooden apparatus that was designed to accommodate the baskets, which were full of groceries. We were told the mule skinner was the husband of the woman who ran the store.

"What's with the burro?" I asked Ramona

"Any purchase of fifty dollars or more comes with free home delivery. I also bought two gallons of gasoline."

"They had gasoline at the store?"

"Well, not exactly. There was a man at the store with a truck. He was buying a sack of flour and heard one of Pedro's boys say we'd run out of gas. He charged me five dollars for each gallon he siphoned out of his vehicle. He would have sold me the whole tank, but his wife would only allow him to give me two."

"I'm willing to bet the house that this is the first home delivery that store ever had," I said.

"Probably so. The whole area seems very poor. The lady who owned the store was surprised to see me walk up with the kids. I made her day."

"I bet you did. Her husband seems impressed also."

The owner of the burro couldn't keep his eyes off Ramona's breasts. I couldn't believe she went to the store wearing a low-cut halter top and short shorts. The sight of her long, curvy, slender legs was dangerous enough. She had no sense of propriety. The woman that owned the store probably sent her son along to make sure her husband behaved.

Ramona had purchased two scrawny live chickens. I was pleased to find that the donkey driver was also a chicken killer and feather plucker. Ramona was a clever shopper. She came home with food, gas, and a butcher. However, she made the mistake of returning with a month's supply of food, causing Pedro to complain that the purchases exceeded the money paid for the cow's services and then to insist that we stay a few days with them. Charlene glared at me when I accepted the offer.

"Don't give me any dirty looks," I said. "Your daughter is to blame. If she hadn't purchased the whole store, we'd be out of here tomorrow."

Ramona overheard me. "I didn't spend all of the fifty dollars on food and gas. I also bought the boys water pistols and yo-yos. You can't believe how cheap things are here."

One hour later, I heard a commotion in the backyard. I went out to investigate and found Pedro mad as hell. He was collecting the water pistols from the kids. As he passed me, he glared and muttered, "Water pistols are totally unsuited for our household. It causes Antonio and Armando to ignore the rules of water conservation."

"You're having a drought?" I said.

"No. But we only have a small cistern."

With a scowl on his face, the old man threw the water pistols into the trash bucket and disappeared into his bedroom.

Pedro didn't stay mad for very long, as the aroma of Ramona's cooking had hypnotic powers. He came out with a smile that said volumes about her culinary skills. I patted him on the back and whispered, "As I said, Don Pedro, you and the boys are in for a special treat."

We made small talk and ate to our hearts' content. Ramona prepared too much food, and there was some left. Pedro looked at the leftovers with righteous anger.

"The main difference between our cultures has to do with the fact that you gringos have too much and we Mexicans have too little. You cook without regard to how many people are eating. We count heads and take into consideration the appetite of those sitting at the table. There is never any leftover food."

Charlene was bristling with anger. I was hoping Mata Hari would control herself, but she didn't. She snarled and defended her way of life.

"With all due respect, Don Pedro, the main difference between our cultures has to do with electricity. Everyone in the United States has refrigeration. If we cook too much, we put the leftovers in the fridge. In our culture—especially in Texas—it is considered bad manners to prepare barely enough food to cover the guests' appetites. It is always better to have too much than not enough. Besides, we have dogs to feed."

Pedro became outraged. Charlene's contempt toward poverty made him puff up. He slammed his fist on the table, knocking the plastic tumblers to the floor. I braced for an outright brawl. Charlene was out of booze and seemed to be in a nasty mood. Before the old man could come up with a reply, Ramona's sharp sense of awareness kicked into gear. She jumped into the fray and told Pedro there was enough leftover stew to give his skinny dogs a nice meal. Pedro got up. I prepared for an all-out battle. Obviously, he misunderstood her comments.

To my surprise, the expected brawl didn't materialize. Pedro looked at Ramona and then at his hungry dogs. He agreed to her suggestion, thanked her for the nice meal, and left the table. He entered his room and closed the door.

I admonished Charlene for insulting our host. "I can't believe you behaved so badly," I said.

"Up yours, Alex. Education is everyone's duty. Don Pedro needed to need to have a class in Texas culture. Now he knows why we are different. You are nothing but an ass-kisser."

After the women cleaned the kitchen, we agreed to bed down early so we could get up at the crack of dawn and help the old man with his chores. We made a pact to accept his hospitality for one more night. Antonio and Armando were gracious enough to offer

Charlene and Ramona their bedroom. It had two cots in it. I took the hammock in the living room. The kids slept outside in our tent.

In the middle of a sexual dream, I heard a loud "Psst." I tried to block the intrusion because I was in the process of removing a woman's panties. I wanted to see if she was a real blonde, but the intrusions continued. Grudgingly, I abandoned the dream, opened one eye, stretched my neck, and saw Junior. He was standing by the open window. "Psst . . . Mister Alex? You better get up. We have a big problem."

I climbed out of the hammock and went outside. "What's the problem, Junior?"

"Look over there, Mister Alex. The cow is dead!"

My heart sank. Pedro's cow, his only source of income, was lying on the ground all stretched out and stiff.

"Oh no! What happened?"

"I don't know. I got up to piss and saw that the cow was dead. I think it died of a heart attack. I think making the old cow pull your heavy American car killed her. I think you're in trouble. What do you think?"

Junior was right. I killed the old man's cow. I felt terrible. I had to come up with an idea, and fast. "I have a plan," I said.

"Is it as good as the last one? Getting an old cow to pull a heavy car was a dumb idea."

"Be quiet, Junior. No need to cry over spilled milk. If we can pull this off, there's a ten-spot in it for you. Now, pay attention and let me explain the plan . . . "

Twenty minutes later, I sneaked into the boys' bedroom. I placed my hand on Ramona's mouth, and she woke up and looked at me with scared eyes. I placed a finger on my lips and slowly removed my hand from her mouth.

"What's going on, Alex?" she whispered.

"We have a big problem. Wake your mother and meet me outside. Get your gear and be ready to ride."

"What? What's going on?"

"Don't ask any questions. You'll know why we have to leave as soon as you come outside. Wake your mother and get dressed without making any noise. Be quick about it."

"The cow's dead, isn't it?"

"What made you think that?"

"Mother told me you talked the old man into hitching his old cow to the car instead of the young oxen. The cow's dead, isn't it?"

Shit, Charlene is going to level dirt on me. I hated to give that grisly woman ammunition with which to abuse me, but hell, I deserved it. The stiff-legged cow in the backyard was damaging testimony.

"Yes, the cow's dead. Get your mother up. We are running away."

In no time at all, (and I must admit it, I had never seen Charlene move so quickly before) we were in the car and out of there. I left a note for Pedro apologizing for the good deed going bad, and attached a hundred-dollar bill to it. Once we were a distance away, Charlene dove into me. First, she yelled at me about getting an old cow to pull a heavy car, and then, she scolded me for leaving the tent behind.

"Now we don't have a tent. What are we going to do if we get stranded somewhere?"

"Losing the tent was unfortunate," I said, "but Armando and Antonio were sleeping inside. Junior was lucky to get Raúl out without waking them up. What was I supposed to do . . . wake them up and then tie and gag them?"

I tried unsuccessfully to defend myself by pleading a momentary lapse of reason. Ramona decided to throw fuel into a roaring fire and told everyone that I once forgot to tie a piano I was transporting on the back of a pickup truck, and it fell off and broke into a million pieces.

Charlene's eyes gleamed at the revelation. I felt betrayed. Junior's eyes showed disappointment.

"You don't know about ropes, Mister Alex?"

I kept quiet. I could tell I was losing his reverence. For some unexplainable reason, keeping the ragamuffins' respect seemed important. We drove for a while in silence. The women and Raúl slept in the back seat. Junior was sleeping in the front. I glanced down and checked the gas gauge and became worried, because Chetumal was still sixty kilometers away, and the Mercury was good for about sixteen miles to the gallon if it was going downhill with a good wind on its back. I was going to run out of gas . . . again. Junior must have sensed my discomfort, because he woke up. He bummed a cigarette and asked me in Spanish (so the women would not understand) if I really forgot to tie the piano.

"Look," I said. "I did it on purpose. I was bringing home a piano for Ramona, and she's a terrible player. She was going to drive me crazy playing the stupid thing, so I dropped it accidentally on purpose."

Junior looked at me for a minute, trying to digest my statement. Then, he slowly smiled. "You're a smart man, Mister Alex. What a good way of not coming home with the piano."

Soon, we were smoking and bonding. So what if I lied to him? One liar always deserves another, and between us, it was difficult to tell which one was the biggest liar. He was no more the son of Jimmy Buffet than I was.

I looked at the gas gauge again and began to sweat. Junior followed my eyes and noticed the dilemma.

"What are you going to do about that?" he said, pointing at the gauge.

"I'm not sure, but when I think of something, you'll be the first to know."

A few miles further I noticed a car parked on the side of the road. I stopped behind it and climbed out. Ramona woke up.

"What's wrong, Alex?"

"We're almost out of gas. I'm going to try to buy some from the person that owns that car."

She stretched, mentioned she needed to see a man about a horse, and left the car. Charlene was still asleep, and so was Raúl. I counted my blessings, grabbed the empty five-gallon gas container, and went to find the driver. Junior left in the direction of Ramona.

I looked inside the car and saw a man sleeping. I woke him up and negotiated a deal for some gas. He siphoned five gallons out of his tank. I put it in the Mercury. When I was done, I went to see what was keeping Ramona. I made a turn through a gap in the trees and saw Junior crouching behind some bushes whacking off. I looked again and saw the reason. He was peeping at Ramona, who had removed her pants and was washing herself in a creek. I picked up a rock and threw it at him. He looked at me and took off running. I gave chase. He stumbled, and I caught up to him. I grabbed the squirming kid by the arm and thumped him on the head with my knuckles.

"I'm sorry, Mister Alex," he pleaded. "Please don't give me another *coscorrón*, they hurt."

"You were whacking off while spying on Ramona, you little twerp. I have a mind to tell her."

"Please, Mister Alex! Don't say nothing to her. I couldn't help myself. I went out to piss, and then I saw her take her pants off. When she began to wash her bush, I lost control. I am a man . . . I have needs."

"You're a dirty kid. You shouldn't be doing that."

"Don't *you* play with yourself, Mister Alex?"

"Yes, sometimes."

"I do it sometimes, too, especially when confronted with such a sight. You're a lucky man, Mister Alex."

I grabbed him by the neck of his shirt and walked him back to the car. Charlene was awake and talking to the man that sold me the gas. I wondered if she realized he didn't speak English. Raúl was pissing on the car tire. Ramona showed up, and Junior gave me a pleading look.

"Mister Alex, please don't tell her nothing."

Oh, what the hell. I masturbated plenty while looking at naked girls in magazines. Junior's action was understandable. Ramona's physical attributes were indeed tantalizing. I let go of the shirt and patted him on the back. "Don't do it again," I said.

Finally, all was well, and we were on the road again. Feeling smug, I told them that I was surprised the man sold me five gallons' worth. I figured since Chetumal was at least sixty kilometers away, he would only give up one, maybe two gallons.

"How much did he charge you?" Charlene wanted to know.

"I got a better deal than Ramona. I offered him three dollars per gallon. We can't be spending money like drunken sailors. That cow ordeal cost me a hundred bucks."

"You only gave that poor, nice old man a hundred dollars for a two-hundred-dollar cow?" Charlene said. "What a cheapskate you are. It's a good thing I left him another hundred under my pillow."

"You only left him a hundred dollars for a two-hundred-dollar cow? What a cheapskate you are," I said.

"I didn't kill the damn cow."

"I left him two hundred dollars under my pillow," Ramona said.

"Mama Mia!" Junior bellowed. "Let me see if I can understand this . . . you guys gave the old man four hundred dollars for a two-hundred-dollar cow?"

Before he could say another word, I made a curve, and there was a PEMEX gas station. I felt hustled.

"That man knew there was a station here and didn't tell me," I said, feeling the fool.

"Let me see if I understand this," repeated Junior. "You paid three dollars a gallon for gasoline that cost only sixty-five cents a gallon?"

"How was I supposed to know the station was around the corner?" I said. "I am a damn tourist. I don't know the layout of the land."

"Okay," Junior said. "If you guys want to make it to Chetumal with money, you need a business manager. I'm not a damn foolish tourist but a Mexican kid with a good idea of where things are, what they cost, and how they work. I'm applying for the job."

"How much will it cost us?" Ramona said.

"I can't believe you're considering it," I said. "I am more than capable of handling things."

Sensing an opportunity to humiliate me, Charlene agreed we would be better off with Junior in charge, but she demanded to know how much his services were going to cost.

"Five dollars a day," he said.

"Good," Charlene said. "Alex will pay you."

"What? Five dollars a day is highway robbery. You're no better than the guy who sold me the gas."

"Mister Alex, for five dollars a day I will keep you from buying cows, getting hustled to buy expensive gas, and getting into trouble with the police. Besides, with a job, I can pay for my way and Raúl's way. I can give you five dollars a day for our expenses."

I couldn't believe it. The street urchin was offering me my own money back again. This kid was good. Ramona smiled and put her arm around his neck and said, "All in favor of hiring Junior to be our business road manager, please say 'aye.'"

Charlene, Ramona, and Junior said "Aye." Raúl raised his hand.

"How come Raúl raised his hand?" I asked. "I thought he didn't understand English."

"Just because he doesn't have words doesn't mean he does not know what's going on. He's not stupid, Mister Alex."

Charlene and Ramona had a good laugh. Junior smiled, and Raúl crawled unto Ramona's lap. Feeling like a fool, I kept quiet and bit my lip.

Soon, everyone was asleep again. I drove, trying to think of ways to get revenge. No twelve-year-old was going to get the best of me.

Chapter 5

We finally made it to Chetumal. I had never been so glad to see a hotel and an air-conditioned restaurant in my entire life.

When we walked into the lobby, the man at the front desk gave us a disapproving glare. We certainly looked like a motley group. However, the gold American Express card that Charlene flashed soothed his sense of propriety. We booked a suite with two bedrooms. One had a queen-sized bed, and the other came with two double beds.

Any idea I had of getting laid left me when I understood I was sharing the room with the kids. I complained to Ramona, but it didn't help. Charlene was paying for the room, and she was not sleeping with the kids. She was sleeping with Ramona, and her answer to my complaint implied we were going to do without sex until after we became husband and wife.

In the morning, Ramona and Charlene went shopping. They asked the kids to go with them, but Junior refused the invitation. He said he needed to work on an itinerary. He did tell them to please remember he wore small adult clothes. He also wanted a pair of one-toe ring leather sandals, size seven and a half.

The Mayan Plaza Hotel had a small refrigerator in the suite. Junior and Raúl were fascinated with it. They kept opening it, looking inside, and eating the cheese and sausages. They also enjoyed the Coke and orange sodas.

When the women and Raúl left for the open market, Junior and I went down to the restaurant for breakfast. After the morning meal, a couple of cigarettes, and scowls from several American tourists who obviously misunderstood our relationship, I asked Junior if he wanted to join me on a walk around the square. He declined, saying he had other plans.

I spent part of the morning walking around and turning away annoying peddlers. Unable to enjoy the walkabout, I went back to the hotel. When I opened the door, I found Junior sitting on the window ledge smoking a joint and enjoying a cold drink.

"Hola, Mister Alex. How was your walk? Want a Scotch and ginger ale?"

"It's eleven-thirty in the morning! What are you doing drinking this early? It's not even noon yet. Where did you get the reefer? Don't you know it is against the law to burn one of those?"

"Don't be so uptight, Mister Alex. I'm getting on higher ground so I can advise you on your problem."

"Which one? I have several."

"The marriage to the woman with sharp edges," he said.

"I'm not marrying Charlene . . . I'm marrying her daughter. Also, I am not taking any advice from someone who doesn't know the difference. That must be some good shit you're smoking. Where did you get the stuff?"

"Whichever one you marry, you get the other. It's a package deal. Those two are attached at the hip." Then he looked at the joint and said, "Yes, this is primo stuff. I bought a bag in Matamoros some time ago. I sell one joint at a time to the American and European tourists. I have to make ends meet."

The brisk walk I had undertaken had given me a powerful thirst. I went to the fridge and pulled out a small bottle of Bacardi rum. I grabbed a Coke and mixed a drink. I searched my bag for something to spray the room and only found my cologne. Hoping it would mask the smell of pot, I sprayed the whole place. I paid Junior a dollar for a joint but stashed it for later. I wasn't going to stoop so low as to share reefers with a kid. I heated up a Marlboro and joined him at the window.

"Tell me the truth about Raúl. What's his story?"

"Raúl can talk . . . he just doesn't want to."

"Why?"

"In the beginning, it was because that was his job. When I met him he was a bottom feeder. He was selling chewing gum, pencils, and begging from tourists. I told him if he wanted to work for me, he needed to lose his speech. Tourists were easier to hit if he was handicapped. But now, he doesn't speak because he likes the attention."

"Where's his family?"

"He's an orphan."

"What about you? Where's your family?"

"I told you, my father is Jaime Buffet, the American singer. My mother died several years ago. After she died, I spent eight months in San Cristóbal's Orphanage in Mérida. That's where I'm taking Raúl. There's a priest I like called Padre Humberto who runs the place. He will take him in. Then, I can go to the United States. I have learned to speak English very well and can take care of myself. I have some money stashed in my underwear. Want to see how much?"

"No, thank you. I don't want to see your underwear."

"I have some more buried under a rock at the orphanage's cemetery, too. I'm saving to go north."

"Trying to catch the American Dream, huh?"

"No . . . trying to find my father. He lives on an island off the coast of Florida."

"Oh, brother," I mumbled. "I asked you for the truth, and you give me another cock-and-bull story."

He gave me the bad-eye, put the joint out, and left the window ledge. He dug into his sack and pulled out a snapshot.

"Here, Mister Alex. This is a picture of my parents."

I grabbed it. Sure enough, there was a man that looked like Jimmy Buffet, and he had his arm around a pretty Mexican woman.

"This is your mother?"

"Yes, that's my mother and my father. She's dead, and as soon as I take Raúl to San Cristóbal's Orphanage, I'm going to find my father. Why is that so hard to believe?"

"Okay, I'm sorry. It just sounds like a tall tale. What makes you so sure he will accept you when you knock on his door?"

"Would you turn your son away if he knocked on your door?"

"Okay, well, you got me there."

Not wanting to deal with Ramona's disappointment over my parental abilities, I grabbed the cologne and sprayed the room again. She had become a bear since Raúl entered her life. Now she disapproved of everything including my mannerisms. Hell, I'm the same guy she fell in love with.

The women and Raúl finally came back loaded with merchandise. Ramona took one good look at us and understood we were drunk. She sniffed the air, smelled the cologne, and scowled, but kept quiet. Charlene went right for the fridge. She grabbed the Oso Negro Vodka, a can of orange juice, and poured herself a stiff one. She spread the merchandise they had purchased on the bed. Junior was pleased with his one-toe sandals. He put them on immediately and began to walk back and forth. "I want some of those," I said.

Ramona shot me a disapproving look and threw me a white cotton shirt and brown leather belt. "If you wanted sandals you should have asked for them."

Women are so difficult to understand. I didn't order a white shirt but got one anyway.

We left Chetumal the following day and stopped at the archaeological sites of Cobah and Tulum. Instead of continuing on to Cancun, we spent the night in a local campground called Hotel Cocotero, about a mile and a half from Tulum. The place was located in the midst of a coconut grove. It had areas set aside for hammocks and tents. It also had four large round wicker cabins with sand floors. These huts had a double-bed frame made out of small logs that hung from the ceiling with ropes. The reason for this contraption (as I soon found out) was not to give you a swinging bed, but to keep the creepy crawlers that lived in the sand off the bed. On top of the log frame was a thin mattress, and the bed came with a long mosquito net. We were told to keep an eye out for scorpions. The manager said they liked to live in the thatched rooftops and fell to the ground regularly. We were reminded to shake our shoes before putting them on. When the manager left, I grabbed the can of bug spray we had in the car and sprayed the whole roof. I'd been stung by scorpions before, and it's no fun.

These cabins were unusual in the sense that you could see the outside area from the inside by looking through the cracks between the wicker walls, but you could not see from the outside into the room unless you pressed your eyes to the walls. Ramona, going against Charlene's wishes, decided to bunk with me. She said she was afraid of the creepy crawlers, but I knew better. She was ready for a little love action. What a self-serving bitch. If I wasn't horny, I'd have turned her down.

The cabins were primitive but affordable, so Charlene rented three. Aside from the scorpions that fell off the thatched ceilings and then crawled around on the sand, the main deterrent to staying here again was the annoying sand flies that came out when the wind stopped blowing. The large blood-sucking mosquitoes were no big deal. Hell, we lived in Houston, and our flying pests came in an extra large size. You never know what fright is until a huge Texas tree roach flies straight at you and lands on you.

Hotel Cocotero's cabins were strewn on a strip of white sand beach. We appreciated the rustic ambiance of the campground, as well as the friendliness of the people working and staying there. We enjoyed it so much we spent four nights and three days.

We took the time to worship the sun, collect shells, and play in the resplendent Caribbean Sea. The campground boasted a communal bathroom—a large square wicker cabin with a thatched roof. It had one entrance. The toilets were private, but the wash sinks were not. Neither were the showers. I hadn't showered with men since gym class in high school.

The room where the showers were located had two hallways. A wicker wall separated the men from the women. If you looked really hard, you could see the females on the other side, a fact that galled Charlene. The showerhead was nothing more than an open pipe that poured cold, brackish water. Junior and I showered whenever there was a woman showering.

The hotel had a dining room that doubled as a cantina. The place had no electricity, so everything we ate was fresh and everything we drank was warm. A fisherman with his three sons came by early in the morning and sold his catch to the manager, meaning fish with eggs and bread for the morning meal and fish with rice and beans at night. At lunch, we had to find our own fish. There was a store close to the ruins of Tulum. We walked there and bought sweet bread, hot beer, and sodas.

The hotel cantina opened after dinner and remained open until the bar candle burned out. It was a nice place to spend a couple of hours talking with fellow adventurers. We met a hairy German girl at the bar named Gertrude who gave holistic massages for five dollars an hour. We also met a quiet American couple from Iowa, on their honeymoon. We tried to befriend them, but they didn't show any interest. They spent most of the time lying out in the sun or staying in their cabin. The wife showered twice a day, as did Junior and I. There was a friendly Japanese man who smiled a lot but spoke no English or Spanish. He was fond of taking early morning walks in the nude and took photos of everything.

On the afternoon of our second day, Junior came to me and whispered, "Mister Alex, do you know that for an additional price, Gertrude will massage your winkie?"

I gave him a stern look. "Don't you know that if you keep whacking off, you will go blind?"

Personally, I had an aversion of getting close to any girl who could braid her armpit hair. I made a point to keep my John Henry a safe distance from that German woman.

On the third day, Ramona stayed out in the sun too long and fried. It was time to head out. We bid our hosts and guests adieu and then drove in the direction of the archaeological site of Chichen Itza, which was located in Yucatán. However, before we were barely out of Quintana Roo, I became tired of Ramona's loud discomfort and Charlene's lethal farts. The old woman's diet of fish, eggs, and beans was playing hell with her bowels. By now, I was having problems with this whole gig. I didn't think I was going to make it to the pyramids without first losing my mind. Ramona kept behaving like a baby, crying and complaining about her third-degree sunburn. Desperation overpowered me, and I decided it was time to seriously consider Junior's plan.

"I can't believe she fell asleep on the beach for four hours," I said to Charlene with indignation. "Where were you? Didn't you warn her about the dangers of overexposure to the sun?"

"Screw off, Alex. She made a mistake. Don't start getting superior on me. She's been good to you all these years, and now it's time for you to be good to her. She's in pain, and you need to take care of her. I can't do it . . . I don't feel well."

That was an understatement. Charlene had been killing us with her smelly farts. Before long, she began to scare us by complaining loudly that she was having severe stomach cramps. Every time she cut one, we were afraid she was going to shit her pants. She kept apologizing, telling us it wasn't her fault. We suspected she had caught a case of "Moctezuma's Revenge" and prepared ourselves for the worst. Sure enough, a fart came, and we smelled it. The grizzly had soiled her underwear. We stopped the car. She got out and cleaned herself. Before she climbed back in the car, I made her bury her shitty drawers. Then we made her ride in the back seat while the rest of us rode in the front. We kept the air conditioning on and drove to Chichen Itza with all the windows down.

The visit to the archaeological site was short. Hell, we barely saw the place. Charlene, who by now had become accustomed to using the seat-less Mexican toilets, kept complaining about having cramps and severe diarrhea. On the way out, I proposed to the group that we postpone our excursion to Uxmal. They agreed, and we made a dash for Mérida. Ramona needed a comfortable hotel room with air conditioning, and Charlene needed a private toilet.

I decided it was best to book separate rooms. The women had become bears to be with, and they needed to be isolated. There comes a time when a man knows he is not getting lucky, and this was that time for me. A woman with a third-degree sunburn was not going to put out, period, so I was bunking with the boys.

Chapter 6

"*¿Estás seguro que esta idea va a trabajar?*" I asked Junior, while enjoying a rum and Coke in the hotel bar.

"*Sí*, Mister Alex, I'm sure it will work. All I have to do is make a few phone calls. I need five dollars."

I gave him the money. He took it and then looked at me with a serious expression. "Are you sure you want to go through with it, Mister Alex?"

"Is there any reason I should be wary?"

"Sometimes when you open Pancho's Box, things get a little crazy."

"You mean Pandora's Box, don't you?"

"You gringos think you own everything, including the sayings."

"First of all, Junior, I am not a gringo. Second, the saying about Pandora's Box has been around for centuries. Third, my mother's four-slice toaster is not worth a lifetime with Charlene."

"*Bueno* . . . if you are prepared to deal with the consequences and if you trust me, I'll handle everything. You know, Mister Alex, well-made plans seldom go bad."

Even though I had developed a certain amount of skepticism in the kid, I worried for days over that statement. Little did I know that putting your future in a kid's hands would be so unsettlingly rewarding . . .

We spent four days in Mérida getting Ramona's sunburn and Charlene's gastric malady under control. Junior confessed that the orphanage was not in Mérida but in San Cristóbal de las Casas, in Chiapas. When I asked him why he lied, he told me it was because he needed to come to Mérida. I didn't ask him why. I blew him off and decided to enjoy this beautiful place the Mexicans call the "White City," as most of the buildings are painted white.

When the women were feeling better and we were done sight-seeing, we left Mérida and visited the Mayan pyramids of Uxmal. Later, we drove toward the jungle state of Chiapas, where I expected to meet Padre Humberto, hand over Raúl, and slip out of my marriage promise.

The drive to the archaeological site of Palenque was long, so we spent the night in Villa Hermosa. The following morning, we found the pyramids. It was the best of all the sites we had visited. The beauty of the place mesmerized us. We marveled at the oriental-style King Pacal's palace and wondered about the connection. We were able to walk down a hidden, cramped corridor with hundreds of tiny steps to visit the king's tomb. He had been buried in a small room deep inside the pyramid, and his tomb was covered by a stone sarcophagus that was about a foot thick and barely two inches from the surrounding stone walls. The intent was to guard his remains from tomb robbers. Obviously, the builders never expected the intrusion of laser technology. The sarcophagus had been cut open, and King Pacal's bones and ornaments had been inspected and moved to the National Museum in Mexico City.

After spending a couple of days at this magnificent site, we drove toward San Cristóbal de las Casas in search of Padre Humberto and the orphanage. Raúl seemed to understand that something bad was about to happen. He became unusually clingy, and

Ramona began to have separation anxiety. She kept looking at me with eyes that asked for a reprieve.

I was also having difficulties, but they had nothing to do with getting rid of Raúl. His stay at the orphanage would be far better than his education at the hands of Junior. My problem had to do with being an accomplice in a low-down, unpardonable double-cross I was about to perpetrate on Ramona, the girl I loved. Hell, what could I do? I could not accept Charlene in my life as a permanent fixture. If I arrived in Panama and introduced the Creature from the Black Lagoon to my mother, she would chastise me. Regardless of Ramona's beauty, Mother and Aunt Margo would think of me as an imbecile and berate my father's genes.

We drove to San Cristóbal de las Casas and found the orphanage on the outskirts of town. There was a broken sign that hung sideways on a pole that read: "Asilo para los Huérfanos de San Cristóbal."

We were welcomed by Padre Humberto, who, to my surprise, greeted Junior with some reverence. We were given a dilapidated cabin with two small beds for all three of us to share. Junior and Raúl had other accommodations. I decided against sleeping with the women. I found a hammock hanging on the inside of the back porch of the main building and claimed that spot for myself.

The orphanage turned out to be nothing more than a ragged group of wooden cabins set up in the courtyard behind the main building, which was old and constructed with cement blocks. It had a roof composed of rusted zinc sheets. There were many broken windowpanes, and the place hadn't seen a coat of paint in years. The orphanage looked as if it had been abandoned. The interior of the building was sparsely furnished, but it was clean and orderly.

Padre Humberto gave us a tour of the place and introduced us to his assistant, a pretty young woman who worked the greeting desk and coordinated the activities of seventeen children. Her name was Rosita, but she preferred to be called Rosie, and she seemed very fond of Junior.

When my future mother-in-law entered the orphanage, her nasty temperament lost its edge. Even this awful woman was touched by the appalling conditions. The poverty of the place roused her Christian sense of duty. Needless to say, we stayed a while.

Padre Humberto was a good Catholic priest. He was well-schooled in ways of separating the flock from their money. He spoke enough English to hustle Charlene and used his learned skills to work her for all she was worth. She purchased building materials, and I worked like a dog.

Charlene drove to San Cristóbal de las Casas every day with Padre Humberto in an old truck that had no floor. Whenever I rode in it, I had to place my feet on parts of the frame. I could see the road beneath and kept an eye on the family jewels, lest a rock fly in and do ghastly damage. Also, I had to keep the windows open, or the road dust became unbearable.

The trips to town were to buy the materials needed to repair the main building. We replaced the rusted zinc sheets, painted the front part of the building, erected a new sign, and hired a couple of local men to help re-thatch the cabins. Ramona took over the kitchen duties.

I could tell she was happy. She drove to town with Rosie every morning in the now-bedraggled Mercury Marquis station wagon. They went to buy food and clothing material. Then, to my amusement, all three females sat on the porch at dusk for sewing sessions, determined to make clothes for the orphans. I couldn't understand why they just didn't go buy garments for the kids from a store. They were certainly cheap enough.

Charlene's Christian sense of charity was at full throttle. It was a good thing the place had no electricity; otherwise, they would be sewing on machines and using a refrigerator instead of an icebox. They did have a gas stove. We picked up a block of ice every day and made sure we had an extra ten-gallon gas container stored in reserve.

Two weeks after our arrival, Junior finally reappeared. He looked tired and ragged. I asked him to explain his long absence.

"You were supposed to help me with my problem, Junior. How can you help when you are never around?" I implored.

"In order to help you, I had to go and open Pancho's Box," he said. "Everything's in place now. You owe me . . . big time."

"What exactly is in Pancho's Box?" I wanted to know.

"Fairies," he said, smiling.

"What kind of fairies?"

"There are many different kinds—some are good, some not so good. I hope that in the end, Mister Alex, after you have felt their work . . . you will not think less of me. You wanted me to help you, so I had to do it in a way that would benefit me. I hope that's okay with you."

"Do these fairies look like bandits?"

"Yes. There's one that steals from the rich, and two others work on making particular wishes come true. There are several with matchmaking skills. Then there's one that brings good luck to the person that opens the box, and there's one that specializes in putting a smile on those in need of one. Don't worry, Mister Alex. You'll get your wish."

"How about you . . . what's your take on the deal?"

"I'll get four wishes."

"Why four? Why do I get only one wish and you get four?"

"Because only two have to do with me. The other two have to do with Raúl and Padre Humberto."

He gave me that sheepish smile of his, and I could not help but admire the little rascal. Junior's brown hair and eyes and capricious facial countenance gave him a handsome look. Still, his keen eyes were his best feature. They spoke volumes about what he was . . . a grown man in the body of a boy.

Two weeks later, Ramona came to me and announced that Charlene wanted to leave right away.

"Why the rush?" I asked.

"Mother slept with Padre Humberto last night."

"So, she bounces the mattress with the priest, and now we have to leave? Why is that fair?"

"Get serious, Alex. Mother is a Protestant, and she just seduced a Catholic priest! We have to leave right away. You can get your things or you can stay here. Suit yourself, but we're leaving."

"Are we going to see the ruins of—"

"No! We're going home! Mother is afraid that her lustful behavior will bring us bad luck. We can't continue on our journey."

"Are you telling me our wedding trip to Panama is off?" I said, trying to suppress a smile. Ramona broke into tears. She wiped her eyes with the back of her hands and then looked at me with puppyish eyes.

"Yes, Alex, the wedding trip is off."

When she noticed I was not moved by her statement, she became angry. I was surprised how quickly the tears disappeared. She puffed up and developed a challenging stance.

"The ticket to mother's precious Mercedes Benz is a wedding ring on my finger. I'm sorry to have to say this, Alex, but without a ring and a marriage certificate, you are going to feel the brunt of mother's sense of loyalty."

"What does that mean?"

"Mother will ask her handyman to persuade you to take your clothes and leave my house."

"You can't be serious. That man breaks legs for a living!"

"I'm sorry, Alex, but mother blames you for her tryst with the priest. You were the one that demanded a wedding trip, and you brought Junior and Raulito into our lives. She's traumatized by her evil deed. Mother feels the devil has infected her with an uncontrollable lust. She's despondent over the fact that she went down on a priest, and she believes God will punish her for luring Padre Humberto into breaking his vow of celibacy."

"Great," I mumbled. "She loads up on ecclesiastical wine and blows the priest, and I lose my home and Mercedes Benz."

Ramona's nostrils flared, her face contorted, and her eyes squinted. Recognizing that expression, I reacted quickly and dodged the punch she threw at me.

"You're an asshole, Alex! My heart's broken, Mother fears the imminent hand of God's wrath, and all you care about is a damn car!"

I walked away before she had a chance to throw another punch. I wanted to tell her it was not just a car—it was a Mercedes Benz 190SL convertible with a hardtop—but Ramona was not a girl you wanted to mess with. Once, during a fierce argument at home, she hit the wall with her fist and broke through the sheetrock. I learned to keep my cheekbones a safe distance from her steel knuckles.

I wondered as I made my getaway, what else was going to come out of Pancho's Box. I was expecting a certain amount of trouble. Hell, letting a kid with Junior's take on life handle my affairs was stupid. The old saying "Be careful what you wish for" kept haunting me. I tried to remember all the evil that came out of Pandora's Box as I started packing.

One hour later, I was ready to go. I looked for Junior, but he had disappeared again. Padre Humberto was nowhere to be seen. Raúl and Ramona were having a tearful good-bye, and Charlene had the look of a condemned woman. I had to pry Raúl away from Ramona's leg and give him to Rosie.

We finally drove away from San Cristóbal's Orphanage. As I made a turn and passed the freshly painted block sign, I forced a smile. I wondered if we were going to be remembered as benefactors or troublemakers.

I drove through the town of San Cristóbal looking for the fork in the road that would lead me to the main highway. I came to it and stopped to read two handpainted signs that caught my eyes. One had "God's Road" written on it, and the other read, "Pancho's Road." I felt the hand of fate was about to touch me again.

"Okay, girls, decision time," I said.

The women stared at the signs with curiosity. Charlene broke into tears. I felt sorry for the old woman and allowed myself a measure of regret for the pain she was going through. But I soon got over it.

"Which one do we take?" I said, knowing quite well that Junior was giving me one last chance to walk away from trouble.

I looked at Ramona, then at Charlene. Neither one said anything, so I made the decision.

"Since God is mad at Charlene, let's play it safe and take Pancho's Road."

They agreed without saying a word. I felt sorry for both of them, but what could I do? I was a writer without a story. I knew one road would lead me back to my mundane life, and the other, I was certain of it, would give me a story.

"Charlene," I said, "do you feel the passion of Humberto to be a sin, or do you feel it was nothing more than a testament to the weakness of the flesh?"

"Bedding a priest is a sin," she said. "God will punish me for my actions. I knew when I unfastened the top button of my blouse and then unpinned my hair that I was courting trouble. I saw the admiration in his eyes and trousers and became aroused. Padre Humberto is like no other priest I have ever met. He is all man. His eyes and soft voice bedeviled me since I first met him. I can't believe I lost my head and gave him head."

"Mother, please! It's not necessary to go into details. The thought of you blowing a priest makes me sick."

"What else did you do?" I said.

"Stop it, Alex," said Ramona, clenching a fist. "Don't you edge her on . . . she's miserable."

Enjoying their misery, I turned the steering wheel, gunned the engine, and headed down Pancho's Road. Ramona touched my hand in support. She knew that I would somehow save the day.

Half a mile later, we came across a log that was blocking the road. When Ramona and I left the car to move it, a man wearing a bandana over his face and holding two pistols came out of the brush. "*¡Manos arriba!*" he shouted.

I raised my hands immediately, and Ramona became frightened. Charlene came out of the car with her hands up.

"*¿Qué quieres?*" I asked the masked bandit.

"My name is Pancho, and I want your car and money. You can keep your *pinche* credit cards."

We did as we were told, and he was gone in a flash. He left us stranded, but with our passports, drivers' licenses, and credit cards. Ramona broke down and began to cry. I cursed my luck, as I saw the merchandise-laden Mercury going down a dusty road with the armed man inside. Charlene smiled. I demanded to know why she felt so good about our misfortune.

"We have been robbed, for heaven's sake," I said. "The damn thief took my mother's toaster!"

Charlene placed her hand on my shoulder. "Screw the toaster, screw you, and screw your mother. The road to misfortune was not God's road, so He has forgiven me. He was showing me, testing my understanding of His greatness. I should have trusted Him and taken His road. After all, he made Eve. He knows our weaknesses. I have been forgiven for my sin."

Charlene opened her arms and summoned Ramona to find comfort. Soon, both women were hugging, laughing, and enjoying what they called a "divine adventure." I scolded them for making light of a dangerous situation.

Minutes after I predicted doom and gloom, a flatbed truck appeared. The driver stopped and offered us a ride into town. He said one of us could ride in the cab with him and his wife, but the other two would have to ride in the back. Since I was the only one that spoke Spanish, I climbed in with them. The driver's wife became incensed. She looked at me with scornful eyes and vacated the cab, climbing in the back with Charlene and Ramona. I asked the driver what was the deal with his woman, and he mumbled something about females needing to bond. He bummed a cigarette, and I told him what had happened to us and where we had been these last few weeks. He said it was odd that we came from the orphanage. I asked him why, and he said because it had been abandoned years ago. He said he knew of three priests in San Cristóbal de las Casas, and none were named Humberto. I cursed, realizing we'd been hustled. He asked me where I wanted to go. For a fleeting moment I wanted to go back to the orphanage and confront the thieving bunch, but then again, what for? We were in Mexico—certainly out of our element. It was better to take it on the chin, cut our losses and run. To bring the police into our lives would only complicate matters.

"*La estación de autobuses, por favor,*" I said.

When we arrived at the bus station, we thanked him for the ride. The driver's wife spat on the ground when she passed me. She gave me the bad-eye and called me a *pendejo.*

"What did she say to you?" Ramona wanted to know.

"She called me an asshole."

"It's amazing how quickly people get to know you," Charlene said with a smile.

We produced our passports and purchased tickets to the border town of Reynosa. We found some empty chairs, sat, and waited for our departure time. A half hour later, a ragged-looking kid came into the bus station carrying a box. He looked around, made eye contact with me and came over.

"*¿Es usted el* Señor Alex Perez?"

"*Sí,*" I said, "*Yo soy* Alex."

The boy handed me the package.

"*¿Es para mí?*" I said, surprised.

He said no, that the box was really for a boy named Raúl, but he was told by the person who gave it to him to put it in the hands of a man traveling with two gringo women; one old and one young. He looked at Ramona's bosom with admiration before he left.

I explained to the females that the box was for Raúl, but for some unexplained reason, I was to have it. They were curious and asked me to open it. When the toaster became visible, my future mother-in-law threw a fit.

"I smell a Russian in the kitchen," she said. "Let's pay a visit to Padre Humberto."

When Charlene was out the door, I asked Ramona what in the hell a Russian in the kitchen had to do with anything that had happened today.

"For a man who claims to be worldly, you are very naïve, Alex. Russian cooks are the antithesis of Italians. Do you get it? Mother smells a skunk."

"You mean to tell me she feels defrauded?"

She looked at me with her big dark eyes. "Alex, sometimes you amaze me."

Looking at a finger missing a wedding ring, I smiled. Hell, sometimes I amaze myself.

Chapter 7

Fairies Galore

Charlene cursed when the new sign we had erected for the orphanage came into view. I couldn't help but wonder if the jails in Mexico were as bad as we had been led to believe. I was sure we would be in one before the day was over. Keeping my freedom was important. The fact that the women smelled a rat and were mad as hell worried me. I paid the taxi driver two dollars and asked him to please wait. We hadn't moved twenty feet when he drove off. He probably smelled trouble too.

Junior came out to greet us. He was accompanied by Rosie. The crooks are still here . . . how cheeky of them. I bet they didn't expect to see us. To my chagrin, they both looked happy to see us. However, the grin on Junior's face quickly faded as Charlene grabbed him by the ear, shook him, and asked where she could find Padre Humberto.

Raúl came out and shrieked when he saw Ramona. He ran into her arms. I couldn't help but notice that her anger had been replaced by joy. Other than the occasional "psst," that shriek was the first real sound the boy had uttered since we picked him up in Tampico. Ramona was beaming with pride.

"Tell me the truth about the orphanage, Junior," said the old woman, tugging at his ear. The ragamuffin broke under pressure and told the story. I was disappointed but I didn't think I could have sustained the pain Charlene was inflicting on his ear either, so I remained cool.

"The orphanage was closed several years ago because the priest in charge died," he said. "When the police started to put the children with local families, I decided to rescue Raúl and take him with me. We were going to go out into the world and make our fortune."

"What can you tell me about Padre Humberto?" said Charlene.

"He's not a Mexican. He's from Guatemala. He was a good priest there, but they kicked him out of the church because he complained to the bishop about the way they were collecting money."

Sensing an opportunity to get on my future mother-in-law's good side, I grabbed the bull by the horns and went on the attack.

"Give me a break, Junior. No one gets defrocked because he complains about irregularities. There has to be more to this story than you are letting on. Charlene has been the orphanage's benefactor, and she deserves the whole truth."

Before he could reply I approached him, grabbed his other ear, and gave it a twist. "Ouch! Mister Alex, you are hurting me," he said with wounded pride.

Ramona glared at me. I let go of the boy's ear. With a look of bewilderment, Junior moved away from me.

"Tell me more," said Charlene.

"Padre Humberto was given a second chance by the church bosses, but when he got caught in bed with the bishop's woman, his job as a priest was over. Padre Humberto left Guatemala with a plan to enter the United States. He wanted to get a new life away from the church. On his way to Texas, he came upon the abandoned orphanage. He stayed long enough to learn about the trouble the children were having; some of them were being forced to work in the fields, others had to work as servants. Wanting to make things right with God, he became involved with reopening the orphanage. He told me it was his ticket into heaven."

"Where did you meet him?" Charlene wanted to know.

"I met him in Mérida where he was trying to collect money. I gave him a ten-dollar bill a gringo had given me for taking him to a house that kept women without panties. I have been helping him ever since."

I couldn't believe the cock-and-bull stories this kid came up with. I was about to chastise him for thinking we were fools when I realized both women had bought his story, hook, line, and sinker. This kid was good.

"Where's our car?" I asked, trying to impress the old woman.

"Pancho has it."

"Where's Pancho?" Charlene wanted to know.

"I don't know where he is. We haven't seen him, and that's the truth. He is a bandit, you know. They don't tell you where they hide."

Rosie held up Junior's hand and kissed it; then she placed a finger on his lips, cueing him to stop talking. It was time for her to take center stage.

"Pancho used to live here when he was a boy," she said. "Like Junior and Raúl, he is part of this place and one of its main bene-factors. Pancho robs the rich and gives to us. Your car will be sold in Mexico City, and part of the money will be donated to the orphanage. Do you have insurance?"

"Yes," Charlene said in a cold tone of voice.

"Well, there you are. All is well that ends well. You will get your money back, someone will get a good deal on your car, Pancho will be able to feed his family, and we will get some money to start our next project."

I grabbed my wallet. This girl was way smooth. As a matter of fact, I strongly suspected that these people were professional flim-flam artists. Junior had marked us right from the beginning as an easy touch. We were like sheep being herded to slaughter. Still, I felt a tinge of admiration for their skill and audacity, but I was not going to make it easy. I was going to see how good they really were. Ramona took the bait Rosie put on the hook. "What project are you talking about?"

"The building of a chapel," she said. "We need one because the closest one is forty miles away in San Cristóbal de las Casas."

Refusing to be swindled again by these cheeky people, I turned my attention to Junior. "If Pancho has gone to sell the car, and if you haven't seen him since the robbery, how come I got my mother's toaster back?"

"I took it from the car before you left us. I understood from the very beginning that the toaster is very important to you—that you would die for it. And when I saw that Raúl was heartbroken when Ramona said good-bye, I knew I could use it to bring you back."

Ramona broke into tears. She didn't care that we'd been lured, robbed, plucked, and skinned. All that mattered to her was being with Raúl. She was happy to have the little rascal back in her arms. Charlene had lost the anger in her face. We were doomed.

When the wayward priest finally made his appearance, I expected trouble and braced for a fight. Again, to my vexation, the scene went in a different direction. Charlene had been moved by Junior's tale and had already forgiven Humberto for his sins. I suspected his prowess in bed and the fact that he had already broken his vows of celibacy with a Guatemalan girl were reasons enough to forgive him. That girl had freed Charlene from any guilt. She was not the perpetrator anymore—only the caretaker.

I assumed that she was contemplating having another lovers' tryst. I found the hammock, rested my tired body, and started to think things out. There had to be something about priests and prisoners that seemed to elude me. What is it that propels women to get involved with them?

My keen sense of observation was rewarded when her eyes sparkled as he entered the courtyard. Padre Humberto came and greeted us with enthusiasm. He shook my hand and hugged Ramona. He kissed both of Charlene's hands and acted as though nothing bad had happened. He thanked us again for all the help we had given him with the orphanage. Junior told him we had been robbed by Pancho. The priest apologized for his friend and explained that Pancho was a sort of Mexican Robin Hood, although robbing us was not a Godly thing to do. Padre Humberto then promised to do what he could to get the car back.

"Your presence in our lives has been a blessing," he said. "I have been impressed by your kindness, your creativity, and your love."

This last part, the one about love he said while looking at Charlene and holding her hand. I was disgusted. What a scam artist.

"I want to build a chapel," he said. "However, I will not do it with money from the sale of your car. I cannot repay your love with thievery."

I couldn't believe it. Charlene was blushing. She was hanging on to his hand like her life depended on it. Then she uttered words that upheld my belief in the nonsensical saying, "God behaves in mysterious ways."

"That's all right, Humberto. I purchased automobile insurance before I entered Mexico, but I must report the robbery to the police in order to get my money back. Can you help me with this matter? The insurance company has a lot of money. They can afford to pay for my car, and I feel honored that I can be of help building your chapel."

Humberto kissed her hands again. She blushed again. I felt like puking. What a load of crap. What a hustler. I was about to protest when I noticed that Raúl was sitting on Ramona's lap, and her eyes were oozing with love. I could sense Charlene's lust from where I stood. What the hell . . . only a fool stands in front of an avalanche. I left things alone.

It took six weeks to build the chapel. I kept busy carrying lumber, hammering nails, and writing in my notebook. It seemed that everyone obtained what they wanted. I was pleasantly surprised that there were two wishes in Pancho's Box for me: I had a story, and by the looks of it, I had dodged marriage because we weren't going to Panama. Raúl had Ramona and vice versa. Padre Humberto's chapel became a reality. Charlene enjoyed the priest's amorous disposition, and Junior and Rosie had each other. I felt confident that the fairies had done their duty and were all back in the box.

One day, I took Junior aside and thanked him for releasing the fairies. "They did a good job," I said. "Now we can move on to other things."

"They're not all back in the box," he said.

"What do you mean 'they are not all back in the box'? I don't understand, but is that a problem?"

"Yes, I'm afraid so. There were two fairies for each person in the box, plus an independent one. Charlene and Humberto's are accounted for. She found a worldly purpose and love. He has his chapel and has reopened the orphanage. Charlene has been generous with her money. She knows all there is to know about everything. The woman is a saint. Together, they will make this place the envy of the region. Raúl is happy with Ramona, and she with him. However, they still each have one fairy out. You have your toaster and have avoided the trip to Panama. Your fairies are back in the box. I have helped rebuild the orphanage. It was one of my missions in life. I have something else I want very much and still have one fairy out there working for me."

"So, there are three left? What's the big deal?"

"No, there are four still out. One of them is the *diablito*. He is the worse one."

"You mean a rogue, don't you? What kind of a fairy is that?"

"It's a fairy that messes with you."

"What are you trying to tell me, Junior?"

"Please forgive me when I say this, Mister Alex. You know that I am very seldom wrong, but I don't think you are out of trouble yet. You must keep your guard up. The *diablito* may get you."

I was about to ask another dumb question but decided I had enough Mexican riddles to last the day. Still, I was curious about something. "What is the other wish you are trying to coax into your life?" I said.

"The other is for my father. I want to find him."

"You're not talking about Jimmy Buffet, are you? You can't expect me to believe he's your father, do you?"

Junior gave me a cryptic look, and then I saw a tear roll down his cheek. He turned his back to me and walked away.

Several days later, while we were having a quiet dinner on the veranda of the main building, Padre Humberto treated us to his story. It was similar to the one we had heard from Junior, but to Charlene's distress, it had a twist. Humberto had not been officially defrocked as we had been led to believe. And, the story about bedding the bishop's mistress was not true either.

"I fell out of favor with my bishop for complaining about the church's methods of raising money," he said. "The bishop had warned me several times to stop my public assault on the church or face severe consequences. Of course, I did not listen. There is a part of me that likes to rebel. Anyway, the bishop had a mistress; she was a beautiful young woman named Cecilia. She had wanted to break off the affair, but the bishop was a powerful man, and she was afraid of what he could do to her. Cecilia had a very young daughter she had conceived during an affair with a married man, who refused to accept the child as his own. She was having trouble making a living, and His Eminence, taking advantage of confessional information passed on to him by a village priest, called upon her and made her an offer she couldn't refuse. Once the relationship started, she was placed under his protection. The bishop was a controlling man. He made it impossible for her to get away. Eventually, Cecilia became mortified about the affair. She was sure God was going to punish her or her little girl for sleeping with a priest, especially one of high rank."

Padre Humberto leaned back in his chair, drank the last of his warm lemonade, lit a cigarette, blew a few circles of smoke into the air, and continued, "One day, she came to me with her problem. Since I was already in trouble with the bishop and disillusioned with the church, I decided to get involved. I planned our escape, and when the opportunity presented itself, we left Guatemala. It was our hope to reach the United States. Along the way, Cecilia developed a bad fever from an infection due to a barbed wire cut on her leg. I brought her to the hospital in San Cristóbal de las Casas, where she died. I had her daughter with me, so I visited the church and asked for asylum. At first, we were well received. They took us in, and I was able to help. When the priest learned who I was, the little girl and I were both sent away. Desperate, I approached the priest running the orphanage, and he accepted the little girl, but not me. That girl is Rosie. I abandoned the idea of going to the United States. Instead, I left for Mérida, where I earned a living doing many different things, always returning to see Rosie. When the priest died and the orphanage was closed by the authorities, I decided to reopen it. Although I do not practice the rite of celibacy, I am still a priest. And now that I have a chapel, I can conduct regular Sunday services and marry people."

Padre Humberto's last words stung me to the quick. I saw the look of complicity in Charlene's eyes. I looked at Ramona and knew the rogue fairy had just dumped on me. I knew there would be wedding bells in my immediate future after all. I had just been outwitted by a needy priest, a wily kid, and a vengeful woman. Three days later, Ramona and I were married in the new chapel.

After the wedding, we said farewell to all and boarded a bus for the island of Cozumel, where we planned to enjoy a short honeymoon. The plan was to take it easy, return, pick up Charlene, and say good-bye to everyone at the orphanage. I dreaded the separation of Ramona and Raúl, but was determined to leave the ragamuffin behind. I needed to get used to being a husband first; fatherhood was for later.

The trip was fruitful. Ramona and I had a chance to reconnect. I understood that I did love her and felt comfortable being her husband.

Seeing her lying on the Cozumel sand in her skimpy bikini bottom with her long dark hair covering large unclothed breasts brought unbridled passion to my loins. Not only was she a beauty, but she also came with a wealthy mother, and was a fantastic cook. From here on, life was going to be good. I was sure of it.

When the time came to leave the island, Ramona told me that she had received a wire from her mother.

"What does the old battleax have to say?"

"I don't believe that statement fits my mother anymore. I was hoping that you, being the observant person you claim to be, would have noticed the change in her behavior."

She was right. I knew better. Charlene's sharp edges had dulled. Ever since she hooked up with the wayward priest, Jackie the Ripper had developed a niceness never expected.

"I'm sorry. I was out of line. Please accept my apology. Charlene has turned over a new leaf. What's up?"

"Mother has left the orphanage with Padre Humberto. They have gone to Mexico City on business. There is no need for us to go all the way to San Cristóbal. I want to fly home from Cancún. Can we do it?"

"Yes, of course, but I thought you wanted to say good-bye to Raúl."

"I do, but it will only upset me, so it's best that we go home from here."

Counting my blessings and assuming that Raúl's fairy must have failed him, I agreed.

Chapter 8

The Last Fairy

Back in Houston, my life with Ramona had become dull. The adventure in Mexico had been wonderful, ruining for me what had previously been a mundane but enjoyable existence. I consoled myself by devouring my notes and writing my new novel, *Mexican Fairies*.

The guys at La Dolce Vita coffee house were envious—a sign they believed my novel was good. I felt a bestseller coming up.

One morning, as I was preparing Ramona's herbal tea, I saw Charlene driving the white 190SL into the driveway. "Ivanna the Terrible has returned to us from Mexico," I yelled. "We have a Mercedes!"

I opened the door, and there stood Raúl with Charlene. I was dumbfounded. He had a bouquet of flowers and a smile. Ramona shrieked with delight when she saw him. He handed me the flowers and then ran into her arms.

"Hello, Alex," said Charlene. "How is married life treating you?"

I could not speak. Seeing the little urchin in my house gave me a fright. After I regained my senses, I decided to investigate. "What is he doing here?"

"He came to visit Ramona. I hope that's okay with you."

"How the hell did you get him across the border?"

"Pancho moonlights as a *coyote*," she said. "Raulito crossed into McAllen yesterday. We flew out of Harlingen last night."

"You met Pancho?"

"Yes, and he is quite likeable for a bandit. He became careless and was arrested in Mexico City. Padre Humberto and I went to pay his bail and get him a lawyer. He is free now, and I'm happy to tell you he is back practicing his trade."

"You mean to tell me you sprang that crook out of jail so he could continue to rob innocent people? Are you crazy?"

"No, I am not demented. On the contrary, I understood very quickly that I needed help with the funding of Humberto's orphanage. You can't even begin to imagine how expensive it is to keep that place running."

I gave her the bad-eye. She returned it and shoved me aside. Then she opened her arms to give Ramona a hug. I prepared myself for what was to come, and when Ramona asked me if we could keep the boy, I just nodded. What the hell . . . at least he would be a quiet kid.

Ramona cried and jumped into my arms. The little rascal understood that he had been accepted and gave me a hug.

"Jeez," I mumbled, "A husband and a father, all within two months."

Charlene slapped me on the back. "You are a good man after all, Alex. I'm proud to be your mother-in-law." I gave her a civil nod.

"Did you see Junior before you left?" I asked.

"Yes. He came by and stayed for a week."

"Did he ask about me?"

"Yes . . . and he said to tell you he was trying to get his fairy back in the box. Do you know what he meant?"

"Yes, I do."

"Well?"

"Well, what?"

"What did he mean by putting his fairy back in the box?"

"I'll tell you later. Right now, I want to enjoy my entrance into fatherhood." Charlene, with a mischievous grin, turned to Raúl and told him to say something. The boy looked at Ramona and said, "Mamá, I love you." Ramona and I looked at each other in disbelief.

She dropped to her knees and began to cry. I looked at all the gush coming from her and understood what I'd done. I had unwittingly allowed Junior's apprentice into my house.

Several weeks later, I received an envelope from Miami, Florida. I opened it and laughed. Inside was a photo of Junior. He was standing next to a man that looked a lot like Jimmy Buffet. On the back of the photo was a lone sentence. "If Raúl and Ramona are together, the last fairy is back in the box."

Sometimes I allowed myself a measure of hope that the scoundrel would find his way to my home. Junior would have been proud of Raúl's progress. He had found his speech and now spoke two languages. His company had made a difference in our lives. Ramona was as happy as a lark being a mother, and Charlene and I now fought only eight or nine times a month.

I was still not sure about Junior's parentage. I was hoping the story about Jimmy being his father was factual for Junior's sake, but deep down I didn't want it to be true—for my sake.

I felt empty. Ramona had Raúl, and I wanted Junior. With an entrepreneurial son like him, a father could rest assured that he would pasture well when old. If Buffet had any sense, he'd hang on to that boy. I bet Junior could be one hell of a songwriter. I can already hear the tunes and see the song titles: "The Killing of Don Pedro's Cow," "Ramona's Chocolate Chi-Chi's," "Dancing with a Sharp-Edged Woman," and "Ballad of a Wayward Priest." And, what would certainly have to be my favorite song: "There are Fairies in Pancho's Lunchbox."

I understood (too late) that Junior did not want to be an orphan, which is why he claimed Jimmy Buffet as his father. My insensitivity to that need caused me to lose him, a cruel testament to the fact that words can hurt more than sticks and stones.

In my need to find Junior, I wrote several letters to the Jimmy Buffet's fan club asking about a Mexican kid named "Junior." Their reply was unfavorable, and no one knew anything about him. To this day, whenever there's a knock on my door, I hold my breath and hope to see his smiling face. I know that one day he will find his way here . . . I know he will. And when he does, I will have found a son.

Chapter 9

A Peeper Up a Tree: Houston 1977

"**H**oly cow, Ronson, do you see what I see?"

"No. I'm on the ground, Alex. You are the one up in the tree. What do you see?"

"She's taking off her clothes and she has huge tits."

"Damn it, Alex. Why is it that you always get the visual end of the assignment?"

"Because I'm a voyeur, and you're a listener. Do you have anything worthwhile on tape yet?"

"No, not yet, Alex. All I have is a bunch of gibberish. I hope we can wrap this up before they start screwing. I hate it when they make all those sexual noises."

"You know what's wrong with you, Ronson? You're Swiss. Sex noises are good, and so is . . . wait a minute . . . bingo! Our unfaithful husband has just come out of the bathroom in his birthday suit. Man, you ought to see the size of his boner. There's nothing like a new woman to make a man proud, huh?"

"You bet, Alex. I hope you have the long-eye lense on him."

"Yeah, buddy. The camera's doing its thing."

"If she gets on top I'm climbing the tree. I like it when the woman gets on top."

"I'll keep you informed if anything weird happens, Ronson."

"Oh no, Alex. You are not going to believe this . . ."

"What? What's going on? What is it?"

"We have a big problem. A cop with a dog and two women are coming our way."

"What do you mean, 'a cop and a dog are coming our way'? Have you given our position away, Ronson? Are we in trouble?"

"Quick, Alex! Drop the long-eye and climb down."

I dropped the surveillance camera; Ronson caught it and took off running. I tried to climb down, but the dog made it to the tree first and started to growl and bark. Shit, busted again. Kermit's going to be pissed.

"There he is, Officer," said one of the women. "The Peeping-Tom is still up in the tree."

"What? I'm not a peeper . . . I'm a tree doctor," I said with indignation.

Two hours later, I was standing in line at the River Oaks police station getting booked by Sergeant McGowan.

"Ah, Alex Perez, you're back. Caught peeping again, eh? You are incorrigible. It's the third time this year. Don't you know it's against the law to masturbate in public? You're developing quite a rap sheet. This time it's going to be expensive."

"Give me a break, Sergeant. I wasn't playing with my John Henry. I was working. I can't help the nature of my business."

One hour later, my boss, Kermit Laarsen showed up and paid my bail. This time though, instead of giving me the usual bitch session about my clumsiness, he fired me.

"I don't want you to take this personally," he said. "You know I like you, Alex. Please understand that letting you go pains me, but I can't afford you. You have become a liability. Stealth is not your thing, is it? Ronson never gets caught."

"Cut me some slack, Kermit. Sneaking around people's back-yards and taking photos is not easy work. The cops think I'm a pervert. You should see my rap sheet. My wife keeps harassing me to get a *real* job. Ramona has become a bear to live with."

"Why? What's wrong with working for Laarsen's Security Services? I have a reputable company. Or, well, I did until I hired you. You are giving me a bad reputation. You need to find employment elsewhere."

"I can't believe you're firing me. You know I love my work."

"Let's get real, Alex. You're not meant to be a private eye. You get too involved in your work. I'm not paying you to peep. Your job is to take one or two incriminating photos and get out. You'll be fine. You're like a cat, and you'll land on your feet."

I drove home feeling downhearted, betrayed by a man I respected and considered to be a friend. Hell, he was right, though, for stealth is not my style. I got off the freeway, made a right turn on Wesleyan Street, and came face-to-face with a most familiar, but distasteful sight—zillions of cars going nowhere. Man, I hated Houston traffic.

I sat in my car wondering how Ramona was going to react to my getting fired. Will she smile and give me pussy? Hell, she should kiss me. The damn woman had repeatedly admonished me for my choice of profession and I was now fired. Yet I didn't feel lucky today. I suspected there wouldn't be any love action in the cards for me. What was probably in store for me would be the dreaded out-of-a-job-again look. I hated that. Ramona had a way of berating me with those dark eyes that cut me to the quick. Although she didn't think it was morally correct to make a living peeping into people's windows, she did believe in kicking a dog when it was down, so I expected to be chastised. What a pain in the ass she had become.

Since I was stuck in traffic and time was the only thing I had plenty of, I began to prepare my defense. I was going to remind her of her complaint about how Raúl couldn't be proud of his father because the job lacked decency. What a joke. She didn't know that during one of my days off, while I was babysitting the kid, Kermit called and sent me on an emergency assignment. I couldn't leave Raúl home alone, so I took him with me to check on a doctor who had a thing for one of his patients. The man was meeting the woman at her house for lunch. She was single and lived alone. I paid a friend of mine forty bucks to lend me his Houston Power and Light work shirt and truck for an hour. I took a king-sized T-bone steak from the fridge and fed it to the guard dog the woman kept in the back yard. Then, with Raúl in tow, I climbed a tree that offered us a good view of the back bedroom window. You should have seen the little bugger's eyes pop out when the blonde walked in naked. Raúl keeps asking me to take him along ever since, but I have to refuse. His education had to be monitored.

I was not enjoying my life these days. Ever since Ramona became a mother, she stopped being the girl I loved. In the old days, she would give me plenty of love action. I got plenty of discourses these days on proper behavior for a man my age. Hell, I'm only thirty. I am acting my age.

The traffic started to move. I turned right on Richmond Avenue. When I got close, I crossed my fingers, hoping Ramona was off shopping with Raúl. I didn't feel like explaining why I was home early. Nevertheless, any hope I had nurtured of avoiding unwanted conversation faded. Her damn car was in the driveway. Not only was she home, but she had company. I didn't recognize the Cadillac that was parked on my side of the garage. Usually, I'd make a ruckus if someone parked in my spot, but today I wanted to keep a low profile. I parked the Mercedes next to the sidewalk.

The fence door was unlocked. I walked inside and looked for Poppy, but the stupid mutt was nowhere in sight. Some guard dog. I sneaked a peek through one of the front windows to see who had dropped in for a visit, and, to my mortification, Charlene was sitting with Ramona in the living room.

I held my breath and opened the door. "Hello, Alex," said Charlene. "I understand you were fired today."

The hairs on the back of my neck stood up. I clenched my fists and prepared to battle, but Ramona quickly interfered.

"I'm glad you don't work there anymore, Alex. That was not suitable work for a man like you."

Before Charlene could take that statement and abuse me with it, Ramona cut her off at the pass. I was impressed, as she usually fanned the coals while Hanna the Cannibal roasted me.

"Mother is back from her Jamaican vacation," she said with winged words. "Be nice . . . she caught a bug and doesn't feel well."

Ramona made a quick exit to the bathroom. Charlene sneered at me. I looked for a meat cleaver.

"Listen to me, Alex. I have a proposition for you. I suggest you accept it, since you have no job, and there's money in it for you. Stop by my house after dinner today, and I'll give you the details. Come alone." She smiled, stood up, and left. Good riddance.

As the new Cadillac pulled onto Richmond Avenue, I smiled. She has a bad time on her vacation and buys a new car to soothe her frayed feelings. How nice it must be to have an ample supply of money.

The proposed meeting she had suggested smelled of trouble. The job offer would undoubtedly be difficult and would not pay enough. Charlene's generosity always stopped short of my pockets. I had a mind to stay home and say screw her. Nothing good would come of it, anyway.

"Did mother leave?" said Ramona from the safety of the bathroom.

"Yes, thank God. That woman has such an abrasive personality."

"Being grateful is not your thing, huh?"

"Give me a break, Ramona. Everything she does for us comes with a price."

"That may well be, but she takes care of us. You can't seem to be able to hang on to a job . . ."

That attitude galled me because I was chasing a literary career, and steady employment interfered with my creative process. How can a person write when he's up to his ass in work? I ignored her.

Unfortunately, my position was precarious; the private eye job I was fired from was the third one in the last eight months. I was walking on thin ice.

The time to meet with Charlene arrived. I told Ramona I was going out for an evening ride. The fact she didn't question me showed her complicity. Grudgingly, I took the bicycle out of the garage and pedaled down Kirby Street toward River Oaks. It was easier to deal with the Houston traffic on a bike. When the House of the Living Dead came into view, I cursed my luck.

The large iron gate was open. I was expected, an ominous sign. Feeling the hand of fate upon my shoulder, I prepared for the worst and walked the bike inside the mansion.

To my surprise and chagrin, blocking my path was Ramona's dog, Poppy. The animal had developed the bad habit of walking between both houses. One day I was going to see his body splattered on the street. Poppy saw me and took a menacing stance. As I came closer, he began to growl. I could never figure out what his problem was; you would think that after three years of living with me, he would stop treating me like a stranger. Keeping a leery eye on the stupid mutt, I walked past him and toward the green door.

I cursed my luck, inhaled deeply, and rang the bell. I was surprised to see Charlene because the maid usually opened the door. Charlene had curlers on her head and was wearing her housecoat. She gave me her usual crocodile smile and invited me inside.

"What's up?"

"I have a problem you can help me with," Charlene said.

"Is it dangerous?"

"Yes, there is some danger involved, but I can assure you it's minimal. The job requires some travel and pays five thousand dollars plus expenses."

"What's the deal?" I asked cautiously.

"I need you to break a man out of a foreign jail."

"Oh, is that it?" I said sarcastically.

"Yes. I figured that a man with your disposition and idle time would be perfect for the job."

I looked at her. I couldn't believe that a good Hispanic man like me was stupid enough to marry into that crazy family. The Addams Family had nothing on these weirdos.

"Won't Ramona object?" I said.

"Only if you fail to return, but we both know that is an improbability, don't we? You're like a bad penny, Alex. You always turn up."

What a bitch. "You are correct, Charlene. I will always be around because I know it chaps your ass."

Chapter 10

I'm not going. I don't care if mother is going. I'm not going back to Mexico, and neither is Raulito. You can go with her if you like. It's your skin. I'll give you my blessing."

"Listen, Ramona, I'm not crazy about going to the corner grocery store with Charlene, but she's determined to see Padre Humberto again. He's in a Guatemalan jail. Do you understand how far that is? We'll kill each other before we get across the Texas border. You need to come. Besides, I need Raúl for . . ."

"No way, Alex, he's not leaving my sight, and I am not going anywhere that requires a passport, period."

"Fine. Let your mother go on alone, then. It's no sweat off my brow. She can get herself killed for all I care. If you are not going, neither am I."

Disgusted with the whole affair, I jumped on my bicycle and rode to the café. I needed to work out some tension over coffee and a newspaper.

I smiled when I saw my good friend Carlos Laughing Crow sitting at our usual table. Actually, Carlos' last name was "Mansfield." His grandmother was a descendant from an Apache Chief named "Running Wolf." She was the one that gave him his Indian name.

Carlos had an identity problem, though—a matter that annoyed him. Not only was he a white man sporting green eyes, but his hair was light brown and curly. He didn't look at all like an Indian, yet he was intent on being one. Carlos loved to promote his indigenous culture. He wore his hair long, tied to his forehead by a brown leather strap. He carried a leather pouch and never used mainstream shoes. He preferred what he called "more traditional" footwear, such as sandals or moccasins. Carlos was also a product of the fifties Beatnik era. He was forty-nine, a published poet, and a homosexual.

"Hey, Kemo Sabe, how's tricks?" I asked.

"Fuck off, Alex."

I smiled, pulled a chair up, and sat down. "Hey, chief, I have a problem to discuss. You got a minute?"

"Don't call me 'chief,' and cut the 'Kemo Sabe' crap. You know I hate it when you mock my heritage. You don't hear me addressing you, *Hey, bato, ¿qué pasa?* I treat you with respect, and I expect the same."

I looked at him and wondered what was wrong. We were buds. Although I knew he hated the Indian-baiting thing, he usually let me slide.

"What's wrong, Carlos?"

"I'm about to get evicted from my apartment," he said. "The fucking landlord has given me till the end of the month to get out."

"Can he legally do that?"

"I'm three months in arrears. I have no legal leg to stand on."

"What are you planning to do about a place to stay?"

"I have no money or job and no intention of imposing on the few friends I have left."

"Well, what does that mean?"

He opened his jacket; I saw a pistol stuck in his belt.

"Are you crazy? What are you going to do with that? Rob a convenience store?"

"You've been reading my mail? Yes, that's what I'm going to do. I'm going to hit a Lone Star convenience store. Everybody robs them, so why can't I?"

"Which one?"

"What difference does it make?"

"You're right . . . it makes no difference. The fact that you're planning to rob one is what's important. Can I talk you out of it?"

"I need twelve hundred dollars right away. Do you have it?"

Twelve hundred dollars was a small fortune for an unemployed man. When Kermit fired me, I barely had two hundred in my bank account.

"No, I'm sorry. I'm temporarily low on funds."

He mumbled something and stood up.

"Where are you going?" I asked.

"I have to see a man about a horse," he said, then mumbled some more and left for the bathroom. I've often wondered where that saying came from and what it had to do with taking a piss. Everyone in Texas uses it, including me, but it makes absolutely no sense. It must have its roots somewhere in cowboy lore.

I tried to figure out what I could do to help Carlos. Then I saw a poster of Uncle Sam on the wall. The bearded man was pointing my way, telling me he wanted me. All of a sudden, his face became that of Charlene. Bingo! An idea shot through me like a burning bullet. I knew how to keep my friend from becoming an inmate at the Texas Correctional facility in Huntsville and at the same time take care of the un-scratchable itch that had been bothering me. When Carlos returned, I had a major grin going.

"What's your deal, Alex? Is my misery making you happy?"

"Listen up, Carlos. I have a way out for you. Come close and listen to what I have to say, and please don't interrupt until I'm finished. I have been offered the lead role in an adventure."

He gave me his stoic Indian look.

"Okay," I said, "Here's the deal . . ."

He sipped his cappuccino without speaking. When I finished, he grabbed me by the shirt and pulled me to him. His eyes were on fire, and his left cheek kept twitching.

"You're crazier than a loon, Alex. Here I am thinking of robbing a convenience store barely four blocks from here—a dangerous enough task—and you have the audacity to propose saving my ass by asking me to go to a foreign country and help you break a priest out of prison? It's a crazy scheme. Do you think I'm insane?"

"Cut the drama, Carlos. It's less dangerous."

"Less dangerous, my ass. In the convenience store, there will probably be one, maybe two unarmed Pakistanis behind a counter. In Guatemala there will be a contingent of soldiers with automatic weapons guarding the place. I'll take my chances with the local stick-up. Thank you very much, but I believe I'll have to pass."

"You need to trust me on this, Carlos. You really want to sign up for the jailbreak. A good foreign adventure will do wonders for your attitude. I have all the angles covered. Besides, if you enlist, I'll have an advance for you in a couple of days. You can save your place. What do you say, old friend?"

"I'd rather bathe in boiling oil than go with you to Guatemala."

"Cut it out, Carlos. You're not taking this proposition seriously. This deal is good for both of us. You need to trust me and sign up. I need you."

I spent the next day fine-tuning the plan. I had promised Carlos up-front money, and I wanted to make a good profit. The task was worth more than the measly five thousand Charlene was offering. Armed with numbers, I paid Cinderella's evil stepmother another visit.

"You have a lot of nerve asking me for eight thousand dollars, Alex. Do you think money grows on trees? I offered you five thousand plus expenses. That's plenty. You better accept it."

"Yes, I believe money grows on trees, and I know you have at least one in your back yard. I'm disappointed, Charlene. I figured you'd be jumping all over this offer."

"Why would I? It's more than I care to pay. Let's face it, Alex, I can fly to Guatemala, hire a private detective, and bribe a judge for half the amount you are asking."

"Maybe you can, or maybe you can't. First of all, you don't speak the language. Second, you have no clue about the culture. Third, you don't know a soul in Guatemala City. Fourth, the head of the Catholic diocese, his eminence Bishop Omar Ramírez brought charges against Padre Humberto. Your priest was arrested in Mexico for operating an orphanage without a license. He entered the country illegally, was arrested, and then extradited to Guatemala. Your Padre is now facing what amounts to first-degree negligent homicide charges. Plus, he has been blamed for the death of the bishop's squeeze, Cecilia. That carries a stiff sentence. If he is convicted, you can kiss him good-bye. By the time he gets out, both of you will be too old to enjoy board games. Now, let's throw in the fact that you have a lousy personality, no sense of character judgment, and look rich to boot. I can tell you with a good degree of accuracy that every conman in the area will be trying to help you spend your money. You need to take my offer."

She gave me the bad-eye, but refrained from insulting me. She knew I was right on all counts. I smiled, for I had managed to get my hand in her purse. Her eyes told me I had gotten the raise.

Charlene had made the mistake of falling in love with Padre Humberto; that, in itself, was a bad deal. Not only is fooling around with a priest bad business, but it has no future. They are married to the church, and they drink bad wine.

"After all he did for those kids," she said with sarcasm, "I can't believe the Mexican authorities arrested him and closed the orphanage."

"Charlene, be serious. Your wayward priest messed with the bishop's squeeze. He helped Cecilia escape from his bed. Now, the long arm of the church is messing with him. It's a clear-cut case of tit for tat. Humberto should have kept to his original plan of coming to the United States. Here, the power of the church is not so influential. It's strong in Mexico, and it's really powerful in Catholic Guatemala. Your Padre can kiss his freedom good-bye unless you can find a really good lawyer that can bribe someone to let him out of jail. Once he is released, we can work our plan and spirit him out of the country. You need to be aware that this whole affair is going to cost you the better part of fifteen thousand dollars. We will probably spend six thousand between bribes and the lawyer's alone. Do you want your priest back? Is he worth fifteen grand?"

"What do I get for the first eight thousand?" she said.

"I need the money to put together a team. You don't expect me to do it alone, do you? I have two individuals in mind, and they don't work for free. I'm only charging you eight thousand plus expenses, for heaven's sake. In any book, the fee is cheap at twice the price. It's a son-in-law discount as it is, so take it or leave it. I'm not going to cut the fee down any further."

"Tell me again, Alex. Besides you and me, who else is crazy enough to be a part of this escapade?"

"I have recruited a half-breed American Apache Indian. His name is Carlos Laughing Crow, and he will be our scout. I also have a Mexican national in mind because I need an inside contact."

"Sounds like a motley group to me."

"Listen, Charlene, what do you expect for eight grand? Charles Bronson and Sylvester Stallone?"

She gave me a cryptic look, shook my hand, and showed me the door.

"Who else is dumb enough to go traipsing with you on this madcap escapade?" Ramona demanded to know.

"If you must satisfy your sense of curiosity, your mother hired Carlos Laughing Crow. Our job is to find Padre Humberto and free him."

"When did you get involved in this ludicrous scheme?"

"Your mother hired me a week ago."

"Does she know that Carlos is a pot-smoking, old hippie, faggot kind of guy?"

"Well, no, not exactly."

"What does she know?"

"I told her he was an ex-Army Indian scout."

"And she believed you?"

"Yes, she did. I didn't lie. He is an Indian. He was in the Army. And, he is in the Boy Scouts. He holds the rank of Eagle Grand Master or something like that."

"I can't believe they let a homosexual into the Boy Scouts."

"Hey, what's with you? All of a sudden you've become a member of the Moral Majority? Give the guy a break."

"I suppose you expect me to keep quiet while you swindle Mother out of eight grand. Are you nuts? I'm not going to let you do it. I'm going to tell her. Who's the third partner in the group? You said there were three going with her."

"Junior," I said.

"Junior?"

"Yes."

"Our Junior? Are you serious? But how—"

"Yes, ma'am, as serious as a heart attack."

"You've got to be kidding!"

"Why?"

"He's a kid! You're going to break a priest out of jail in a foreign country with an old hippie and a kid? I'm telling Mother."

"No, you're not."

"Why not? She's my mother, and I need to protect her interest. I have the right to tell her what's going on."

"If you do, I will file for divorce, and you'll have to explain Raúl's presence in the States. He has no papers because Charlene sneaked him into the country. Your mother and you will be fined for harboring him, and Raúl will be deported."

Feeling smug after that verbal barrage, I continued to express my demands: "You will stay here and prepare yourself to come to our aid with bail money. Something might go wrong with the plan."

"Something might go wrong with the plan? Have you lost your mind, Alex? At best, it's a Mad Hatter's Delight. You will all end up arrested! I'm not going to Guatemala to bail anybody out. You might be able to blackmail me into remaining quiet, but you can't make me leave Texas."

"Don't be so sure of that," I said.

"I'm as sure of that as I'm sure of anything. No one in this house except for you will be leaving town."

She went into our bedroom and slammed the door. I heard the lock click and knew she was in for the night. Good riddance. I sat at my desk and began to make more adjustments to the plan. I needed Raúl with me, and there had to be a way to get him away from Ramona and out of the country. I worked on every detail.

The following Wednesday, when the clock hit eleven, I packed my traveling bag and put the plan in motion.

"Psst . . . psst . . . Raúl, wake up."

"*¿Qué quieres*, Papi?"

"I want you to get dressed quietly and meet me outside. We're going on a trip. Don't wake your mother, for God's sake. She's not coming with us."

"*¿Adónde vamos*, Papi?"

"We're going to Mexico."

"*¿Para qué?*"

"We're going to find Junior."

"Papi, *¿sabes dónde está* Junior?"

"No, I have no idea where he is."

"Papi, *¿cómo lo vamos a encontrar?*"

"I'm putting you back on the streets, son. You need to earn your keep. You are going to find him."

"*¿Cuanto me vas a pagar?*"

"I'm not paying you anything. You are my son. You work for free."

"*Yo quiero cien dólares.*"

"A hundred bucks! That's highway robbery. You're worse than Junior. I'm not paying you that kind of money. I'll give you fifty, and that is my final offer. Take it or leave it."

"*Cien dólares o me quedo aquí.*"

"Okay, okay . . . I'll pay it. You are a swindler, Raúl. I'm ashamed of you. I'm not taking you with me to peep at naked women anymore. Hurry up and pack some clothes, but whatever you do please do not wake your mother."

Chapter 11

On the Road Again

As we drove down State Highway 59 South, I kept mulling over the plan. First and foremost, we needed to find Junior, and I was banking he was still in Mexico. I never bought the story about Jimmy Buffet being his father. The photo he sent me was indisputable evidence that an encounter had taken place, but it had to have been brief—nothing more than a photo-shoot between the star and a young fan. When no one in the singer's fan club knew of the kid, I knew his efforts of latching on to Jimmy failed. Poor kid, all he wanted was a father. By God, he was going to get one. I missed him.

I assumed finding Junior would prove to be the toughest part of the plan. Once we snagged the ragamuffin, the second stage would be simpler. All we needed to do was hook up with Charlene, who was going to meet us at the Hotel Pacaya in Mérida.

Originally, she had planned to fly to Guatemala City and wait for us there. She wanted to interview a few lawyers and have one ready when we arrived. I nixed that suggestion. I was of the opinion that if we were to be successful in this clandestine operation, my cohorts needed to acclimate themselves to the Latin American way of life. It was important to travel within and get a handle on the culture. To my surprise, she agreed.

Charlene had not lost her sharp edges. She still cut me whenever possible. I was hoping her love for the wayward priest had dulled them, but that was not the case. She was still a bitch. However, docility from a woman like her was repugnant to me. I missed the verbal jabs we used to have. Life is simpler when things remain the same.

When I told her I planned to recruit Junior and when I introduced her to Carlos Laughing Crow, she did not berate me. Charlene confided that she had a touch of Indian blood herself from her mother's side of the family. She felt confident that Carlos was going to be an asset, even though he seemed to be a tad older than she expected and appeared to be out of shape for an adventure of this nature. She understood the wisdom of finding Junior and had no problem with kidnapping Raúl. She thought that was a capital idea.

"Not only will the kid find Junior, but it will force Ramona out of Texas," she said. "She'd be mad as hell, but so what? If the final goal is a good one, all avenues to get there are allowed."

"I'm with you, Charlene. You need to leave Ramona some money so she can take on the role of the U.S. Cavalry, just like in the old Western movies, and come to our rescue just before danger deals us a deadly hand."

"I thought you said the plan is foolproof?"

"I'm speaking hypothetically. Don't get all worked up."

The plan, in theory, was a good one. We had already bought a big used American car—a blue 1969 Chevy Impala. We were going to drive it through Mexico, Belize, and Guatemala. Once we reached Guatemala City, we'd hire a lawyer, set bail, and flee.

I was amazed that Charlene had been willing to spend a small fortune and then risk her freedom in order to spring her lover from the clutches of the Catholic Church. The Reverend Martin Luther would have been proud of her; for striking a blow against the Catholics was every Protestant's duty.

Once we freed Padre Humberto and were back in Mexico, we'd get in touch with Pancho and have him put his *coyote* hat back on so he could sneak Padre Humberto and Raúl into Texas.

Feeling good about things, I drove until we reached the Texas-Mexican border.

Before we made it to the border bridge, I stopped the car and told Raúl to get in the trunk. There was a long line ahead of us. Carlos started to worry about the kid in the trunk.

"Aren't we going to get into trouble if the U.S. border guards find the boy?"

"Yes, if they open the trunk we're in trouble," I said. "Raúl can't ride in the front seat because he has no papers. We have to take that chance."

"I don't want to get arrested before we begin this mad-cap escapade," Carlos said.

"Don't worry, my friend. No one sneaks *into* Mexico *from* the States. Don't you know anything?"

We crossed the U.S.-Mexico border at McAllen and began our search for Junior in Reynosa, Mexico. He was nowhere to be found, so we drove to Tampico and called on the owner of El Pelicano Loco, but he had not seen the boy since we were last there. We continued on to Veracruz and scoured the tourist areas without any success. Tired, we booked a hotel room at the Papagayo. That evening after supper, we gathered at the hotel bar to discuss where to go next. I wanted to look for Junior in Villa Hermosa, but Raúl insisted we go on to Mérida. After quizzing him, the boy dropped a bomb on me. Junior had family there.

"I thought Junior was an orphan?" I said.

"No, Junior *tiene una tía que vive en Mérida.*"

"What's with this kid anyway?" asked Carlos. "He won't speak to me, and he speaks to you only in Spanish."

"Raúl has always been a strange kid. If you want to get anywhere with him, offer him a Marlboro . . . he loves them."

"How old is he?"

"I'm not sure. He claims to be ten."

"Claims to be? Isn't he your adopted son? Don't you know his age?"

"No, I don't know how old he is. And no, he's not my kid. He's Ramona's kid. Raúl is more of a young friend. He's peculiar and lies a lot. You have to take what he says in stride. Offer him a cigarette, and you'll make his day."

"I'm not offering the kid a cigarette. It's not proper. Besides, I only have two smokes left."

"That's two more than I have. Why don't you give me one?"

"I'd rather not. If you want to smoke, why don't we fire up some reefers?"

"You smuggled pot into Mexico! Are you crazy, Carlos?"

"No, I didn't bring any. You think I'm stupid? No way I'm smuggling dope into a place where it grows wild. I was hoping you had."

"I'm not stupid either. Listen, Carlos, I have spent plenty of time in Mexico lately, and I can tell you that I've never seen any marijuana growing in the wild. I'll get the kid to score some for you."

"The kid smokes dope?"

"He's been pinching my bag on a regular basis. I wanted to complain, but the urchin would have told Ramona, and she would have flushed it down the toilet."

"I don't want the kid to score any grass for me. It's not proper. Why don't you tell him to get it for you? Then, if you like, you can share it with me."

"I'll ask him to do it when we get to Mérida."

That being settled, I turned to Raúl. "Are you sure Junior has an aunt in Mérida?"

"*Sí*, Tía María *vive en Mérida.*"

"Where in Mérida does she live?"

"*Ella trabaja en el Hotel Roma en la calle Cuarenta y tres.*"

"What did he say?" Carlos wanted to know.

"He said Junior has an aunt that works in a hotel in Mérida."

"And you believe him? I thought you said he was a liar."

"Listen to me, old friend. I said the kid lies a lot. I did not say he was a liar, and there is a difference. You obviously don't have any experience being a father. If the story turns out to be a lie, we will be in Mérida, a nice place to hang out while we wait for Charlene. While we are there, I'll get him to score us some pot, and I'm sure he can take us to a place where they keep women without panties."

"I'm not going into a whorehouse to pick up any disease," he said. "Besides, I'm not inclined to go that way."

"I'm sure they have male prostitutes," I said. And as soon as I said it, I regretted it because Raúl's eyes bugged out. He quickly moved away from Carlos.

"Papi, ¿ese hombre es un maricón?"

"No, he is not a queer. I was just kidding."

I gave Carlos a stern look. "He will not travel with *maricones,*" I said. "The kid is weird that way. He has a phobia of faggots. Tell him you were kidding about not wanting a woman without panties."

"I'm not telling him any such thing," he said, as he crossed his arms over his chest.

"Yes, you are."

"No, I'm not."

"If Raúl refuses to travel with us, we will not be able to find Junior, and he is the key to this operation. Are you with me, Carlos? You and I—we—need to be on the same page for this operation to succeed. Please concentrate on the money."

He gritted his teeth and looked at the boy with fire in his eyes. "Okay, Raúl, I want a woman without panties."

"Good man," I said.

"Papi, ¿estás seguro que no es un maricón?"

"Yes, I'm positive. Carlos is not a queer."

We finally made it to Mérida. I was glad to be there again. We found a hotel, parked the car, and booked two rooms. After a short rest we waved down a taxi. I was tired of driving, so we asked the driver to take us to Hotel Roma. By the look of displeasure the cab driver gave us, I felt that going to this hotel with a kid was a problem, so I asked him what type of hotel it was. He said it was a whorehouse.

When Raúl called me Papi and asked if he could buy a woman, too, the driver glared at me through the rearview mirror. I gave the cabbie a fiver for a two-dollar ride and hoped that by overpaying him he would think me to be a better man.

We walked inside Hotel Roma and met Junior's aunt. María was a portly woman of about forty. She had a thick coat of makeup on, and her dark roots could use another shot of blonde hair dye.

"*Buenas tardes,* Señora María," I said, "I'm looking for your nephew, Junior. Do you know where I can find him?"

She smiled and escorted us into her office, informing us she was the brothel manager and that she wasn't Junior's blood aunt. She seemed glad to see Raúl. María gave him a bear hug and planted a kiss that left a bright red lip mark on his cheek. After greeting the boy, she turned her attention my way and stared for a moment. When she made the connection, the fat broad broke into a grin.

"You must be Señor Alex Perez. How good to meet you. Junior has spoken about you. He is very fond of you."

"I am fond of him," I said, "Where can I find him?"

"He is upstairs with Carmen. I will send someone to tell him he has visitors."

The fat woman looked at us and grinned. "While we are waiting for Junior to come down, can I talk you two handsome and virile men into enjoying some female affection? Our girls are clean, friendly, and very young. It will only cost you fifty dollars each for an hour of immeasurable pleasure."

"Okay, I'm in." I said, trying not to sound too eager.

"*Yo también,*" said Raúl. All three of us stared at Carlos, who was visibly upset. I glared at him, and Raúl whispered to María, "*Creo que él es maricón.*"

"He's not a homo," I said. "He's shy."

I glared at Carlos again and took him aside. "You need to buy a girl. I don't care if you only play tiddlywinks with her, but it's important to Raúl."

Carlos glared back but nodded in agreement. That being settled, I was happy to pay María one hundred and fifty dollars. I made a mental note to charge this escapade to my expense account. María smiled and gave me back twenty-five.

"Raulito is not a grown man yet, so he only pays half price."

As we left her office, I whispered to Carlos, "Child rates at a brothel? Man, are we out of our environment." Then I noticed he was wet with perspiration.

"Don't worry yourself to death, old friend. If anything, you can get a good hour-long body massage."

"Fifty is a lot for a body massage," he said. "I'm glad you're footing the bill."

"Listen, Carlos, a plain massage cost forty in the States, more than that if you want them to play with your John Henry. Don't you know anything?"

We walked into the hotel bar and were immediately approached by a dozen women that weren't as young as we had been led to believe, but heaven-sent nonetheless. We picked one each and climbed the stairs to find a room. One hour later, we were back downstairs in the lobby, and Carlos had a grin on his face.

"What's with the smile?" I said.

"I didn't think I had it in me," he said. "It's been a lifetime since I've loved a woman."

Raúl looked at him with pride in his eyes. I gave him the thumbs-up sign. María came and escorted us back into her office where we found Junior. Raúl shrieked and ran into his arms. They hugged for a moment, and then Junior turned his attention to me.

"Hola, Mister Alex. You don't know how good it is to see you." I opened my arms and gave him a hug. I had found my son.

The following day, we made arrangements to meet Charlene after lunch at the air-conditioned bar in Pacaya Hotel.

"Well, well . . . I can't believe it," she said to me on the sly. "You actually found the little rascal."

"I told you I would."

"Hello, Junior," she said. "It's good to see you are alive and well."

"Hola, Señora Charlene. How's life in Texas?"

"Lonely . . . I miss Humberto. Are you aware of his situation?"

"Yes, I am. I know everything about everything that matters to me. He is the reason I am in Mérida. I'm trying to raise money for a rescue attempt. I have managed to get some, but I need more."

Oh brother, here we go again. Once a hustler, always a hustler. I put a hand on my wallet instinctively. As expected, Charlene took the bait.

"How much money have you raised? How much more do you need?"

"I have three hundred, and Carmen has five, but I need one thousand more."

"Who's Carmen, and what is your plan?" Charlene wanted to know.

"She's a hooker," I said, speaking out of turn.

He looked at me with hurt eyes. "She's my sister, and she works at Hotel Roma."

"I thought you were an orphan," Charlene said. Before she could continue with her inquisition, a matronly looking waitress came, and we ordered a round of margaritas plus a cherry Coke for Raúl. Trying to spare Junior the third degree, I tried to change the conversation, but Charlene was focused.

"I thought you were an orphan?" she repeated.

"I'm a private person. There are a lot of things about me that you don't know. Like everybody, I have a business life and a personal life. For business, I am an orphan. In real life, I have a sister, and her name is Carmen. When our mother died, she became responsible for taking care of me. We left our home and tried to make a living in Mérida, but she had no money-making skills, and I was too young to be of any real help. Eventually, she found work at the Hotel Roma, but I could not stay with her, so she placed me in the orphanage where I met Padre Humberto and Rosie."

Charlene looked at me. "Why did you call Junior's sister a hooker?"

"Hotel Roma is a brothel," I said.

Suddenly, Raúl's bug eyes popped out and he shrieked, "¡Mamá!" I turned, and, to my horror, I saw Ramona entering the bar. I was in big trouble. How in hell did she find us so quickly? She came in and hugged Raúl, sat down, greeted her mother, Junior, and Carlos and gave me the bad-eye.

The waitress came back with our drinks and took Ramona's order. She wanted two tequila shots with a Sangrita chaser, which is mescal mixed with tomato and lemon juice. I knew she was spoiling for a fight, so I kept a cautious eye on her.

Without having the decency to first make small talk, Ramona dove into the reason for her arrival. "Were you involved in the kidnapping of Raulito?" she asked her mother.

"Certainly not," said Charlene. "Bringing Raulito along was Alex's idea. I was under the impression that Junior was to be the only kid involved."

What a lying bitch. I couldn't believe she said that. "That is not entirely true," I protested.

"Well, he's not going any further, I'm taking him home," said Ramona.

"No, you are not." I said.

"Yes, asshole, I am. And I dare you to try and stop me."

"Señora Ramona," interjected Junior. "You gringos think you own everything, including Mexican citizens. Raúl belongs here. This is his country. You can't force him to leave with you, and you can't take him out of Mexico legally. He can leave on his own free will if he wants. Here in Mexico, no one is forced to do anything."

They stared at each other for a moment. Ramona was measuring Junior's resolve. Understanding she needed another approach, she turned her attention toward her little boy.

"Raulito," she said, "don't you want to go home with me?"

"Yes, Mamá, I would love to go home with me, but I can't do it right now. I earned one hundred dollars from Papi for sneaking out of the house and finding Junior. Now I want to help him find Padre Humberto. I want to go on the rescue mission."

As soon as the boy finished staking me to a burning cross, Ramona lunged over the table, knocking the drinks and breaking the glasses. I had been sold out by my very own son.

I didn't react fast enough, and the damned woman managed to grab hold of my shirt. I tried to pull away, but she wouldn't let go. In a flash, a man with a club came and hit Ramona on the shoulder, bringing Charlene and Raúl into the fray. My mother-in-law jumped the bouncer from behind, and Raúl started to kick him. The waitress came back with Ramona's order and saw the melee. She set the tray down on an adjoining table, drank one of Ramona's tequila shots, chased it with the Sangrita, and then pulled Charlene off the bouncer, knocking her down.

Thinking this was a prime opportunity to endear myself to my wife and Charlene, I jumped the waitress. Carlos and Junior stayed out of the fracas. Someone called the cops, and we were arrested for brawling in a bar.

Inside the crammed rickety paddy wagon, Charlene was bristling with indignation. "I can't believe you paid Raulito one hundred dollars. You charged me eight thousand!"

Raúl's eyes bugged out. "You got eight thousand dollars and gave me only one hundred? I can't believe you called me a thief."

I couldn't believe it. The boy had actually spoken to me in English. I beamed with pride.

"You only asked for a hundred, son. I can't help it if you work cheap."

Ramona cursed and lunged at me again. When the wagon arrived at the station and they opened the door, I had Ramona in a headlock, and Charlene in a scissor-lock with my legs. Raúl had me by the throat from behind. The policeman hit me with his nightstick. I complained about the blow and explained that one woman was my wife, the other my mother-in-law, and the kid was my stepson. He apologized for interfering in a family matter.

We were brought before the officer in charge of the station. Junior and Carlos were already there waiting for us. We were chastised for being ugly gringos. The officer said that we were forbidden from having anymore family reunions in a bar, and if we ever violated that order while in Mérida, we would be locked in a jail cell. He told us our friends had paid the fines, so we were free to go.

As we filed out of the station, Junior approached me. "Mister Alex, I can't believe you let that old waitress beat you up. I was so embarrassed."

"That was not an old waitress, Junior. That was a man dressed as a woman. She hit me with the force of a mule kick. However, you would have been proud of me, had you been inside the police wagon. I defended myself very well in there against what appeared to be immeasurable odds."

Carlos took me aside and immediately started to complain about how much this adventure was costing him.

"You owe me six hundred and fifty dollars. Junior told me his money was hidden under a rock in a cemetery and that his sister would only give us her money if she could come along. She was working, and we couldn't wait for her shift to end, so I paid the fines."

"What? That's a fortune! I can't believe it cost that much to fight in a Mexican bar! How did they arrive at that figure?"

"The fine for fighting in a bar is one hundred dollars for each adult. There was an additional charge for being a foreigner. That cost another hundred each. They charged fifty for the local kid."

"Juvenile discount. I love this country." I said.

We cleaned up and met for dinner. Charlene refunded Carlos his money. She paid for mine also, given the fact that I had gotten into trouble by coming to her rescue. Before we met for dinner, Junior and I managed to have a few minutes together in private. I wanted to ask him what happened with Jimmy Buffet but decided against it. I had already hurt his feelings when I called his sister a whore. I did ask him if he would consider, after this escapade was over, coming to Houston and staying with us for a while. He told me he would sleep on it and let me know later. We ordered our meal and washed it down with lemonade. When Junior started to explain the plan, Ramona groaned. He looked at her. "Don't you like him?"

"Who are you talking about?" she asked.

"Padre Humberto. Don't you like him?"

"Yes, I like him fine, but I don't want anything to happen to Raulito."

"Nothing will happen to him, I promise. His job in the plan is to be just what he is—a kid. Nobody pays any attention to kids. He will be the perfect lookout."

"Hey, I'm running this show," I said.

Ramona, sensing an opportunity to humiliate me, went on the offensive: "All in favor of hiring Junior to be group leader say 'aye.'" They all said "aye," including Carlos. I was pissed.

"Okay, everybody, please pay attention," said Junior. "Ramona and Charlene can take a flight out of Mérida for Guatemala City tomorrow. Raúl can't fly without a passport, so he will go with us. When the women arrive in Guatemala City, they need to get a hotel, preferably an American one. Once there, they need to find a lawyer named Miguel Garza. Padre Humberto told me he was a good friend of his."

He looked at Charlene. "The lawyer's job will be to arrange for Humberto's freedom. He will know who to pay. We will be there as soon as we can, and then we will help him cross back into Mexico."

"Hey, that was my plan," I said. "You stole it." Junior ignored me, and everyone else hissed at me.

"I need money to arrange the escape," he said. "Pancho wants an advance, and I'm short. My sister and I barely have enough money together for the down payment."

Oh, no, here comes the long arm of Junior. I waited for the right moment and then decided to strike first. "If I'm allowed to pry, you need a down payment for what exactly?" I asked suspiciously.

"For a private airplane," he said matter-of-factly.

"What a capital idea," said Charlene.

He smiled at her and proceeded explaining the plan. "Pancho's flying Padre Humberto out in an airplane. It's too dangerous to get him out in a car. He will deliver Padre Humberto to a safe house in Villa Hermosa, where Rosie will be waiting for him. Then, when the time is right, Pancho will smuggle Padre Humberto and anyone else that wants to go into Texas."

I beamed with admiration. This kid had been reading my mail, and he was good. I needed to make sure that once Padre Humberto was a free man, Junior would follow him and come live with me.

Chapter 12

Before Charlene boarded her plane, she told Junior that if he needed money, he was to get it from me. She told him she had paid me eight thousand dollars to fund the escape, and I was to share it with him.

Junior immediately wanted his cut. To make matters worse, Raúl demanded five hundred to continue with the rescue. I had already given Carlos a two-thousand-dollar advance in Houston and I had planned on keeping half of Junior's share. I had a financial crisis on my hands.

Junior demanded two thousand for himself and one thousand for Carmen. That left me with barely two grand. I had no choice but to pay him the money. He would cut me off the adventure completely, and I would lose the eight thousand I received from Charlene. I bit my lip and grudgingly paid Raúl the money he asked for after deducting the one hundred I had already given him in Houston.

I figured that by the time I crossed back into Texas, I'd be lucky to have one thousand dollars left. The math was not working out. Somehow, this whole thing had gotten away from me. I needed to pick up a little side money if I wanted to remain in the black.

The following day, Junior showed up with his sister, Carmen. We checked out of the hotel and left Mérida. Instead of going toward Quintana Roo and then crossing into Belize, Junior pointed us in the direction of Chiapas. He said there was one more thing that had to be dealt with before we left Mexico. I argued the point to no avail. In a somber mood, we drove out of the Yucatán.

After a long trek through familiar ground, we made it to San Cristóbal de las Casas. I smiled when we passed the bus station and felt at home when I saw the sign pointing us to the orphanage. However, any feeling of joy I had left me when I took a gander at the place. It looked abandoned again, full of weeds. Obviously, no one had been living there for some time. The grass was knee-deep in places.

"Okay, Junior," I said. "You promised to tell me why we were coming here when we got here. Well . . . I'm all ears."

"Mister Alex, what we are going to do in Guatemala is very important and very dangerous. If we fail, Padre Humberto might stay in prison, and we could join him. We came here to receive a special blessing. We are in Mexico. Raúl, Carmen, and I, we are Mexicans so we are going to do this our way. I hope you and your friend don't cause any trouble. Everything has been arranged. You will leave here a different man, I promise."

I remembered the fairies in Pancho's Box and wondered what kind of cockamamie scheme the boy had in mind.

We drove the Chevy Impala to the front of the main building and, to my surprise, Rosie came out to greet us. I felt a warm, fuzzy feeling as I hugged her. I was flabbergasted to see she was genuinely glad to see me.

Rosie showed us to a cabin that was to be our lodging for the night. Carlos and I spent the better part of thirty minutes getting rid of scorpions, spiders, and cobwebs. After making sure we rid ourselves of all the creepy crawlers, we laid on the cots.

"Tell me again, Alex, why are we letting a kid lead the prison break?"

"Because everybody, you included, voted for him. That's why," I said.

"Sorry about that, Alex. Don't take it personal. It was just a knee-jerk reaction. What are our chances of succeeding? Will we go back home or should I prepare myself for life behind bars?"

"Listen to me, my good friend. You were going to rob a convenience store in Houston, remember? You were depressed and suicidal. You were going to risk your life and freedom just to pay your rent. That was asinine. What we are about to do can be classified as courageous, just, and maybe even glorious."

"I feel like a fish out of water," Carlos said. "I don't know how much good I'll be to the operation."

"Don't worry. I'll watch over your safety. Panamanians are almost Mexicans. I will use my knowledge of the culture to make sure this comes off safe. Like you, Carlos, I'm also without experience in these types of things, but I need the money to get Ramona off my back."

"You're risking your life to get your wife off your case? Why don't you just file for divorce?"

"The idea has crossed my mind," I said.

"You're a piece of work," he said as he closed his eyes.

We woke up from our nap to find a note on the cabin floor. Next to it was a sack. Carlos opened it and removed two ponchos, two mangos, two bananas, and two corn tortillas. The note was in Spanish, so Carlos gave it to me. I read it and put it in my pocket.

"Well . . . what did it say?"

"That there's a ceremony taking place in the chapel at nine tonight, and we are to be present. We have to put these ponchos on our naked bodies and be hungry."

"Hungry? There's food in the sack."

"We're supposed to fast so that we enter a state of holiness. The food is temptation. If we touch it, we will not be allowed to participate in the ceremony."

"I'm starving," he said, looking wantonly at the food. "I wish I had robbed that convenience store in Houston. This is pure madness."

Evening came, and we readied ourselves for the ceremony. Having dealt with Junior before, I knew to expect the unexpected. Feeling ridiculous with our ponchos, we left the cabin, and headed to the chapel. Junior and Raúl were waiting for us at the entrance. They, too, were wearing "holy garb."

At exactly nine, the chapel door opened and we all walked in single file. I was floored by the reverence of the place. There must have been at least two dozen candles lit all around. The smell of incense was strong but gratifying. Standing in the middle of the altar was an old woman dressed in a white tunic. I was hoping she was not naked. Close to her were four women dressed in white tunics, standing on the right side of the altar. I wondered if *they* were naked. I recognized Carmen and Rosie. The other two were unknown to me.

A bell rang, and the priestess spoke in a language I did not recognize. I figured it was probably a Mayan dialect. She went on about this and that, and then she motioned for us to come toward her. Halfway there, she raised her hand and stopped us. I took the opportunity to look around. There were about two dozen people sitting on chairs flanking the main walkway.

We stood in silence, waiting for the old woman to give us directions. She motioned to the robed women, and they came and escorted us to the altar, where we were made to kneel. I was hoping the woman that led me was naked under her tunic like me.

The smell of incense became strong, and I began to have difficulties breathing. The glow of the many candles created huge dancing shadows on the chapel walls. The place began to take on a surrealistic atmosphere. I looked at Carlos, and he seemed dazed too. Junior had a serious countenance, and Raúl looked like he was on his first Communion. He seemed to have been injected with a heavy dose of religion.

A short, fat woman came out of the shadows carrying a large pottery bowl that put out a lot of smoke and placed it next to Rosie. I identified the smell . . . cannabis. Carlos and I looked at each other and smiled.

The priestess called Junior to come before her. She placed a crown of flowers on his head, then put her hand on his right shoulder and uttered more gibberish. He was led to the bowl by Rosie, where he refreshed himself by inhaling the smoke. When he had enough, he was escorted to a chair, where he sat down. Rosie stood directly behind him. This ritual was repeated until all of us were seated with our escorts standing behind our backs.

The old woman uttered more nonsense and then finally spoke in Spanish. I was able to translate her words to Carlos: "By the power of life and everything in it that is holy, I have ordained you four men Knights of San Cristóbal. Go now and fight the evil that exists in Guatemala and bring back what has been taken from us. May the light show you the path and keep the fear of darkness away. Go now and enjoy the pleasures of the night."

She finished, turned around, and vacated the altar. We understood the ceremony was over. Junior, with Rosie at his side, started the parade by passing through a room filled with people who were applauding. I was accompanied by my escort to my cabin for what promised to be a nuptial night. I figured Carlos spent the night with Carmen. She had become fond of him. Raúl was led away by an older woman. The urchin had a grin on his face.

Morning came, and I found myself alone. I remembered the lovemaking and I felt like I had been given a last meal. Now, it was time to grab the bull by the horns. Carlos seemed in good spirits. He began to brag about how he was able to love Carmen twice. What a sorry excuse for a homo he was!

We ate a good, hearty breakfast, bid Rosie adieu, and drove out of the orphanage toward Belize.

Earlier, Carlos and I had scored a few joints from Junior. When we arrived at the border crossing, Carlos threw his last joint out the window. I had my reefer hidden in a round metal container for safekeeping. Refusing to part with them, I gave Raúl the container attached to a leather string and placed it around his neck to wear as a necklace. Junior, Carmen, and Raúl hid in the trunk. Carlos became nervous as we approached the border crossing.

"Why can't we drop them off at the border and let them find their way inside? If we get caught smuggling them, we'll be arrested. I don't want to spend years in a prison in Belize," he said with anguish.

"Because we need them. They are important to the success of the operation. Besides, their chances of getting caught are less with us. Trust me on this, Carlos. No one from Mexico is going to sneak into Belize," I said. "Belize is a poor country."

Chapter 13

Earl, the Pearl

We passed Orange Walk and drove all the way to Belize City. There was some kind of festival going on, and the hotels were full. We scoured the city but there were no vacancies. Desperate, we followed a man's advice and drove out of town. We were looking for a place called "Paradise Cabins."

The stranger told us the cabins were rented by the hour until midnight, after which you could get one till morning. Not having any choice and wanting a bed for the night, we drove in search of a resting place. We found the cabins an hour later. I knocked on the one that had a hanging sign with "Office" written on it. The door opened, and I was met by a most unusual man. He introduced himself as Earl, but told us to call him "Pearl" like his friends did. His lips showed signs of having been painted, and his cheeks still had a touch of rouge. Earl's hair was curled up in rollers, and his eyebrows were plucked. He was wearing a pink nightgown with matching slippers. Raúl climbed out of the car, tugged at my shirt, and whispered, "Papi, *ese hombre es un maricón.*"

I looked at the boy with eyes that confirmed his opinion. Still, *maricón* or not, I was tired, and we all needed to rest. I continued with my negotiations. Raúl went back to the car, grabbed Junior, and returned. The boy's eyes shot up as he took a gander at the flaming queen standing by the doorway.

"I'm staying out here with Raúl," he said. "A man does not go into a *maricón*'s house. You need to be careful, Mister Alex. You never know what can happen in there. He may like you, and then he will not let you leave."

"Suit yourselves, boys. I'm not afraid of queers. They put their pants on one leg at a time."

Carlos and Carmen joined us, and we all walked inside the *maricón*'s home. Earl the Pearl developed an immediate liking for Carlos. Yet, in spite of his attraction, he refused to give us a free room. He said that his cabins rented by the hour until midnight. I looked at my watch; it was only fifteen minutes after ten. Grudgingly, we accepted his hospitality. We had no choice. It was either we waited there or spent the night in the crowded car.

The boys were correct to be apprehensive. To the naked eye, the Paradise Motel looked like a low-rent disease-ridden flophouse.

Earl was a gracious host, though. He offered us cookies and cold Coca Cola. I tried to get the boys to come in, but they refused, preferring to take their refreshments outside. We were making small talk, waiting for the clock to strike twelve, when Earl floored me with a question: "Do you have tarps or sleeping bags, Alex?"

"Why do you want to know?" I asked suspiciously.

"Because the maid quit a couple of days ago, and the washing machine broke this morning. I'm out of clean sheets."

Carlos stood up and crossed his arms over his chest. I knew the stance, for I had seen it before. It was Indian for "I'm not staying here." We thanked Earl the Pearl for the drinks, declined the offer he made us for the room, and quickly vacated the premises.

Discouraged and tired, we drove around trying to find a place to park the car. I finally found a suitable location off the main road by the banks of a river.

"Okay, amigos," I said. "It's the car or the ground." Carmen snuggled with the boys in the back seat. Carlos and I slept in the front. The accommodations weren't great, but the sound of the river had a soothing effect. We were all asleep in a matter of minutes.

Hours later, I developed a need to find a tree. I woke up and noticed that Carlos was not in the car. For that matter, neither was Carmen. I walked outside to answer the call of nature. In the middle of relieving myself, I heard a familiar noise and knew straightaway what was going down—or maybe who was. I followed the sounds of the sweet melody of love and found Carlos lying flat on the ground totally naked with his arms crossed behind his neck. Carmen was on top of him churning for butter. Jeez, what's up with this guy? I made a mental note to chastise him for being unfaithful to his homosexuality.

The next day, we drove to Guatemala in good spirits. Along the way, we ran into a checkpoint manned by policemen. They were stopping all traffic. I casually looked at Raúl's neck and went into panic mode. The necklace with my pot was missing.

"Where's your necklace?" I interrogated.

He looked puzzled. "*No sé,* Papi, *se perdió.*"

"What did he say?" Carlos wanted to know.

"He said he doesn't know where his necklace is. He thinks it's lost."

"What's in the necklace?" Carlos said.

"My pot," I whispered in his ear.

"He thinks it's lost in the car?" Carlos asked.

"Where did you lose it, Raúl?" I asked.

"*No sé,* Papi. *Se perdió.*"

"He doesn't know where he lost it." I said.

"He doesn't know if he lost it in the car!" said Carlos, getting agitated.

"What was in the container?" Carmen asked me.

Junior kept quiet. I said nothing, but Carlos double-crossed me. "He gave his marijuana to Raulito," he said.

Carmen shot me a look full of disdain. I killed the engine. We were fortunate to be far from the impromptu checkpoint. We casually climbed out of the car and searched the entire vehicle as inconspicuous as possible. We never found the damn metal container. When our turn came to cross the checkpoint, one of the three guards came over and grinned. He told us they were looking for four men who had robbed a bank. He removed his hat and wiped off a sweaty brow. Then he grinned again. We smiled back but kept quiet.

"Did you find what you were looking for?" he asked with a sheepish grin.

"No," I said, trying not to sound nervous.

"Well, if you didn't find it, it's a good bet we won't find it either, so no need to search your car." He waved us across. We thanked him and God at the same time and drove on.

Ten miles from the Belize-Guatemala border stations, we came across a river that divided the road. There was a flat-bottomed boat that had a long cable attached to an apparatus that was hooked to two pulleys. The boatman had to crank the wheel that turned the pulleys, moving the boat to the other side. The river was moving too fast for my taste, and I feared the crossing would not be easy. We decided to look for another venue. Much to my discomfort, there was no other place to cross. I couldn't believe there was no bridge. Disgusted with all this third-world bullshit, I drove back to the boat landing and waited for someone to appear. Forty minutes later, we were still waiting. I looked at my watch, and it was half past noon. I cursed. It was siesta time. Knowing the boat captain would not appear for at least another hour and needing to get across, we scattered out and began to inquire as to where the boatman could be found. Unable to find anyone who would give me a straight answer, I returned to the car to find Raúl sitting by himself on a sidewalk. I walked over and sat beside him. Before I could say anything to the little urchin, he put his finger on his lips and pointed at the car. The springs were bouncing.

"*El maricón se está cojiendo a la hermana de* Junior," he said.
"You're right, Raúl. He's banging Junior's sister. See? I told you, and you didn't believe me. Carlos is not a queer . . . he is just confused."

I walked toward the car and tapped on the back window. Carmen looked up and told me to wait two minutes. Pissed, I went back, sat down by Raúl and waited. I couldn't believe it. The homo was the only one getting pussy.

When Junior arrived with the boat captain, Carlos had already finished refreshing himself with Carmen's charms. The boatman charged us five American dollars to pull us across. As expected, the crossing was difficult. The cables were bending due to the strong current. I kept thinking that the cable was going to snap at any moment, and we would be off floating on a raging river. Fortunately, other than dealing with major stress, nothing bad happened.

We drove through the countryside in relative peace until we reached a sign that said the border was two miles ahead. Not wanting the Guatemalan border agents to find the missing metal container, we stopped the car, climbed out, and searched the car, again. The damn thing was not inside. I began to suspect the scoundrel was probably ripping me off, so I asked Junior to look in Raúl's underwear.

He refused. "Men don't look in other men's underwear," he said.

When I asked Carlos to look in Raúl's underwear, Raúl's eyes widened, and he immediately allowed Junior to look in his pants.

"*Mira,* Papi, *no tengo nada en mis calzoncillos.*"

We all looked at him. He was right . . . there was nothing in his underwear—the kid wasn't wearing any. Carmen squealed with delight, embarrassing the urchin. The boy was hung.

We resigned ourselves to our fate and crossed the border, hoping the missing metal container would not rear its ugly head at an improper time. Just like before, we put our three passengers in the trunk. Again, as we approached the border station, Carlos started to show signs of agitation.

"I wish we had gotten them their papers before we started on this crazy adventure. We're pushing our luck. How long do you think we can get away with hiding them?" he asked.

"Relax," I said. "No one sneaks into Guatemala from Belize. Guatemala is a poor nation."

Chapter 14

After driving for the better part of a day, we came upon a village situated across a huge lake. On the other side was a town called Castillo de Oro. The map showed it to be big enough to have at least one good hotel with air-conditioned rooms and several real restaurants. However, there was a problem. The only ferry the place had was broken and out of service indefinitely. There was no bridge either, and the map showed no other way to get across. By now, I had adjusted my keen sense of readiness to match the countryside. Hell, I was in Central America. To expect things to work here as they do in Texas was ludicrous.

There was a dock where we could hire a water taxi, but we were driving a big American car. Needing to find a way to get to the other side with the vehicle, we spread out on foot. Carlos, who didn't speak Spanish, stayed behind to guard the car.

We talked to as many people as possible, hoping to find a way to get across. To my displeasure, there was no other way. Someone told Junior if we drove a little further down the lake we would find a gringo that had a large flat-bottomed boat that could possibly carry the car. Filled with hope, we followed the road, looking for the American ferry. Ten minutes later, we found the boat. On it was a dark-skinned Indian. He was standing erect with arms crossed, wearing sunglasses and a feathered hat. He kept looking at us. Raúl and I stepped out and went to negotiate passage.

"Ahoy there, mate," I said. "Can we hire you and your boat to take us across?"

"We don't take Australians or Englishmen anywhere," he said in a brusque manner.

"I'm not Australian or English," I protested.

"You said, 'ahoy, mate.'"

"I am only pretending to be an Australian or an Englishman. Can you forgive my impertinence?"

"Which one are you pretending to be?"

"What difference does it make? You don't take either one."

"Hmm," he said, as he scratched his cheek. "You're right. It makes no difference. What do you want?"

"My companions and I would like to book passage to the other side."

"Who are 'your companions,' and how many?"

"Three Mexicans and an American Indian."

"The Indian can ride. The rest of you can swim for all I care."

Jeez, what rotten luck—an indigenous imbecile is in charge of the boat. Where in hell is the gringo? Not being easily dissuaded and being particularly enamored with verbal titillation, I attacked. "Would you take us if we paid handsomely and if all of us pretended to be Indians instead of Australians or Englishmen?"

"He wouldn't take you if you were smugglers and wanted to trade gold bullion for passage," said a rough voice coming from underneath a dirty blanket. "It's not his boat."

The Indian smiled.

"Papi, *ese tipo es raro*," whispered Raúl.

"What's so strange about the guy?"

"*Tiene anteojos oscuros y ya no hay sol.*"

"He's trying to be cool, son. Wearing sunglasses in the dark is in vogue."

A hand came out of the talking blanket holding an empty bottle of tequila. Soon, a bedraggled man appeared. He got on his feet, stumbled, threw the empty bottle into the water, reached inside a satchel, and pulled out a full bottle.

"Hello, there," he said, as he scratched a scraggly beard and itchy ass. "My name is Captain Chris Thomas, late of Beaumont, Texas. This is Jaime, my first mate. I am the owner of this fine boat. How much did you say you wanted to pay to get across?"

"Papi, *¿por qué está rodeado el bote de llantas?*"

I looked at the perimeters of the boat and noticed that except where the motor was, it was surrounded by old tires. I also saw signs of hard landings.

"The lake must be crowded," I said. "The tires are to protect the boat."

"Papi, *el capitán es un borracho y el otro está ciego.*"

I looked at the Indian who hadn't moved and at the captain who had opened the new bottle and was drinking it like water. I pondered Raúl's wisdom. He was correct. The captain was a drunk, and the first mate was blind. Needing to get to the other side without having to pay a small fortune, I decided to keep Raúl's revelation a secret from the others.

"How much did you say you were willing to pay for a trip to the other side?" said Captain Chris one more time. "What does a pretender mean when he says he will pay 'handsomely'?"

"What is the price of a regular fare?" I said, trying to establish a basis for negotiation.

"You are in luck, because today we have a special," he said. "It's called 'The Guatemalan ferry is broken special.' It will only cost you five hundred American dollars to get to the other side with your car."

"What? Are you out of your mind? I'm not paying you that kind of money. I'll pay you two hundred, tops. Take it or leave it."

"The ferry's broken," said the captain. "It will not be operating for another two weeks, if you are fortunate. You can stay on this side of the lake and live in your car if you like, or you can take a water taxi to get across and leave your car here. Of course, I can't give you any guarantees it will not get broken into or stolen. But if you want a nice meal and a good hotel with a secure parking lot, the price is five hundred dollars."

Full of indignation at his audacity, I clenched my fists and started to walk toward the American bandit. Jaime moved his poncho to one side, showing a long Bowie knife. He tapped the knife and kept smiling.

"Okay," I said. "How much will you charge just for the American Indian and the Mexican woman?"

"Indian and woman ride for free. White man pays out the ass for transporting car to other side," said Jaime.

"I'm not a white man," I protested.

"You look like one to me," grumbled the captain.

"I'm only pretending to be one. I'm really an Indian in disguise."

"Listen to me, Peckerwood," said Captain Chris, getting a mean on. "My boat is the only one on this side of the lake that is big enough to take your car. Jaime and I know the lake well. You need to pay us the five hundred. There is no alternative. My money's on the Guatemalan mechanics arriving late and with the wrong parts."

"Can you recommend a hotel with air conditioning and a bar?" I said, resigned to paying the exorbitant fee.

"Hotel Oasis, but don't mention my name."

Carlos stepped out of the car and yelled, "I got to see a man about a horse. Don't leave without me."

"You pay extra for horse," Jaime said.

I grabbed Raúl, explained the rules of passage, and told him to keep quiet. We walked back to the car and gathered the group in council.

"Listen, guys, this is the deal," I said. "Junior, Raúl, and I will meet you two on the other side. They want too much money per head. It's cheaper if some of us go by water taxi. I will go on ahead with the children. I have to pay for our accommodations. When you disembark, take a taxi and tell him to take you to the Hotel Oasis."

Carmen's female antenna picked up the notion that something was wrong. She gave me the bad-eye and spat on the ground.

"I'll be happy to get in the boat with you, Carlos, *mi amor.* I can feel that this boat ride will not be easy. I will be there to take care of you."

I looked at her. She was not a beauty, but her sense of aware-ness matched her sense of loyalty. If she wasn't a whore, she'd be a good catch. Her light brown skin looked smooth, and the cotton dress she was wearing clung to her body like extra skin. Her breasts were kept in place by a thin brassiere. Her nipples pointed out from time to time. I wondered if Carlos would share her, because I could use a good poke.

Carlos approached me. "Is there any reason why I would need Carmen's assistance on this crossing?"

"No, everything should be fine. She must be menstrual. Don't worry about a thing. I will see you on the other side. Please keep an eye on the car."

When Junior understood we were breaking into two groups, he looked at me with mistrust. The ragamuffin had been fairly docile since we entered Belize. He was allowing me to run the show. I wasn't sure what his deal was. When he didn't ask me or Raúl any pertinent questions about why we were splitting up, I took it as a sign that he was taking on the role of a son, letting his father run the show. I went back and shook hands with the captain.

"We have a deal," I said. "Can I get a discount if I leave the horse behind?"

Four hours later, there was a loud knock on my hotel door. Being the man that I was, I grabbed the half-empty bottle of rum and prepared to defend myself.

"Who knocks on a man's door at this time of the morning?" I said.

"Open the fucking door!" yelled Carlos.

Oh, no, I'm in big trouble. I opened it halfway, trying to meas-ure the anger in my friend's eyes. He seemed mad as hell. So was Carmen.

"You sent me off on a boat with a drunken captain and a blind navigator!" He yelled as he pushed his way into my room. When they both came in, I noticed that besides being furious, they were also wet.

"What happened?" I said, trying to sound innocent.

"We navigated the lake all night long trying to find a place to put in. We were utterly lost."

"You're not making any sense," I said.

He grabbed me by my sleeping shirt. "The captain passed out halfway here. Then we had to wrestle the steering wheel from the first mate because he couldn't drive for shit. He nearly broadsided two boats before we realized he was blind. Carmen tried to land the boat while I wrestled with Jaime. She misjudged the distance upon docking and took a pier out. The owner came out waving a machete. Carmen and I jumped into the water and ran to safety."

"You left our car behind? How responsible is that? Now I'm going to have to pay for the damage to the pier in order to get it back."

When Carlos let go of my shirt, Carmen jumped me. Soon, I had Junior, Raúl, and the owner of the hotel in the room. The man had a club in his hand. When he saw the damage Carmen's aggressive behavior had caused to the room, he glared at me.

"You know, Mister Perez," he said. "You're in plenty of trouble. You can pay me now for the destruction of this room, or you can pay me tomorrow in front of the judge."

The crook charged me three hundred dollars for the damage. Not only did he rob us, but he also had the audacity (after he pocketed the money) to put all of us out into the street.

"Mister Alex, what do we do now?" Junior said.

"We have to get the car back."

"How are we going to do that?" he said.

"Listen up, everyone. I have a plan."

"Is it as good as the last one?" Junior wanted to know.

Just before the break of day, we approached the site of the shipwreck and inspected the damage caused to the pier. It was extensive. Not wanting to be seen, we crawled on our bellies and found Captain Chris. He and the blind Indian were tied to a tree. Two men were guarding: one had a rifle, the other a machete —father and son team, I presumed. When I saw the car, my heart dropped. The front right fender was smashed, and the headlight was pointing straight up. All four wheels had been removed. The Chevy was standing on cement blocks. The jack and tire tool were next to the man with the machete. Realizing my predicament, I called for the heavy artillery. Carmen and Junior went in.

Junior needed to engage the young man in conversation and then offer him some money so we could get the car out, but he needed to do it away from the father's eyes. Carmen was going to negotiate a price for the repairs to the pier. It was important to split the team up. I needed those two to separate their intended victims, and I needed them away from the car. I was hoping Junior wouldn't get mad at me for trying to pimp his sister. She had instructions to get the man out of his pants. If she managed, and if Junior could distract the son, Carlos, Raúl, and I were ready to implement Plan B, which was to put the tires back on the car. Then, we would wait for Junior and Carmen to return and get the hell away from there without spending any money.

The plan worked out perfectly. One hour later, there were four people gagged and tied to the tree, and we were driving out of Castillo de Oro like a bat out of hell.

Despite fervent pleas from the boys and a diligent lobbying effort from Carlos and Carmen, I left the sailors tied up. Jaime and Captain Chris also pleaded to be cut loose. I was not born yesterday, and I could tell a stupid request when I heard one.

"Are you sure you're not an Indian-hating Spaniard?" Jaime asked just before I duct-taped his mouth shut.

"Listen up, my indigenous friend," I said. "I'm really an asshole pretending to be a Spaniard." Then I came close and whispered in his ear: "Be grateful I'm not leaving you here naked. I left you clothed so you can keep your dignity. That has to count for something."

When Carlos asked me why I insisted on leaving the captain and the first mate tied to the tree, I explained that I didn't want to part with any more money. I reminded him that he and Carmen destroyed the captain's boat, and the man would certainly ask for financial restitution through the court systems, which meant we would not be able to leave and would have to hire an attorney. Luckily for me, he accepted that explanation. I was afraid he might demand that I release the Mayan. Hell, at the rate we were spending money, I'd be lucky to get to Guatemala City with seventy-five dollars.

I began to sort things out. I was responsible for the success of the escapade, as well as the welfare of my companions. I was dangerously low on funds, so while no one was looking, I lifted the price of the boat ride from Captain Chris' shirt pocket.

Driving at a high speed, I was hoping to get to Guatemala City before the cops caught us. In a country where there are only one or two roads to get from place to place, setting up road blocks was easy. I knew we had about a three-hour start before someone would sound the alarm and put the police on our trail.

I was beginning to have doubts about my grand plan. Junior had already reminded me that this trip looked a lot like the last one. I barely had time to dismiss his allegations as being totally unfounded, when we came to a huge four-lane bridge that only went halfway across. The other half had fallen into the river. I slammed on the brakes and stopped the car inches away from the edge.

"What kind of a country is this?" I screamed, getting mad. "You would think there would be at least one sign telling you the bridge is out!"

"There was probably a sign at one time," said Carmen. "Somebody probably took it and used it for firewood."

Upset over losing valuable time and knowing quite well the cops were on our trail, I turned the car around and drove until I found the path everyone had been using to cross. It was a steep drop, but I was driving a Chevrolet. The car seemed up to the task. We did the sign of the cross and said a quick prayer, and then we roared down the slope. At the bottom, we split up on foot, trying to find a shallow crossing spot. Junior found one, and we crossed. We made it to the city ahead of the cops. I drove to the Hilton and contacted Charlene and Ramona. We met them at the hotel eatery and were disappointed to find they weren't paying for a room for us at the hotel. They told us Señor Garza, the lawyer, had made arrangements for bail. They had seen Humberto, and he looked to be in good spirits. They were going to pay for his release the following morning. Hopefully, he would be free. Not wanting to pay a fortune to stay at the Hilton, we booked two rooms at the Tikal Hotel. Raúl stayed with Ramona.

In the morning we met with Señor Garza, who cautioned us against spiriting the priest out of the country. He counseled us in favor of fighting the bogus charges. He felt he could get Humberto off. If we escaped with him and crossed the border into Mexico, Humberto would become an international fugitive.

"Never underestimate the power of the Catholic church," said the lawyer. "His Eminence, Omar Ramírez, is a vindictive individual, which makes him a dangerous opponent. If Humberto flees, the bishop will spend all of the church money to track him down and bring him to justice. He's better off staying here and fighting these ridiculous charges."

Talk about bad news. This advice went against the core of the plan and against everything we wanted. I could tell Charlene was wrestling with the lawyer's advice. She looked devastated.

She had given the attorney the bail money along with her hotel room key to pass on to Humberto. She had moved into another room, wanting some privacy with her priest. I felt sorry for her because I knew what was coming down. She loved him and had to encourage him to stay and clear his name. There could be no happy ending if he ran. Señor Garza was right; the church had deep pockets. Bishop Ramírez could hire an endless army of bounty hunters to look for him. We kept quiet and returned to our rooms. I grabbed Junior and offered to buy him a cold Coca Cola at the hotel bar. Carmen and Carlos went upstairs.

"What are we going to do now?" I asked. "This whole plan was based on rescuing Humberto."

"When he gets out of jail, he is rescued. Our work here is finished," he said. "Did you really give Raúl your marijuana so he could smuggle it into Guatemala?"

"Yes, and don't give me that sanctimonious look. I don't deserve it. Look, Junior, kids get preferential treatment in these parts. Besides, like you said earlier, no one pays any attention to kids. I felt the reefer was safe with him."

"Señora Ramona was right that day when we were hiding from the bandits and she accused you of being a lousy father. I thought she was wrong, but she was right."

"Give me a break, Junior. You and I are cut from the same cloth, so let's not start being pious. I was not abusing Raúl, just taking advantage of the opportunity the culture offered. I could have given you the pot, but you, being older and aware of the consequences, would have refused."

Junior shook his head, refused the cigarette I offered him, and left the bar, returning a few minutes later. He reoccupied his seat, took me up on the cigarette, and said his sister was busy converting Carlos into a regular guy. "Carmen has a caring disposition. She has always been good about giving a helping hand. I love her very much."

"Have you thought about coming to Texas for an extended holiday?"

"Yes, I thought about it. If you had made that offer when we first met, I would have jumped on it. Now I'm afraid I will have to pass. You were right, Mister Alex. Jimmy Buffet is not my father. He's a gringo, and I'm all Mexican. I never had a father. I just wanted one in the worst way. It's every orphan's dream. I was hoping you needed a son, but you treated me badly and left me behind."

He took a puff, slowly let the smoke come out of his mouth, and then sniffed it directly into his nostrils. I was impressed. The kid was a good smoker.

"I may never get a father," he said, "but if I ever do, he will not be like you. Raúl thinks the same."

"I'm sorry you feel that way. I happen to admire you and was hoping you could come to Texas with me. Raúl is a pain in the ass."

"You admire only street smarts, not my heart or my culture. You want to use me, not love me, and I need more than you can give me."

He waited for me to respond, but I couldn't.

The boy had stung me. After a minute, he finished his cigarette, gave me a look that said volumes about our good-bye, and left the bar. I was sorry to see him go, Junior would have been a great son.

Chapter 15

A s expected, Padre Humberto walked out a free man, albeit temporarily. He followed the attorney's advice and decided to stay and fight the charges against him.

Pancho, the bandit, showed up, and after finding that his cargo was staying behind, he talked Ramona and Raúl into flying back to Mexico with him. He had acquired a two-seater crop-duster, and if Raúl sat on Ramona's lap, they could both fit in nicely in the second seat. It was Ramona's intention to hire him as a *coyote* to sneak the urchin back into Texas.

Before my wife left, she told me she was going to file for divorce as soon as she made it back home. She told me all of my stuff would be packed and placed in the garage. She reminded me that the Mercedes had not been titled to me yet, and it would not be, so I'd better leave it there. When I arrived back in Houston, I was to pick up my belongings and move out. Furthermore, if I made any trouble concerning Raulito's illegal status, she would spend her last nickel and hire her mother's handyman to break both of my legs. That being settled, she left with Pancho. Goodbye to a bittersweet love.

Junior and Carmen decided to stay in Guatemala and help the priest. She found employment at a nice brothel called the Zamba

Club. Carlos, Charlene, and I decided to drive back to Mexico via the ruins of Tikal.

The trip to the archaeological site was over one hundred fifty kilometers. We loaded up on fresh supplies. Carlos and Charlene fell asleep as I started to drive—not a smart move. Even though I had managed to do well so far. For me, not getting lost meant having a good navigator by my side, because I can't tell north from south without a compass. I looked at the map and pointed the car in the direction of Tikal. Four hours later, I was in big trouble. I was in the mountains and Tikal as opposed to being in the lowlands. How in the hell did I get us here?

The sun was beginning to peek, and I started to sweat. When I passed a sign that read "Huehuetenango sixty kilometers," I knew I was in trouble. I had driven to the Sierra Madre Mountains. Shit! I was way out of the way from Tikal. Charlene was going to castrate me.

Trying to hide my blunder and knowing quite well she would blow a fuse if we entered Huehuetenango, I took a left turn and went on a steep drop. This radical change of position woke up Carlos.

"Where are we, Alex? I don't recall seeing any mountains on the way to Tikal." I silently cursed him.

That unfortunate remark aroused the bear's curiosity. The beast opened her eyes, stretched, and looked sheepishly at the scenery.

"By the sheer steepness of this drop," said Charlene, "and since we are not in the jungle lowlands, I am willing to bet that we are somewhere in the Sierras."

"What are you," I said, with indignation, "a walking, talking atlas?"

"We're in the Sierra Madre Mountains? This is way too cool." said Carlos.

She looked at him with scorn. "Tell me again, Carlos. Are you really an Indian?

"Don't hassle him," I said. "Of course he is an Indian."

"Butt out," she said. "I have Indian blood in me, but I'm not an Indian, and neither is he. Besides, if I am paying for the pony ride, *I* will ride the pony. Tell me again, Carlos, what did I pay you for? What have you contributed to this whole affair?"

Instead of defending himself and staving off her assault on his heritage and job, Carlos decided to stress my life further.

"Is the gas gauge working right?" he asked.

I looked at it and freaked out—less than a quarter tank. "Quick, Charlene, look at the map and tell me where we are!"

"How can I tell you where we are when I don't know where we are?"

"Don't be difficult, Charlene. Look at the map, and tell me where the nearest town is. If we don't gas up soon, we'll be stranded."

She cursed me and began to scour the map for any telltale signs of where we could be.

"Do you have any idea where we could possibly be? Have you seen any road signs?"

I was doomed to be lost in the Sierras forever. If I told her that we had been some sixty odd miles from Huehuetenango but veered off into unknown territory due to the need to hide my driving blunder, she'd kill me.

"No. I haven't seen a sign anywhere. This country is not tourist-friendly, and they do not believe in signs."

We drove in silence for the next half hour. The mountains kept getting steeper, and the Chevy was sucking gas. Soon, we were forced to stop, lest we end up on empty. Thinking about the unpleasant affair with the Mexican bandits and not wanting to deal with the Guatemalan variety, I drove off the road and into the bush until we came to a clearing. The Chevy plowed through the brush like a John Deere. I love American cars.

Feeling relatively safe, we made camp. Much to our delight, we found the small tent we had stored in the trunk and one of the three lightweight sleeping bags we brought along for the journey. We found it in the spare tire wheel well. There was no tire, but since we didn't have a flat, that was not a problem. I wondered which one of my traveling companions pilfered the tire.

About midday, we found ourselves with company. Unexpectedly, a large crowd of indigenous people appeared from nowhere. They stood about fifty feet away from us in total silence. After what seemed like an eternity, an elderly man with a child in tow approached us. I walked midway to meet them. He smiled and talked up a storm, but I couldn't understand a word. Man, we were in big trouble. We were really lost. These were *real* Indians. They spoke no Spanish.

The elderly man was obviously the chief, and by his gestures and body language, I understood it was okay to be there. They meant us no harm. I tried to convey the fact that we were lost with my best sign language. Maybe it worked, but I wasn't sure. They left us as quickly as they came, and everyone returned early that evening.

Carlos Laughing Crow went through a transformation. Once he realized we were in Indian country, he went into his backpack and brought out his Apache garb. Feeling no need to interfere in Indian matters, Charlene and I left him alone. We had other things to concern ourselves with and trying not to freeze to death was one of them. The wind was picking up, and it was getting cold. Charlene and I were worried. The gas tank was almost empty, so sleeping in the car with the heater on was not an option.

Carlos gathered firewood and twigs. He used his Eagle Grand Master Boy Scout training to get a good fire going. Then he dressed in feathers, put on war paint, and started to do a dance.

"Ay ya yai ya, ay ya yai ya," he chanted as he danced around the campfire. We thought he had gone mad, but the Indians felt a brethren in their midst and came closer. The old chief and the boy joined him in the dance. Then the tribe broke into rank and formed a series of circles around their chief and began to dance. We were being treated to a spectacle. Too bad we didn't have a camera.

Charlene opened the ice chest and brought out a couple of beers. She sat quietly and drank the first one. I stood beside her, mesmerized by the whole scene.

After a while, Carlos stopped dancing. Then, the old chief grabbed him and took him aside. There were a lot of arm waving and hand gestures going on. I knew whatever they were discussing had to be important. When they were finished, he came over to me and dropped a bomb.

"You're going where?" I said.

"I've been invited to partake of their hospitality. I will leave now and return in the morning."

"Since when do you speak Mayan?"

"I do not speak Mayan . . . I speak Indian. It's a universal language. Don't worry about my safety; these are simple, friendly people. I will return in the morning. Have a good night."

We were dumbfounded as we saw him walk away with the old man. Shortly after, the whole tribe disappeared.

We put on extra clothing, crawled inside the tent, and slept using the sleeping bag as a blanket. Two hours later, I was out of the tent and in the car. I turned the engine on and started the heater. There was no way I was going to freeze to death.

I was getting warm when Charlene came out of the tent and yelled at me at the passenger door. She was coughing and screaming that I was trying to kill her. It turned out that I had parked the car in such a way to use it as a windbreaker, but had placed the exhaust pipe by the tent's opening. I had been pumping exhaust fumes into the tent. She cursed me, took the keys away, and zipped the sleeping bag up. Then she ordered me to get in the tent and in the sleeping bag with her. Before she fell asleep, she told me that it was okay to snuggle her. Charlene said our body heat would keep us warm.

I couldn't believe my bad luck. Here I was in the middle of God-knows-where in the embrace of my soon to be ex-mother-in-law. Nothing made any sense to me. This trip did nothing for my self-esteem. Carlos, who swore he was a homosexual, kept getting plenty of pussy. And I, Alex Perez, a man who professed to have a certain amount of charming heterosexual ability, was stuck inside a tight sock wrapped on to a female grizzly bear.

I woke up early with a need to get out of the bag. I had a boner and was mortified about it. I also needed to pee but was afraid to move. Then, to my horror, Charlene felt it. I was horrified.

"Alex," growled the bear. "Tell me what's poking me in the ass is not what I think it is."

I apologized profusely and begged her not to turn around. "Don't worry, Charlene. It's just a morning piss hard-on. I'm not turned on by you."

Several vicious blows later, my bed mate was out of the bag. She kept her distance for the rest of the morning, and I was fine with that.

The morning was cold. I gathered whatever wood I could find, threw in all the books we had (except for the road atlas), and used whatever clothing was deemed expendable to start a fire. We sat across from each other trying to keep warm and waited for Carlos. He finally arrived and so did the indigenous crowd. He greeted Charlene, took me aside, and dropped another bomb on me.

"I'm staying here," he said.

"Why in heaven's name are you staying in this God-forsaken place? This is nowhere!"

"I have been asked to share the hut of the chief's daughter-in-law. His son passed away several months ago, and she needs help raising a boy. The old man is tired and wants to retire, but he needs a son to take over. I am being adopted and will soon become chief. I have accepted the offer."

"Are you sure you want to do this? The Sierras are a far cry from Houston," I said.

"Listen to me, Alex. Here in the Sierras, I feel clean."

I looked into his eyes and knew there was nothing more to say except "Good luck and congratulations." His face was beaming with pride when he gave me the key to his apartment.

"It has an extra month's rent paid," he said. Then he gave me his hand, thanked me for helping him find the love of women again, and said that by forcing him to come on this adventure, I saved his life. He gave me a hug and whispered, "I have found a true sense of purpose. They need me here. Besides, the girl I am to share a hut with is young and attractive. For an old fart like me, this is just too great to pass up."

He gave Charlene a hug and told her to take the road we had been on and continue. He said we would soon find a place to gas up. Carlos smiled, waved, and off he went. I noticed he was walking next to the chief. The tribe walked a distance behind.

I was sorry to see him leave but understood that somehow God had sent me here to deliver a misplaced Indian to a place in need of an American Eagle Scout. I had no doubt that Carlos Laughing Crow had found his tribe. I put a cross on the spot on the map that I thought we were in, just in case I ever came this way again.

We started the Chevy and drove for a while. Just about the time the car started to gasp for fuel, we found what appeared to be a trading post. It had one pump. After filling the tank, buying a few supplies, and feeling good about our role in Carlos' life, we left for the Mexican border.

Chapter 16

A long the way, Charlene told me that if I left Ramona alone and if I promised in writing to make no demands on her daughter's estate or to cause no trouble concerning Raulito's illegal status, she would sign over the Mercedes. She called it her "farewell gift" to me. She mentioned that although I was not the type of man she preferred for her daughter, I certainly was an interesting fellow in an odd sort of way. She also told me that I could keep the Chevy. Being the man that I was, I thanked her immensely for the compliment and accepted her gifts. Hell, I could use the money that the sale of the Chevy would bring, and I was glad to get the Benz. It was impossible to function in Houston with just a bicycle. I was done with Ramona, and I wouldn't dream of ruining Raúl's chance at a good life.

Junior had the wrong opinion of me. He was right as far as a normal father was concerned, for in certain circles it would be a given that I wasn't a very good one. However, if you stepped right across into what is not quite the usual, I was a damn good father. Experience and friendship were far better parenting tools than control and protection. Happily, I drove toward Mexico in a car in need of body work and in the company of my benefactor.

I kept thinking about how good I had it. I had been knighted in a cannabis-laden ceremony, avoided arrest in Guatemala, and had disposed of an unsuitable wife. Obviously, Captain Chris was not able to get loose quick enough to charge me with destroying his boat. I also dodged a lawsuit from the owner of the pier. Neither incident was my fault. Carmen and Carlos were actually responsible for crashing the boat into the pier. I had a clear conscience.

I passed a sign that read, "Quetzaltenango—14 kilometers," and I smiled. Yes, this has been a good adventure. I had been part of a successful rescue attempt, which gave me a warm, fuzzy feeling. I felt bad about losing Junior, but it worked out for the best. I was going to be single again, and I didn't need a son to worry about. I had an apartment with a month's rent paid waiting for me in Houston. I also owned a 190SL Mercedes Benz convertible. To most, that wouldn't be much, but to me, Alex Perez, that was grand.

Rosy dreams aside, I was aware of the danger in counting your chickens before they hatch. Needing to be prudent, I went over the plan. We were supposed to cross into Mexico, drive to Mexico City, drop Charlene off at the airport, and then I was on my own. A nice, slow cruise home through the state of Puebla was just what the doctor ordered. Unfortunately, that simple scenario was not in the cards. Three kilometers from Quetzaltenango, the Chevy blew a tire. Charlene cursed as I navigated the vehicle and got it off the road.

"Oh no, Charlene," I said. "We are in big trouble. There's no spare. Somebody stole the tire."

"Every time we have a problem, it's always someone else's fault. Why is that, Alex?"

I gritted my teeth. She must think I fell off the turnip truck yesterday. "Only a moron would venture forth on a long cross-country journey through Central America without checking the spare tire," I said. "Furthermore, when I bought the Chevy, I made sure it came with a jack and tire tool. We also packed three lawn chairs, three sleeping bags, and two pup tents. I would mention the fact that the toolbox, flashlight, and camera are missing, too, but why? It would only bring attention to my ineptness."

"When was the last time you took inventory?" Charlene asked me.

"Right before we crossed the border into Guatemala," I said. And as soon as I said it, I knew what happened to the stuff. The owner of the pier and his son had removed the goods when they confiscated the car. What a bunch of thieves. "Okay, Charlene. There's no need to argue over lost goods. You either stay here with the car or we hitchhike into town together."

"I'm not staying here alone. You thumb a ride, and I will join you. I'm not fond of standing by the side of the road like a wandering gypsy."

I stuck my thumb out, and we got a ride. The car had three rough-looking men in it, but I decided to get in anyway. Hell, we were close to town. What could possibly happen? I climbed in the front seat with the driver, and Charlene sat between the other two. She was not happy about my choice of ride.

The car suddenly veered off the road. Before I could protest, one of the men behind me stuck a pistol to my neck.

"*Si te mueves, te mato,*" the man said. I froze. I could hear Charlene whimper from where I was. She was scared. Getting a bit of courage, I told her not to do anything stupid.

"We are being held up. All they want is our money. Nobody's going to rape you," I said.

"You're damn right," she said. "No one is getting me out of my underwear today," she growled.

The bandits drove to a spot and stopped the car. We were told to get out and raise our hands. The driver came over to me and smiled. "Sorry to do this, Señor, but my friends and I have families to feed, and we have no jobs. We need all your money, your watch, your neck chain, your ring, and your clothes. Please take them off, except for your underwear."

"Take them all off? Surely you can't be serious?" I said.

"*Sí*, Señor, you and the Señora. You take all your clothes off, but please keep your underwear on. We don't want to see your ugly ass or the old woman's either. What size of boots do you wear?"

"Aah! You're not going to take my imitation ostrich leather boots, are you?"

Charlene started to scream when they tried to remove her dress. She put up a fight, but in the end, they subdued her and stuck a wad of cloth in her mouth. After it was all said and done, we were left tied to a tree practically naked. I couldn't believe that what goes around came around so fast. I had visions of Captain Chris and Jaime laughing at me.

I became despondent over the state of affairs we were in and swore to God that if He got us out of this mess with a minimum of embarrassment, I would light a candle to la Virgen de Guadalupe. A couple of hours later, someone saw us and called the cops. They came, clothed us, and took us to the station.

I told the cops what had happened and complained that the thieves had stolen my car. Like a dumb-ass, I gave them the plate number. It showed up on a list they had. The owner of the pier that Carlos and Carmen destroyed had filed a complaint. We were arrested. You would have thought things could not get any worse, but I was wrong. They stuck me in the same cell with Charlene.

"You are such an imbecile, Alex! I can't believe you wrecked a pier and didn't tell me. I would have covered the damages for you. Now we have to pay restitution plus fines. Is there any more bad news out there?"

"No. What kind of a guy do you think I am?" I asked, hoping Captain Chris and Jaime hadn't reported the damage to their boat.

Charlene made a phone call to her Guatemalan lawyer. Two days later, Señor Garza showed up and made arrangements to get us out on bail. I thanked God, the lawyer, and Charlene. The cell we were being kept in was a small one, and I suffer from claustrophobia. Still, I was going to miss the daily ration of rice, lentils, and plantain.

One hour before we were to be let out, I noticed two silhouettes on the thin curtains coming my way. The two men I was hoping never to see again were coming our way. Their presence sank me into the depths of darkness.

"There he is," said the American seafaring man. "That's definitely the man who wrecked my boat and stole my money." Oh no, now I'm a doomed man. Charlene is definitely going to castrate me.

After insulting me, she paid my new fines, refunded the American bandit the money he claimed I lifted from his shirt pocket, and paid for the boat repairs. She even gave Jaime money to help him cope with the mental abuse he suffered while in my hands. Unfortunately, the Guatemalan police released her but tagged me as a "person of interest" and decided to keep me incarcerated for a while longer. They wanted to see if there would be any other claims against me.

"I'm sorry, Alex, but I need to leave," said Bernadette Arnold. "I gave Capitán Lozardo one hundred dollars for your commissary privileges. That should sustain you for a while."

"What? You gave a cop my money? What makes you think they will give it to me instead of pocketing it? This is not the U.S., Charlene! We are in Guatemala. Things work differently here!"

"Let me tell you something, Alex. It isn't the Mexicans, the Guatemalans, or even the Americans who are precarious and different—it's you. You are the problem. If the rest of the Panamanians are anywhere near as dangerous as you are, I hope Colombia and Costa Rica have enough sense to keep their borders closed. What kills me, Alex, is that I have always wanted to go to Panama—maybe do a little gambling, some fishing, ride a party boat through the canal, spend a couple of days in the Pearl Islands, and visit the famous mountain town of Boquete. But after meeting you, I'm staying clear of the place. I'm not wild about mingling with lunatics. I'm willing to lay a bet that when the Perez family announces a reunion, the police will cordon off the asylum."

"You know what they say about sticks and stones, don't you?" I said, defiantly.

"Now, is there anything else you want from me before I leave you in your cage?"

"Yes, thank you for asking. I was beginning to think you didn't care. I want you to contact Padre Humberto and tell him to tell Junior that I need him to please open Pancho's Box again. Tell him I'm in need of a few more fairies."

"Alex, if you stay in this place long enough, you will more than likely become one yourself. Don't be walking backwards."

"What goes around comes around, Charlene. You won this round, but the fight is far from over."

"Listen to me, asshole. Capitán Lozardo has given me his word that he will release you after he is sure there are no more claims made against you. Please behave and do your time. So what if he keeps you here longer? Give him some credit . . . he's not stupid. You don't have to have a doctorate in Criminology to know the world is better off without you running loose in it."

"And you believed him? You took the word of a Guatemalan cop? They'll probably try to ransom me. Then, when no one responds to their demands, they'll torture me and keep me locked in here for years."

"Screw off, Alex. I'm done with you. You have cost me an enormous amount of money. The hundred bucks I left here is the last money you will ever see from me. I'm going to have to sell the 190SL to recuperate my loss. I'm sorry, Alex. I know I promised you that car, but I am reneging on it."

She paused to measure my resolve. I was down and out. There were no more bullets in my gun. I kept quiet.

"Don't you make the mistake of coming by Ramona's house to make trouble when you get out of here. If you do, whatever these Guatemalan jailers have done to you will feel like patty cakes in comparison to what I have in store."

As I watched her disappear, I wondered what lay in store for me. Hell, a little rest will be good for me. I looked at my jailers and wondered when dinner would be served.

Chapter 17

A Jailbird

Capitán Lozardo kept most of the money my mother-in-law had given him for my support. No surprise there. What did surprise me was that he actually gave some of it to Sargento Moreno. The rogue cop didn't strike me to be the generous type. Nonetheless, as my primary jailer, the man treated me well, considering he seldom spoke to me. The cop was cordial, coming by once a week to make sure I was handling my incarceration in a sane manner.

The sergeant, my secondary jailer, was a more amiable fellow. He thanked me for the money the Capitán gave him, didn't offer me a dime of it, and praised his Capitán's generosity.

Sargento Moreno had been assigned to me. His orders were to stay by my side, which he did, always with a watchful eye. His forte was loyalty; he followed the Capitán's orders without question. I was allowed to do certain things, forbidden to do others, and any deviation from the program was not possible.

The third month came, and I experienced the joy of celebrating a birthday locked up. I began to wonder if Charlene had passed the message I had given her for Junior. I needed to be rescued, and the boy had the ability to release the fairies kept in Pancho's Box. These mystical creatures were vividly engraved on my mind. I remembered they were rough, unpredictable, but fast in achieving the goal assigned to them. I wanted out of my Guatemalan jail.

By the end of the fourth month, I began to suspect my family and friends had abandoned me. Feeling low, I succumbed to my fate and decided to stop waiting for the cavalry to arrive. I was going to make the best out of a jailbird's life. Hell, why not? There were opportunities available for a prisoner with a good disposition and a keen eye, and I possessed both.

The first thing a person learns about a Guatemalan jail is that nothing is free and that includes your room and board. I had to work for it by sweeping and mopping my cell every day. Hallway duty came every other day, and my turn at the hideous bathroom fell upon me every three days. There were opportunities placed on the table for all the inmates. One of them was signing up to work long hours at a privately owned plantation, picking coffee beans every Friday. This seemed like the best deal to me. The pay was lousy, and the work was backbreaking, but weather permitting, I was all for it. Besides, Sargento Moreno, who had become my financial adviser, recommended it highly.

The Guatemalans were not draconian in the manner in which they treated their prisoners. There was a bright ray of sun shining upon the jailhouse; all I had to do was grab it. These people were not at all like the gringos, whose prison system is designed to breed *maricones*. The Guatemalans allowed an inmate a monthly conjugal visit. The last Saturday of every month was set aside for the wives or girlfriends to come in and service the inmates. If you didn't have a woman, the local whores would come in and let you have a good look at their physical attributes. That is how I met Laura. She came to the jailhouse one day, set her sights on me, and won my affection immediately.

Laura was not your typical brothel whore. She was an independent contractor, working a regular gig at a stand that sold American-style hamburgers and hot dogs. She was proud of the fact that she only prostituted part-time. Hell, you couldn't help but admire the woman's industriousness; she had two kids to support and no husband. Her positive demeanor was admirable, and her negotiating skills were right up my alley. She told me she usually charged ten *quetzales* for a quick poke, but since I was a handsome foreigner and because she really liked my manners, she would only charge me seven. Knowing a bargain when it's staring me in the face, I agreed to the price.

Being keenly aware that one good deed should be followed by another, I insisted on doing something special for her. So, when I asked Laura what would give her immeasurable pleasure, she told me it would be great if I could make English love to her. Even though I had no idea how the English did it, a deal was struck, and an amorous association between us began. Whenever I could afford to mount her, I pretended to be an Englishman.

These conjugal visits were a godsend, but they came with rules. If you wanted to have an additional monthly screw and if your behavior qualified you for it, you could get laid twice. If you were flushed with cash and your behavior allowed it, you could move up to *elite* status and purchase the "House Special." For twenty-five *quetzales* you could buy the Caballo Blanco package. This included an hour at the exclusive White Horse Motel. The room came with air conditioning and a soft bed. You also got a basket of salted, fried yucca with ketchup and two bottles of Gallo beer. The twenty-five bucks didn't include a woman; you had to supply your own. Capitán Lozardo supplied the guard that stood outside your door for free.

Everything considered, the special package was a bargain at twice the price. However, it was an expensive proposition for an inmate with limited means. I needed to find a way to make more money. One poke a month on a hard jail bed was not acceptable. I was used to a better life.

Laura's sexual prowess captured my heart. She had experience; her mouth and nipples tasted of licorice, and she had motorized thighs. Making love to her was like spending an hour at the gym. All I had to do was lie on my back, grab on to her ample behind, and hold on. When she was done, every inch of my body had gone through a workout. Her energy level was outstanding.

Another thing Guatemalan authorities allowed an inmate was to buy one bottle of rum and a carton of cigarettes per month. To make extra money I had to get creative, and broom and mop work didn't pay any cash. Breaking my back picking coffee beans for ten hours every Friday only netted me five *quetzales*. I became desperate.

Since I had a keen eye for commercial opportunities, I asked the Capitán for permission to go into the business of writing letters in English and Spanish for people in and outside the jail who had business and relatives outside the country. He agreed, but only on the condition I'd let him collect and manage the money. We split the profits sixty-forty, the forty being for me, of course, which in my predicament was still rather generous. I also had to give Sargento Moreno ten percent of my share.

It didn't take long for my reputation as a scribe to grow. Everyone brought their writing needs to me; not only were my fees affordable, but I was also reliable and discreet. My bilingual abilities and writing style provided an invaluable service to the community. Before long, I was writing love letters for shy men. Our monthly take had grown to over eighty *quetzales*. Netting thirty percent a month was not bad. I continued to work the coffee fields on Fridays. The physical labor was good for me.

The immediate goal was to make enough money for a bottle of rum, a carton of smokes, and a piece of ass at least twice a month. I could almost smell the *elite* status that I was about to reach.

I was celebrating five months of living in Quetzaltenango. This was a cause of concern because I was settling in too nicely in my incarceration. However, the time spent in the company of Sargento Moreno proved fruitful. The simple man enjoyed my sense of humor, and I fell into the habit of reading stories out loud to him. He claimed he could read but had failing eyesight and could not afford glasses. This was a lie, but I didn't mind. These story times helped me pass the time when I was not working and gave me ideas for the letters.

In the middle of one of my scribe sessions, an idea struck me like a bolt of lightning. The jail had several books: two were in Spanish, and those were the ones I read to the sergeant. There was also one in English: *The Celebrated Jumping Frog and Other Stories* by Mark Twain. Obviously, the jail had seen at least one other gringo besides Charlene. This book was heaven-sent because I used it to create stories for the sergeant. I told him that all the stories were about animals, and the protagonists were all frogs.

During one of our storytelling sessions, I suggested to Sargento Moreno that we should go public with our storytelling and charge people to hear the stories. He jumped at the idea. We organized our thoughts, and then we presented the plan to Capitán Lozardo. He agreed because Sargento Moreno bragged about my excellent storytelling prowess. Like before, he insisted on handling the finances.

The enterprise proved to be an immediate success. Capitán Lozardo advertised the readings in the local newspaper, and before long, we were making good money. Being the man that I was, I raised my creativity another notch and read to the audience a story about a frog named Pololo, who happened to live in Quetzaltenango. The crowd was amazed that their town had managed to get into a storybook, especially one in English. Someone actually said he had seen a frog that fit the description of Pololo, and then the crapola took off from there. Soon there were businesses named Pololo springing up everywhere, as well as sightings of the frog. The moola kept rolling in; an accountant was hired, and the sergeant and I started to receive our take in weekly pay envelopes.

Capitán Lozardo was impressed with my abilities. His behavior toward me changed drastically, and he warmed up and made it a point to engage me in conversation. The tedious mop, broom, and bathroom duties were assigned to the other inmates. I was also removed from the coffee plantation list. I was beginning to feel like a celebrity.

At first, I was told not to slack off on my letter writing, but when the storytelling sessions became popular and the townsfolk began to appear in numbers, I was ordered to cut down on the letter writing and spend more time working the story show. Needing to add something different to keep the audience interested, I took a chance and introduced poetry readings into the show. It went over big. We increased the admission fee.

We were packing the jailhouse every Friday night. Sargento Moreno hired a woman to set up a concession stand inside the jailhouse that generated even more money. We started making money hand over fist. I felt like the proverbial Golden Goose, and the sergeant felt like a capitalist.

Before long, the crowds began to get bigger and bigger, outgrowing our abilities to house them. We were turning paying patrons away, a matter that galled us. Needing a bigger facility, we were forced to get involved in negotiations with the town mayor—the Capitán's brother-in-law. We needed a larger hall for the readings, and the mayor had access to the municipal auditorium. However, the relationship between him and Capitán Lozardo was tainted with mistrust. We could not reach a favorable agreement to use the hall, so we remained where we were.

Needless to say, as the fan base grew, so did our visibility. Our successful enterprise became a problem. Not only did influential men become jealous and begin demanding a cut of the action, but also, the mayor started to make noise about the unlawful use of the jailhouse as a commercial venue and complained about the illegal exploitation of the inmates. He threatened legal action. In order to avoid trouble, we either had to cut the mayor into our deal or move the show away from the jail. Sargento Moreno was not happy with his current salary structure, and I wanted my freedom. Not wanting to share our profits, we became obsessed with finding another venue.

Later, Capitán Lozardo came upon an idea. Instead of giving me the freedom I had asked for, he made me a full partner and promised to release me soon. He gave Sargento Moreno a raise, a testament to his value as a moneymaker. We kept an eye on the greedy mayor.

Incarceration aside, my privileges were abundant. Paying for my meals ceased. Pretty soon, the "House Special" became my regular routine. It was only fitting, as I had achieved celebrity status. Laura's standing as a whore shot up as well. Now everybody wanted to buy her, but she kept herself solely for me. All of the other prostitutes were envious.

After my seventh month, the notion that Charlene might have paid my captors to keep me in Guatemala started to consume my thoughts. Although this prison ordeal was turning into a good adventure, I was now beginning to feel like Odysseus without a Penelope. I yearned to reach the shores of my beloved Texas. Escape became an obsession. I missed home and wanted out of Quetzaltenango. Every time I asked the Capitán when I could leave, he only said, "Soon but not yet."

God must have felt my forlornness, because he sent me a couple of young angels to distract me. Mariela and Margarita would come by the jailhouse daily. They would say hello and leave me a covered plate full of rice, lentils, plantain, and beef. One Thursday, the menu changed. Beef was replaced by iguana, lentils by kidney beans, and, instead of plantain, I got fried yucca. To my surprise, the hideous lizard tasted a lot like chicken. On that day, the girls sat directly in front of me and watched me eat. They were sitting in a manner which afforded me a discreet glimpse of their panties. They were obviously oversexed and bored with the duty of guarding their virginity.

Who could blame them? In a small town, a young girl had to control her urges lest she become known as a *puta* and damage her marriage opportunities. And, if putting out was not an option and engaging in heavy petting with their sweethearts was discouraged, where could these sweet young virgins get sexual amusement?

I was pleased to be on the receiving end of the strange attraction these young girls had for prisoners. Romance with an outlaw raised the titillation level. Maybe it was the need to nurture a caged man, or maybe it was the danger factor that turned them on. Anyway, Mariela and Margarita increased their teasing level by decreasing their discreetness. They graduated to sitting in front of me with their legs brazenly open, and I was now allowed to stare at their crotches with impunity.

One day, Mariela turned the game up a notch. She came in wearing no panties, showing me the beaver's moustache. Margarita had her drawers on. I smiled. Hell, I had been waiting for one of them to step up to the plate. It now appeared that I had a player. Mariela had just pushed the envelope further. Now, all I had to do was figure out how to separate them. But there were a couple of things that concerned me: The first was the fact that they were indeed young girls. Mariela was the oldest, and she was barely seventeen. Margarita was an overly endowed sixteen-year-old beauty. The other problem was Capitán Lozardo, Mariela's uncle. I had to be careful. A wrong move on my behalf and I'd be cleaning toilet bowls on a daily basis. Then, to add to my worries, I had the jealousy factor to deal with. I had to make sure I looked at each crotch evenly. I couldn't afford to offend Margarita. The last thing I wanted was to create a rivalry between the girls.

I wasn't sure how knowledgeable Margarita was about Mariela's "no-panties" routine, yet I was willing to bet she knew nothing about it. For Margarita, this was probably nothing more than a harmless game of "tease the prisoner"—a daring but harmless game.

I was well aware of the dangerous nature of the game and knew I was a tad too old to be messing with such young virginal flesh. A thirty-one-year-old guy should be respectful of other people's young daughters. Still, I was in Guatemala, and there a seventeen-year-old girl was in prime marriage age, so she was fair game. She became my target. How to bag the pussy without losing my privileges (or the family jewels) to an irate uncle was of utmost concern.

Mariela became a regular attendee of my story sessions. She would come early to help set up and would stay behind and help Sargento Moreno clean up. If I was ever going to taste forbidden fruit, I had to do it in the jailhouse, and I had to distract the sergeant long enough to raise Mariela's vaginal juices up a degree. The time afforded for fornication would be minimal at best. If the girl wanted to do it, we could. And, if we were to do it, a quickie was in order. The girl needed to be ready for action. I began to work on a plan.

Chapter 18

On the eve of my eighth month of imprisonment, it dawned on me that Capitán Lozardo was never going to let me go. I had become a cash cow, too valuable to turn loose. I also began to give up on Junior. The fairies should have made an appearance by now. I knew he had been disappointed in me, but that was no reason to turn his back on a friend in need. Feeling trapped, I began to work on an escape plan. Now, I had two sets of strategies to contend with, so coordination was important. I needed to prioritize my steps, lest I escape too soon. I did not want to get away before deflowering Mariela, the young virginal girl.

One day Capitán Lozardo came to me with an unusual proposition. He took me aside and laid his cards on the table. "Señor Perez, do you feel welcomed here? Do we treat you good?"

Knowing this had to be a trick question and wondering where the trapdoor was, I pondered the answer for a minute. "Sí, Capitán," I said, "You treat me very well."

"Good, then please no need to be formal anymore. You can call me 'Luciano.'"

"Okay. You can call me 'Alex,'" I said. "What's on your mind?"

"You know, Alex, I've been watching you, and I think you are the right man for the job."

"What job?" I asked. "I'm very busy."

"My cousin Pablo brought six pretty girls from Honduras and El Salvador last week. These girls want to work pleasing men. I have three girls from Guatemala City already working and my other cousin, Rubén, is bringing two from Mexico. I have a brothel here and want to open another one in Huehuetenango. Pablo will run one and Rubén the other."

"Where do I fit in?"

"I need someone to oversee the operations. You have done a good job here with the writing business and the storytelling. I can see you have talent for doing business. The concession stand in the jailhouse is also doing very well. You're popular, and people like you. It's a matter of time before politicians will try to steal you for themselves. I'm already paying my thieving brother-in-law a small fortune to keep his greedy hands off. I need to protect the time I have invested in you. You do understand that, don't you?"

I nodded, but kept quiet.

"I'm going to have to turn you loose soon, and I need someone to be in charge of all my businesses. I can't do it all by myself. The owners of the coffee plantation are putting the arm on me; they need me to supply them with more workers. I have to concentrate on my police work and arrest more fieldworkers. The owner of El Caballo Blanco Motel wants more money, so we're upgrading the deal. We will now supply the girls. If a man wants to make love to his wife or girlfriend, he can do it in his cell, but if he wants to enjoy a nice girl in a soft bed with room service, he will have to hire one of our girls. I want to offer you the position of general manager of Lozardo Enterprises. You will have to continue working your two jobs, but I know you can do it. The money will be good. I am a generous man. What do you say?"

Hell, it's every man's dream to run a brothel. "Will your cousins resent me being their boss?" I asked.

"No. Those two idiots can barely take care of themselves. They need me to provide guidance, security, and to help with the finances. They will be glad to have you in the family. With you watching things, they can concentrate on getting new girls and moving the old ones around. Fresh young whores are very important if you want to keep the customers interested. Besides, the young ones bring a good price. What do you say, Alex? Are you interested?"

Talk about a stupid question. If I say no, he will find a reason to keep me incarcerated. Besides, what sane man wouldn't give up his left testicle to run a brothel?

"The offer is tempting," I said. "I may be interested, but I need to think it over."

Capitán Lozardo stared at me with his cold, beady eyes. I knew what he was thinking . . . You either work for me, or you'll be cleaning toilets. I had to accept the offer. If I wanted to escape, money and freedom were needed. Wanting to impress my new boss, I decided to show my management skills.

"Are the whorehouses operational?" I asked.

"The one here is open for business—a small one-story club on the outskirts of town. It's called El Paraíso. We are looking for a building in Huehuetenango."

I looked at the despicable man. He fit my impression of what a crooked cop was supposed to be like. The man was short, sported a Zapata moustache, and always had a five-o'clock shadow on his face. He had a big belly, bow legs, and wore a ranchero hat to cover his baldness. The only thing missing was sunglasses. The man never wore any.

Physical attributes aside, the lawman was mentally sharp. He was also cold-blooded and had a quick eye for opportunities. His cohort, Sargento Moreno, was totally different. He was tall, gaunt, clean-shaven, and wore a police hat—Kepi-style—that was too small to fit on top of a thick mop of unruly black hair. I often wondered how the hat stayed on.

Needing to impress my boss so a good salary could be negotiated, I prepared to take on my new position. "Luciano, everyone knows you can't run a brothel from a one-story building. It has to have at least two stories. You party with the girls downstairs, and then you take them to bed upstairs. Jeez . . . I can see why I am needed here. Can I get back to you with my answer? I have to concentrate on tonight's storytelling. I'm reading about a frog from Texas that fell in love with a pig. His name is Kermit. It's really a funny story. You should come and accompany Mariela."

"Sorry, I can't waste my valuable time listening to stupid animal stories. Besides, Mariela's father and I are going to do a little business in Guatemala City. We'll leave tonight and won't be back for a couple of days. Mariela's mother is sick, so she'll be coming alone. However, Sargento Moreno will be by her side. If you decide to take the job, please tell Sargento Moreno he has been instructed to let you out of your cell. You can move out right away. The owner of the Caballo Blanco Motel will rent you a room. I've made arrangements already. You and I will make a lot of money together. You'll like living in Quetzaltenango."

"Thank you, Luciano. Becoming a Guatemalan just may be in the cards for me."

As I prepared myself for the evening's storytelling, I thought life was finally giving me a good shot at fulfilling my potential. Running a brothel was way up on the list of things I wanted to do, and bedding Mariela was a close second. That young virginal flesh had to be tasty, and I couldn't wait to get my hands on her sweet body.

Sargento Moreno and I began the usual preparations for the evening reading. We made sure the concession was stocked with an ample supply of frying oil, sliced yucca, sliced plantain for *patacones*, popcorn, and flan. The usual big jars of *tamarindo* and *horchata* drinks were in place, and we had two cases of Gallo beer crammed in wash buckets covered with chipped ice.

I was moving things around in the hall so it could accommodate the crowd when I caught a glimpse of a man looking in through the corner window. Our eyes met, and he quickly turned away. I had a feeling I'd seen him before. When I stepped outside, he was gone.

"Is something wrong, Señor Alex?"

"No, Sargento. I just thought I saw someone spying on us."

"It's probably someone working for the *alcalde*. He's mad because we turned down his offer to rent the municipal building."

"Turning him down was a mistake," I said. "The man can be trouble."

"He wanted too much money for the place plus a big cut of the action. He's a crook, and we have to stay away from him."

"He has a cut of the action already," I said. "Capitán Lozardo had to pay him because he threatened to shut us down. We were running a business from the jailhouse. Hell . . . we still are! He's the mayor, and we'll regret this action. I'm sure of it."

"Don't you worry about him. He's probably just spying on us. I will tell Capitán Lozardo about this matter when he returns."

I made a mental note that if I wanted to ever see Texas again, I needed to get the hell out of Dodge before the greedy mayor grabbed me. Getting away from him would be doubly difficult.

Laura came in as I was putting the final touches on my presentation. She had the look of a woman in the midst of a hormonal bonfire.

"What's up, dear?"

"Papi, my *mono*'s hot. I need you to cool it down. Today you can do it for free."

Sargento Moreno laughed and told me I could use the back room where he took naps. He said the sheets had been changed earlier that day. Laura lifted her skirt, giving me a view of her agitated monkey.

"Aaargh," I said. "Swab the decks, hoist the sails, and load them guns, lads, thars treasure to plunder on them high seas."

"Ooh, I love it when you make English love to me," Laura said.

Chapter 19

"**Y**ou have a visitor, Señor Alex," said Sargento Moreno.

"Oh no . . . it's not Laura coming back for another round, is it?"

"No, it's a young man this time. Can I bring him in?"

"A visitor for me? Are you sure?"

"*Sí.* He claims to know you."

I gave him a perplexed look and nodded in agreement. He came back with Junior. Sargento Moreno raised an eyebrow, showing me a troubled countenance. Oh no! He thinks I'm a switch-hitter.

"Hola, Mister Alex, how are you?"

"Junior, what are you doing here?"

Before he could say anything else, I gave the sergeant a look that told him to please vacate the premises. In a huff, he left and slammed the door.

"I wanted to see you," Junior said out loud. Then he came closer and whispered, "I also wanted to tell you that everything's ready for your escape. The fairies have been let out, and they are doing their thing."

"Now they're doing their thing?"

"Yes. I'm sorry it took so long, but I was very busy with Padre Humberto's problems. The fairies were helping him. But I'm here now, and everything will be fine as wine. You will soon be out of here. Trust me."

I panicked. What does he mean by I'll be out of here soon? How soon is soon? I'm getting closer to poking Mariela . . . I can't be rescued yet. I swallowed hard.

"Listen, Junior, we have to have a long talk, but not right now. I am not quite ready to leave here. Can you put the fairies back in the box and come back to see me in about a month? We can talk some more then. I'm working on a deal, and I need time to pull it off."

He shrugged his shoulders. "Maybe I can and then maybe I can't. Working with them is hard, you know. It is not a science thing with fairies. There's no book about how to work with them. They can be difficult to control. I will try to do it for you, but I can make you no promises. Why do you want to stay here? This is a prison and *maricones* live here."

"It's a long story, and it has nothing to do with *maricones*. I'll tell it to you later. Why don't you stop by the jailhouse tonight? I'm giving a reading about a Texas frog. I'm very popular here, you know."

"Yes, I know. We heard the people in town speaking about you. They call you the 'Storyteller of Quetzaltenango.' What time do you think we should come?"

"Come around seven, and who is 'we,' Junior? You've got a mouse in your pocket?"

He gave me a puzzled look. "No, I'm here with Padre Humberto, my sister, and Pancho. You know, Mister Alex, these fairies surprise me all the time. You cannot believe what they did for you. They brought us some gringos from Europe to help with your escape. This whole thing will be hard to stop."

European gringos? What in hell is he talking about? I changed the subject. "Did Padre Humberto beat his accuser?" I said.

"Yes. The lawyer got him off. We beat the bishop. The good Padre is free to do whatever he wants. We're on our way to Mexico now, but before we get out of Guatemala, we have to help you. You helped us a lot, and now it's our turn. Like I said, Mister Alex, your escape will be hard to stop."

Sargento Moreno came in and announced that visiting hours were over. He escorted Junior out. A few minutes later, the sergeant came back, and with a dubious look, he asked me who my visitor was and what he wanted.

"He's a Mexican boy I met in Guatemala City some time ago. He's in town with an important priest. The holy man wants to come to my reading tonight, and the boy wanted to make sure we had room for them. My reputation is spreading. We better put out a few more chairs, because it looks like we're going to have a really big crowd tonight."

Mariela came early and helped with the kitchen duties. The yucca had to be sliced, as well as the green plantain. When she asked Sargento Moreno to go to her house and bring the case of orange soda her father had left on the front porch, I knew she was ready for me to take her. I looked at the situation closely and understood that the simple-minded woman who worked at the food stand and the two dumb guards assigned to the jailhouse were my only obstacles.

"Señora," I said. "Take these five *quetzales* and buy as many sugar-covered *tamarindo* balls as possible. There are some people from Guatemala City that are coming tonight, and they love to eat them. Go right away."

I called the guards in and told them that Sargento Moreno had heard a rumor that the mayor was sending thugs to disrupt our reading tonight. I asked them to please stand guard outside and to not let any ruffians or foreigners get inside. When they closed the door behind them, I moved in on my prey.

"Mariela," I said, enjoying the sound of her name. "Come here."

She came to me eagerly. I grabbed her hand and placed it on John Henry. He was standing at attention. She touched it, squealed with delight, and put a chokehold on it.

"*Bueno*, Alex, *ahora eres todo mío*," she said in a sultry sensual voice.

Mariela was right. I was all hers, and so was John Henry. He didn't seem to mind the killer grip she had on him. He was full of himself; he wanted to frolic inside her passion bowl. I fondled her luscious breasts and kissed her. Her hold on John Henry intensified. She used her free hand to grab my neck and began to swab my tonsils with a frantic tongue. She finally let go of my swollen and bruised dick. But before I could reach down and soothe his pain, she crossed one leg over my waist, keeping me close to her. She kept on sparring with my tongue. I began to suspect this girl was no virgin. As a matter of fact, by the way she was manhandling me, I understood this young girl had been playing me for a sucker. She was experienced. I was not the first prisoner she had screwed. Encouraged, I tried to force a hand under her skirt. There was a need to feel the readiness of the beaver. But no matter how hard I tried to reach it, the leg wrapped around my waist wouldn't allow me to touch it. She kept on kissing me like there was no tomorrow. When I finally broke through the log jam, my heart leaped. She was ready. With pride, I brought the beast out.

"Papi," she said, "*ponte el sombrero.*"

"What?" I said, "You want me to put a condom on now?"

"*Sí*, Papi, *no puedes entrar sin sombrero.*"

Oh no . . . she won't let me in without a condom. I panicked. The damn things were in my cell under the mattress. Not wanting to waste valuable time going after them, I pressed the point. She applied more pressure and closed the gate.

"No, Papi, *ponte el sombrero.*"

"Mariela, I want you more than life. Give me a little taste first, then I'll go put a hat on John Henry."

"No, Papi, *me vas a perjudicar. Por favor, ponte el sombrero.*"

Knowing it was no use to press the point, I gave in. There would be no getting past her vaginal lips without the damn condom. I ran to the cell, returning just in time to hear the sound of Sargento Moreno's police car drive up. Shit, this can't be happening. I had a boner of major proportion going, and what was I going to do? Baseball . . . think about baseball . . . maybe it'll go away.

"What time do you have to be home tonight?" I asked, with a gasp.

"Sargento Moreno will take me home after the reading, but I can get out again. Where can I meet you? Can you escape?"

"Yes, I can get out. Can you meet me at the Caballo Blanco after the show? I will get a room with air conditioning, I promise."

She kissed me again and straightened her blouse and skirt. I went to the bathroom, cursed my luck, and threw cold water on John Henry.

As expected, the reading room filled up. The customers were in a joyous mood. I was eloquently introduced by Sargento Moreno as a "storyteller extraordinaire." The crowd clapped, cheered, and whistled. When I mentioned that tonight's reading had to do with a Texas frog who had fallen in love with a Mexican pig, they laughed, clapped, and whistled some more.

I was about to begin the reading when the doors opened and three hooded men walked in brandishing guns. "¡No se mueva nadie!" yelled one of them. Oh God, not now, Junior! Don't rescue me now . . . I'm not ready!

"Everybody, please lay on the floor now!" said another man with a familiar Swiss accent. Then, a man with bulging breasts and a moustache walked over to me and placed a pistol on my neck.

"Come with us."

"Carmen?" I whispered. "The disguise looks good on you."

"Cállate, pendejo. Camina rápido que nos tenemos que salir."

I did as told. I kept quiet and moved fast. My rescuers escorted me out of the jailhouse at gunpoint. To give my jailbreak some credence, I resisted their efforts. Hell, why not? If the Guatemalans recaptured me, I could plead total innocence.

We walked outside, and there was Padre Humberto, who had the drop on the two guards I'd sent to keep the thugs away. He was wielding a pistol and wearing holy garb. As I passed by him, I couldn't help but notice the puffy bags and dark circles under his eyes. He looked like a man who had been ridden hard and put up wet.

"Hola, Padre," I said. He didn't respond, and I couldn't blame him. If the fairies actually helped him, he looked the part. I shuddered at the thought of what laid ahead for me. It was bad enough I had to leave without plundering Mariela's physical attributes, but leaving Laura without saying good-bye hurt.

"Alex," yelled a man inside a big American convertible, "just hurry up and get in the damn car!"

"Hello, Kermit! Fancy seeing you here. What brings you to the Sierra Madre Mountains?"

"Your mother-in-law hired my company to mount a rescue."

"Where are we going?" I asked.

"To Mexico," said my Swiss bud Ronson.

"Hey, the gang's all here. Thanks for coming to get me, but if you guys think you can outrun the Guatemalan police, you are all crazy. Ever heard of radio? We'll be caught before we get close to the border."

"Don't worry, Mister Alex," said Junior. "Pancho's stealing us a plane."

I breathed a sigh of relief. Okay, this escape might actually work. Then I realized that theoretically, I was a free man. All I was doing was running away from Laura, a seventeen-year-old wanton girl, and a job auditioning whores. Damn fairies.

We hadn't gone very far when a set of lights and a siren began pursuing us. I figured it was Sargento Moreno. If I did manage to escape, his ass was going to be mud. His boss was going to be mad. I felt sorry for him and secretly wished him success in his pursuit.

Actually, I felt good about things. Either way, I was going to come out a winner. If I did manage to escape, I would see Texas again. If I did not, then I'd be general manager of Lozardo Enterprises. Kermit turned a sharp corner, screeching the tires. My adrenaline began to flow. I gave him a thumbs-up and shouted, "Graham Hill has nothing on you!" He grinned, obviously enjoying the race.

We passed a sign that read "Aeropuerto Esteban Jiménez." It figures. Where else do you steal a plane from other than from an airport? Junior talked to Pancho on a walkie-talkie.

"Mister Kermit, turn right on Avénida Bolívar," he said. "Pancho's waiting there with the plane."

Kermit had his Norwegian blood boiling, and he was driving like a man possessed by devils, trying to outrun our pursuit. The cops behind us fired two shots, unnerving Carmen. Soon after that, we saw Avénida Bolívar and did as Junior ordered; we made a sharp right turn, screeching tires again.

"The plane, the plane, there's the plane!" shouted Junior.

He was correct. There was the plane all right, coming straight at us. It was being followed by another cop car. They were having a good time with the siren, which was blaring constantly.

"All right, boys and girls," said Ronson, "we've got to get into the plane while it's moving. Don't everybody jump out of the car at the same time."

"It has propellers," I said. "The plane has propellers, and we are heading right toward them. We can't approach it from the front. Haven't you guys ever seen John Wayne do it? He catches up to the plane from behind, then he jumps into an open door."

Kermit took my advice to heart, slammed on the brakes, turned the steering wheel, and the car turned around. We cheered.

"I saw Burt Reynolds do that during a chase scene in the movie *Smokey and the Bandit*," he said. "I always wanted to do it. I can't believe it actually worked." We patted him on the back.

The plane passed us by; we saw Pancho grinning from the cockpit. The cop car chasing us also passed us by. I saw Sargento Moreno's big eyes flash by me as we passed him going the other way. The two dumb jail guards were riding with him. They pointed their guns at us but did not fire. I smiled. They were probably out of bullets already. The sergeant obviously saw the Burt Reynolds movie, too, because he tried the same maneuver but failed. The cop car spun around in circles several times and crashed.

Kermit floored the gas pedal, and we passed the cops chasing the plane. They turned to looked at us, and Junior flipped them the bird. A pistol shot rang out, shattering the rearview mirror, unnerving all of us. We caught up to the rear of the plane, came as close to the door as we could, and prepared to jump. We heard another pistol shot; the cops were obviously upset over Junior's behavior.

"The plane door is closed!" I yelled.

"Junior, call Pancho and tell him to open the door!" said Carmen.

Like magic, the door opened, and there was Charlene and some dude I had never seen before. "Jump, Alex!" she said. "Don't be a coward!"

I pushed Carmen aside and jumped into the open door. The guy grabbed me and pulled me inside. I looked at Charlene and smiled.

"Nice to see you," I said. "I thought you didn't like me."

"Don't be smug," she said. "I'm paying a fortune to rescue your dumb-ass. You owe me big time."

Everyone made it into the plane. The car crashed, and the lone Smokey on our trail was left behind. The plane roared up into the sky. We cheered again.

Pancho circled the town and headed north. I looked at Quetzaltenango, said a silent good-bye to Mariela and Laura, and cursed my rescuers.

Charlene opened two bottles of champagne. We toasted the successful escapade and drank our libations. A few minutes later, I heard Kermit say, "There's a helicopter following us."

Ronson went to look out the cockpit window. "It's a military helicopter," he said. "The army's after us."

"I can't believe the Guatemalans are making this much fuss over an imbecile like Alex," growled Charlene.

"Hey, you took away their storyteller," I said. "What do you expect?"

"Can we outrun them, Mister Ronson?" said Junior.

"Yes, we can outrun the helicopter. It's those jet planes they will scramble to intercept us that worries me. They have missiles," said Ronson.

"Can we just throw Alex out the door?" suggested Carmen. "I don't want to die for this *pendejo.*"

I gave her the bad-eye and was about to tell her a thing or two when I heard the sound of gunfire followed by the ominous sound of bullets hitting the plane. Ronson started yelling from the cockpit, "We've been hit! We've been hit! Hang on . . . we're gonna make a crash landing!"

Some rescue. I left a good job offer and a sweet young body in need of attention behind in Quetzaltenango, for this? So I can die in an airplane accident somewhere in the Sierras? *Me cago en Judas.* I need to find new friends.

"Hang on . . . we're trying to find a place to land," said Ronson.

"Where?" I said, "Where are you going to land?"

"There's a clearing up ahead between two mountains. It's gonna be tight, but we have no choice," he said.

"We're losing altitude!" yelled Kermit.

I looked out the cockpit window and saw a jet coming from behind, and then I looked to the front and saw the mountains. It looked like suicide any way you sliced it. I left the cockpit, grabbed one of the two parachutes stuffed in a compartment, and put it on. The jet passed us, made a circle and came back firing. Bullets kept hitting the plane.

"We're hit again!" yelled Kermit. "We're going down!"

"No shit, Sherlock." I said, "I'm too young to die. Open the damn door . . . I'm jumping. You guys can crash land if you want."

"I'm going with you," said Ronson.

"No, you are not," said Kermit. "You work for me, and I need you here. I could break a leg or something when we land, and I may need you to carry me."

"I'm not paying anyone if I get hurt," said Charlene.

In the middle of all this fuss, I opened the door and readied myself to jump.

"Are you sure you don't want to take your chances with us, Mister Alex?" asked Junior. "We have some fairies still doing stuff for us. They will not let us down."

I pinched the ragamuffin's cheek. "You may be right. The fairies will probably not let us down. It's the pilot in the jet shooting at us who's going to bring us down."

"You need to have faith, Mister Alex. We have a Padre with us, and Pancho is a good driver," said Junior.

"The holy man has a gun, and Pancho's a road bandit. I'm willing to bet that the man who is going to crash us down doesn't have a license to fly. Are you sure you don't want to take your chances with me? There's one more parachute left, and you can put it on. The plane is probably full of gas; it will surely explode upon impact."

No sooner had I predicted doom and gloom, when I heard the engines sputter and choke. Then the propellers stopped whirling.

"We're out of gas!" yelled Kermit. "We're going down!"

I gave him the bad-eye. Before Junior had a chance to say anything, I screamed "Geronimo!" and the wind spirited me away from my friends. The chute opened, and I was heading down fast. To my chagrin, there was a thick forest beneath me. I was going to crash into a bunch of trees. Damn fairies.

I looked at the plane, and it was heading down fast. Soon it disappeared. I looked for a ball of fire or an explosion to pinpoint the crash site, but neither materialized. In a matter of minutes I shot into the middle of a forest. Luckily, I missed hitting any big branches, thus avoiding any broken bones, but I did get cut and scraped up pretty bad. After the joyless ride was over, I ended up dangling from a tree. The parachute was stuck in the branches and I was left swinging about five feet from the ground.

I thanked God for keeping me alive, wondered about the fate of my mates, and hoped there weren't any hungry carnivorous animals around. It was dark, and I was bleeding. I glanced at my watch. Shit, it's eight o'clock—feeding time in the jungle. I crossed myself, kept an eye out for hungry pumas, and said twenty Hail Marys and ten Our Fathers as I hoped God hadn't forsaken me.

Chapter 20

An Angel Up a Tree

"Ladies, please be kind enough to take off all your clothes. My employer has given me explicit instructions to hire three good-looking women, and I'm going to employ the best ones from the group. I need to see everything before I can decide who I'm employing," I said.

"Papi, ¿cuál es el apuro? Me tienes que amar a mi primero," said Mariela.

"You're right, sweetheart, there's no need to hurry with the inspections. First I need to make love to you. Okay, girls, I need to take care of some unfinished business here. You're free to stand around and watch if you like. Mariela's young, and she may be in need of technical advice."

"Papi, si te gusta . . . ellas se pueden meter en la cama con nosotros," said Mariela.

"Yes, of course they can. I'm glad you thought of it. You can all get in bed with us. First one gets a prize. Thanks for suggesting it, Mariela. It will make our lovemaking a bit spicier. Listen up, ladies, the last one to get naked and jump in bed with us has to use the video camera. I want this group-grope on tape."

"Oye, Papi, no es necesario ponerte el sombrero. Tú eres mi hombre, te quiero mucho."

"You are an angel, Mariela, thank you. I will throw the condom away. I love you, too."

This scene was too perfect to be real, but I was going to milk it for all it was worth. Mariela buried her body in the bed and assumed the spread-eagle position. Her heavenly thighs made me quiver with anticipation. However, before I could do any poking, I felt something poking me. Oh, no, there's a *maricón* masquerading as a whore, and he's in bed with us.

"Okay," I said, "the *maricón* has to leave."

I went back to Mariela, whose sweet lips were calling me. As I reached for her, I felt another sharp poke. Annoyed, I turned around. "Okay, girls, I'm the only one doing any poking. I can't concentrate on the business at hand if I have to guard my ass. Everybody off the bed. I'm checking to see which one of you has a dick."

Mariela grabbed me and pulled me down on her. She wrapped her legs around my waist. "Papi, *aquí no hay ningún maricón. Ven, ámame.*"

"Okay, baby, maybe you're right," I said. "Sorry about the distraction. I'm on you like white on rice."

I felt another sharp poke and heard a voice, "Señor, *¿está muerto?*"

I opened one eye and looked down. I saw a kid with a dog standing underneath me holding a long pole. He poked me again.

"Señor, *¿está muerto?*"

I ignored the kid, closed my eyes, and tried to get back to the dream. I was determined to love Mariela. However, no matter how hard I tried to go back to the dream, it didn't work. The stupid kid kept poking me with the stick. Aggravated over losing Mariela, I turned my attention to the boy.

"No, I'm not dead. Stop poking me!"

"Aah, you're not dead. That is good for you," he said. "You fell from the sky. I saw you float down last night. We have been looking for you. I'm glad you did not die. You must be a lucky gringo."

Oh, brother. "Listen, kid, can you help me down?"

"You're lucky that I speak English, otherwise I would not understand you, and then you would be stuck in the tree all day. This is my dog Cacho. He also understands English. Go ahead and say something to him."

"Listen, kid, I don't want to talk to the dog. What I really want is to get my feet on the ground. Why don't you go get your father and tell him to bring a knife so he can cut me down from the tree?"

"My father has gone to San Antonio, Texas, to work. My mother's looking for you by the *quebrada*. Wait here, and I'll go get her."

The creek must have been fairly close, because the kid returned quickly with a woman who I assumed was his mother.

"Mamá, *ahí está el gringo. ¿Crees que es un ángel?*"

"Why are you hanging there? Don't you have any place to go?"

I bit my lip, assuming there was no sense being sarcastic. I was in trouble and needed help. Instead of berating the woman's intelligence, I used the kid's imagination as a bargaining chip.

"Your son's right, ma'am. I am an angel. I was sent here by God to do a good deed for the first person that found and helped me down."

"One good deed? Is that all? Most of the time, when the genie comes out of the bottle, he gives the person that let him out three wishes. I'm not sure I want to cut you down if you're going to give my son only one wish. You need to offer us more wishes."

Jeez, I can't believe this. "Señora, what's your name?"

"Why do you want to know? I don't think I want to tell a man who's hanging from a tree."

Shit, this is not going to be easy. "Señora, I need it in case I want to give you a wish."

"My name is Twila Hernández, and this is my son Julio. The dog's name is Cacho. Who are you?"

"My name is Alejandro Perez. You can call me Alex. Can you cut the straps of my parachute so I can get down?"

"What kind of a gringo are you with a name like 'Alejandro Perez.' You're making fun of us. You must think we are stupid. I will not cut you down unless you admit that you're a gringo, and even if you say you are one you must promise to give us three wishes. We want one each."

"You want me to grant the dog a wish? Are you serious?"

"Yes, Cacho gets one, too. Can you be a gringo and give us three wishes?"

"Look, Twila, I am a Panamanian angel, not some stupid genie stuck inside a bottle. Those genies in the storybooks are Arabs. They are wealthy, and they can give three wishes. Panamanian angels don't have much money, so we can only do one. Sorry."

"*Dice que no es gringo, Julio. Dice que es un pinche panameño. No nos quiere dar tres deseos; nada más nos quiere dar uno.*"

Julio came closer and poked me again with the sharp pole. "You're trying to cheat us, Mister Angel. You don't fool us for a minute, for we are smart. I saw a *panameño* once in a newspaper. His name was Mano de Piedra Durán; he was a strong man. You look nothing like him. You look like a gringo. One wish is not enough. We want three wishes, or you stay in the tree."

Man, this can't be happening. "Okay, I'm making a new rule. I am now a gringo, and everyone standing here gets one wish each and that includes the dog. Now, would somebody please cut the straps so I can get down?"

Twila handed the boy a knife; he climbed the tree, cut the straps, and dropped me. I tried to walk, but my legs refused to hold my weight. Several tries later, I was finally able to stand, but only with the help of a nearby tree. My legs were tingling. Twila, Julio, and Cacho kept looking at me with interest. Since I had time to kill, I began to size everyone up, including the dog. Passing for a gringo was going to be easy. I'd been accused of being one all my life. Hell, my father thought I was a gringo. I could easily imagine the unpleasant surprise my grandfather, father, and uncle had when they went to Amador Guerrero Hospital in Colón City to see me get born and were handed a white, green-eyed blonde kid. I bet mother had a lot of explaining to do.

The difficult part was fullfilling the damn wishes. The mother and the boy seemed sharp, so getting something by them was going to be hard. The dog was going to be easy. Cacho had been hanging around wagging his tail, and he was not wearing a collar. There was wish number one.

The way the portly woman's eyes kept checking me out clued the second wish. I bet she wants to get laid. I can do that. I have made love to fat, ugly women before. All I needed was a heavy dose of rum, and a couple tokes of reefer and voila—wish number two. The kid's wish was worrying me. He looked like he wanted a father, not an easy role for me to fill.

I was finally able to walk so we headed out. They were taking me to their home. I was hoping they weren't weird or cruel like those people in the movie *Deliverance*. The notion of them locking me in a shed and making me perform husband and fatherly duties for months on end terrified me. I specifically hated the idea that I could be forced to walk the damn dog every day.

Chapter 21

Three Wishes

My fears of being imprisoned were unfounded. I was treated well. After all, I was an angel, therefore a special entity. I was fed regularly, went for long walks with Julio and Cacho, and Twila allowed me to wear some of her husband's clothes. However, she would not let me wear any of his underwear. Whenever my one pair of shorts was being washed, I had to go around free-balling.

The house was small but clean. It was a good cabin sequestered in the forest. Staying here suited my sense of comfort. All that was expected of me was to be civil, helpful around the place, and working on their three wishes. Usually, a task of that magnitude would worry a person of lesser abilities, but not me. I was Alex Perez, son of my mother. We could handle anything thrown our way. She had prepared me right from the get-go. She gave me a boat-load of advice and kept shoving it down my throat.

"There are two things you must know if you plan to do well in life, son," she once said to me. "One is to never admit anything that will bring trouble into your life. The other is when faced with a problem of great magnitude, grab the bull by the horns and take control."

Those were words of wisdom, and they had served me well. She had done a good job of raising her son. I made a mental note to give her a call next time I had access to a telephone. In the meantime, I was going to make the best out of this unusual situation.

"Okay, listen up," I said, trying to sound authoritative. "Let me tell you how this wishing thing works. The rules are simple and must be obeyed. Those who are getting the wishes can't say them out loud or even write them on paper. The only way they can get their wishes is by wishing them. I will know what you want. I am an angel, and we have telepathic powers. You don't have to say anything. If you do, you will lose your wish."

"What if you are wrong and give us the wrong wish? Do we get another one?" asked the naïve boy.

"Angels are never wrong. If I give you a wish, it is because you are wishing it. It is not my fault if you have two or three wishes swishing around in your brain. Angels can get confused, you know. We're not perfect. I will try to give you the wish you think about the most, so clear your mind of extra wishes."

That was a brilliant move. I had bought myself a way out of my predicament. Moreover, my inquiring mind and keen sense of awareness had given me hints about what to give them. By the end of my first week, I had the wishes down pat.

During one of my searching sprees of the cabin, I stumbled upon Twila's dildo. It was hidden under the mattress. Obviously, the woman was obsessed with sex. The vibrating apparatus was huge. I turned it on, but the batteries were dead. Poor woman! I knew what she needed, and it wasn't me. There was no way I could compete against the foot-long titillating machine.

At the beginning, I had actually contemplated doing the wild thing with her, but there was no rum or tequila in the house. Libations were needed because she was not very appealing. She was short, fat, ugly, and she never shaved her legs. A hairy woman that does not like rum or tequila and expects me to make love to her is in big trouble. I'm not that easy. In order to make love to her, I needed lots of booze and a strong vision of Mariela's thighs.

Who was I kidding? I couldn't muster up any enthusiasm for Twila even if I had a gallon of alcohol. She had more hair on her legs than I had on my entire body. She was getting a six-pack of D-sized batteries from this angel and nothing more.

When dealing in wishes, being right on target is not that important. You just have to get close enough. John Henry would get a reprieve, for he would not have to stand up for me; he was going to give way to the battery-operated masturbator. I returned the enormous dildo to where it belonged and washed my hands with kerosene.

Cacho and I became friends. He was the only dog I could remember that actually liked me. I understood very early during my stay at Twila's place why I was trusted. The dog was the reason. Cacho's good sense of character and his awareness of my where-abouts afforded me the freedom I enjoyed. The dog tagged me as an angel from the beginning. He knew I was going to deliver the three wishes.

I tried to figure out what kind of dog he was. I knew he had to have some Golden Retriever in him; the thick coat of brown hair was singular to that breed. He had a face that resembled a Great Dane, and his huge paws were webbed like those of a Labrador. He reminded me of the Texans and their Heinz 57 culturally diverse family tree.

After Julio was done with the day's chores, he, the dog, and I would go on long walks. The boy took these opportunities to ask a million questions. He wanted to know why God had sent me to help his family, how long I was going to stay with them, etc. He always ended the conversations with, "When are we going to get our wishes?"

Tiring of this, one evening I removed my belt, used a hunter's knife the boy had loaned me, and cut my money belt to fit the dog's neck. I placed my last American ten-dollar bill in the money pocket with a note written in Spanish stating the money was to be used for his funeral expenses. I signed it, "Dios."

The following morning Twila and Julio were delighted to see such a nice collar on Cacho. The dog seemed impressed with it; he kept wagging his tail and barking.

"Thank you, Mister Angel, for giving Cacho his wish," said Julio. "He lost his old collar chasing rabbits a long time ago, and we could not afford to buy him another one."

He shook my hand and glued his brown eyes on me. "Is it getting close to the time for Mamá and me to get our wishes?"

I looked at Twila with apprehension. She placed a hand on her breast, playing with the string that kept the front of her blouse together. Then, she sensually ran her hand down her furry left leg. When she locked her dreamy eyes on me, I panicked. Oh no, the woman's in heat. "Okay, it's time to fulfill another wish," I said. "I can't tell you whose turn it is, but the lucky person will know in the morning. First, I have to travel into town and get an amulet. I need it for my incantations. How far is it to town? Does this town have a *curandera*?"

"It's a half day's walk to the town of Arisjaga. The *curandera*'s name is Amalia, and she lives close to Palenque," said Twila. "Julio will take you."

"When do you want to go to the mad woman's house?" asked the boy. "You want to buy something to keep the devil away? What kind of an angel are you?"

"The best type there is, Julio."

"Which kind is that?" he wanted to know.

"The type that plays on both sides of the fence. I hope that transgression is okay with you. I need an amulet to make sure the devil doesn't steal my next wish. When can we leave for the town?"

"If we leave right now, we can return before dark."

We packed a lunch, grabbed our walking sticks, and left for town. Cacho came along. The walk was long and strenuous. We were in the Sierras. I was sick and tired of being in the mountains and longed for the flatlands of Texas. I was also fed up with Central America and began to mull a plan. It had been three weeks, and it was time to go home. By now the rent on Carlos's apartment had long expired. The landlord had more than likely moved his stuff out and placed it in storage. Now I would have to pay to get it out. I cursed.

My situation had gone from great to horrible in a short time. Leaving Texas had not been altogether good for me. I was chased by bandits, became a husband, and then a stepfather. I was knighted, saved a queer from himself, and was promised a Mercedes Benz but the person who gave it to me turned out to be an Indian giver. I was robbed at gunpoint, rescued a dubious man of the cloth, was incarcerated, had to pick coffee beans all day for peanuts, and then was offered a promising career running whores, which I quickly lost. Now, today, I was stranded somewhere in the Guatemalan mountains holding on to twenty-two *quetzales.* I had no place to live, my brand-new wife was divorcing me, my stepson thought I was a schmuck, and I was emotionally fond of Junior—a Mexican kid who was clearly a scoundrel. Then, to add insult to injury, my mother-in-law, who had threatened me with bodily harm, came back into my life. And, oh, yeah, let's not forget that I nearly killed myself jumping out of an airplane that was being strafed by a Guatemalan military jet, and by now, the jailbreak had gone public, so I was probably classified a fugitive. Certainly, things couldn't get any worse.

"Mister Angel," said the boy, reminding me that things were actually worse. I was hanging out with a kid that was clearly mental. "Are you going to give me and my mother our wishes tomorrow?"

The meaning of his question was not lost on me. Twila needed a man. The sandy-haired, brown-eyed, lanky kid needed a father. God was not only testing my resolve, but He was also measuring me for a Guatemalan wedding suit. I had promised the boy a wish, and he wanted a father. I was expected to deliver. The scenario was not pleasant. Again, I was facing crossroads.

As far as I was concerned, things were not totally out of control. One road had an ugly fat woman who treated me very well, a loony kid that admired me, a simple but clean house to live in, and a dog that didn't growl at me. The other had Ramona, a gorgeous and voluptuous woman who didn't like me and was going to divorce me, a dog that barked at me, a house in the Montrose area of Houston, and a soon-to-be ex-mother-in-law whose manners would humble Attila the Hun. The predicament needed attention. There had to be a third avenue. The first two sucked. I was done with Ramona and Charlene, and there was no way I could live in the mountains, I was a flatlander from Texas.

Julio and I stopped at a creek, removed our shoes, and soaked our tired feet in the cold stream. Julio mentioned we were close to town. He cautioned me against buying devil things. "They bring you bad luck," he said.

"Don't worry about it," I mumbled. "I know what I'm doing."

"Mister Angel, if you can only make one wish today, I want you to take care of my mother. She needs something good to happen to her. She's very lonely, you know. My father has been gone a long time, and he has not sent us any money. She used to cry a lot at night, but now she does not cry anymore. I think she knows he will not come back. I think she thinks my father has died."

"What about you? What do you think?"

"I think the same. He's my father, and I know he loves me and my mother. He would not leave us alone here without any money. Something bad must have happened to him. We need to know what happened to him, because we can't live not knowing. I want to go look for him, but I cannot leave my mother alone."

As soon as he said it, he put his hand over his mouth. He knew he had blown his wish.

"Oh, no, Mister Angel! Please don't take my wish away. I didn't mean to say it. You tricked me. Can I have my wish back?"

"You know the rules, Julio, sorry."

"There must be a way to give me my wish back," he said. "You must talk to God. He is great. He will listen to you. You are an angel."

"Well, there is a way you can get it back, Julio, but it is costly."

He looked perplexed. "Listen, Julio . . . back in the old days there was a pope named Gregory. He needed money to build something, so he asked God to help him with the problem."

"Did God help him?"

"Yes, together they came up with an idea to sell something they called 'indulgences.'"

"What are those?"

"It's a certificate that you have to buy. It allows you to make a mistake for free."

"How can the mistake be free if you have to pay for the certificate?"

"You are correct, Julio; your grasp of things is impressive. You have a good future ahead of you. You must always remember that even if it appears to be so, there is nothing free in this world. You eventually have to pay for everything you get."

"Are you trying to tell me I can pay for messing up my wish?"

"Yes, that's exactly what I'm telling you."

"But I'm just a kid. I don't have any money?"

"Cacho does."

"I told you I was a kid. I didn't tell you I was stupid. Cacho is a dog, and dogs don't have money. You're some stupid angel."

"Cacho is a dog with money. He has an American ten-dollar bill inside his collar."

"How did he get it? You told me we had to wish for what we wanted. Cacho does not know about money. Why did God put the money in his collar?"

"Cacho wanted the money for his burial expenses. He wanted to pay for it himself because you and your mother don't have any money. The dog loves you both very much, and he doesn't want to end up in a hole in the backyard."

"You know what I think? I think you're lying to me. I think you think because I'm a kid, I don't know nothing."

"I can prove it," I said, thoroughly enjoying myself. "Look inside his collar."

The boy called the dog over and removed the collar. He was amazed at the hidden compartment, and when he found the money wrapped around a note signed by God, my stock as an angel went right through the roof. He was so impressed he kissed my hand. I felt like a bishop.

"If you give me the money, I can give you your wish back."

"I don't know, Mister Angel. It's not my money. It belongs to Cacho. I don't know if I should take it from him. God gave it to him. I may get in trouble."

"That's the deal, Julio. No money, no wish. Sorry."

The kid gave me a tortured look. Obviously, he was wrestling with his decision. Stealing money from your dog was not an easy matter. I watched him grimace, for he was in a quandary. I let the boy struggle with his decision, my main concern at the moment being to take care of Twila's wish, and for that I needed to get my hands on the money. Those ten dollars combined with my *quetzales* would buy a battery pack for her dildo and a bus ticket out of town for me.

What to do about the boy's wish was troubling me, though. Julio's mistake afforded me an avenue of escape. He had lost the wish, and I had no intention of letting him have it back, even if he gave me the dog's money. I was not about to travel to San Antonio to find a man who by now probably had another family. However, I could not leave him high and dry; there had to be something else he wanted. But I would get to that later. At the moment I had to get the boy to give me the dog's money. If I stole it, I would certainly damage my status as an angel. Planning my escape, I waited for the boy to make up his mind.

"Bueno, Mister Angel," said the boy. "I can't steal money from my dog, especially since it was given to him by God. I will have to find money in another way. Maybe when we get to town, I can get an idea. How much do these free mistake certificates cost?"

"The price depends on how big the mistake is. In your case, the wish you lost will cost you ten American dollars."

We left the creek and walked into town in silence. The boy was deep in thought. I was hoping he wouldn't come up with a solution because, even though I wanted to go to Texas, I was not going to San Antonio to find his father.

I sent the kid into town first, as there was no need to be foolish at this point. I presumed the Guatemalan army had to be looking for me. The pilot on the jet surely reported my jump and noted the location. Sure enough, there was a detachment of soldiers in town. I told Julio God had talked to me and told me today was not a good day to be in Arisjaga. There were too many soldiers. He wanted us to go back home and try again tomorrow.

"I thought God knew everything," said Julio.

"Yes, He does," replied Alex.

"Then why didn't He tell us to stay home in the first place? We walked a lot for nothing."

"God works in mysterious ways. He was probably testing our resolve. We passed the test. Tomorrow, we will find what we want."

Twila was disappointed to see us come back empty-handed, but she accepted our reason and sent us out the following morning. We arrived and found the town clear of soldiers. We walked in. Arisjaga was nothing to brag about. It looked like an oversized village. It had no bank, one restaurant, two *cantinas,* a place to hang your hat called Pension María Victoria, a medical clinic, and several small stores where you could buy food and liquor. I told the boy to take the dog's money and exchange it for *quetzales.* I explained he would not be stealing the money, but exchanging it.

"Mister Angel, I don't know anything about changing money. How many *quetzales* should I get back?"

"Tell the money changer your mother is sick, and you need to buy medicine for her. Give him the American money and then bring me the *quetzales* he gives you."

"You are some stupid angel," he said. "The man is going to cheat me. He will think because I'm a kid I know nothing about money."

"Tell him your mother is dying, and you need to buy her lots of medicine. If he's an honest man, he will not steal too much."

Grudgingly, the kid left to find a money changer. I asked a man walking by where a person could catch a bus going out of town. He looked me over and then pointed to a building.

"*El bus para Huehuetenango viene todos los viernes,*" he said.

Shit, I was snake bit. It was only Wednesday, and the bus did not come by until Friday. I would have to go home again and then sneak out.

In the middle of this quandary, I heard a familiar voice behind me. "Hello, Alex," said Ronson.

Startled, I turned around. "What are you doing here?" I said, sporting a huge grin.

Chapter 22

A Family Reunion

"Stop bitching, Ronson. Drinking warm beer isn't going to kill you. What kind of a Swiss dude are you anyway? I thought Europeans liked warm beer."

"It's never this hot in Switzerland. I need something cold."

"I haven't seen an electrical wire anywhere in these parts, Ronson. If you want something cold to drink, you must wait until later. They start the kerosene compressors around dusk. I can't believe Pancho landed the plane safely. I thought you guys were goners for sure. How did you get away from the Guatemalans?"

"After we landed, we were careful and avoided the Guatemalan soldiers sent to capture us. We walked until we found a road, then we hitchhiked, climbed on the back of a truck, and rode into the nearest bus station. Once we settled in Huehuetenango, I was sent to get you. I've been dodging the army for days. They're still looking for us."

"I can't believe everyone is holed up in a comfortable hotel in Huehuetenango while I'm languishing in a cabin in the middle of a forest. If I had known Pancho was going to do a good job of putting the plane on the ground. I would have remained on board."

He gave me one of his famous blank stares. "Your ability to stand with your friends during times of trouble is nonexistent, Alex. You deserve your troubles because you abandoned us."

"Listen to me, Ronson . . . group dying is not for me. When I go, I want to do it alone. It's nothing personal, so I hope you understand. Besides, you can't blame a guy for making a bad decision. I was under duress. Please buy me another beer."

"They are all waiting for us," said Ronson. "I have been looking all over these mountains for you. Finding you here was pure luck. Please drink up, we need to return."

Needing to think things out, I sipped my beer and began to tell him the story of how I was found. The promise made to fulfill three wishes cracked him up. I told him one wish was already delivered, with another fixing to be put to bed, so to speak. I explained in great detail the problem with the third wish.

"Well, what do you plan to do?" he wanted to know.

"First things first," I said. "Please come with me."

We vacated the *cantina* and immediately ran into Julio and Cacho. I introduced Ronson and asked the boy how much money he had gotten for the American currency God gave the dog.

"A man took the ten dollars and tried to give me eight *quetzales*. He must have thought I was stupid. Even with the story about my dying mother, he still wanted to give me eight. I said, 'No way.' I told him I needed more than eight, but he would not give me any more. I demanded he give me my American money back."

"Where is the ten dollars?"

"It's not your money. It belongs to Cacho. I put it back in his collar."

I asked Ronson to loan me twenty *quetzales*. Then, with the boy and dog in tow, we walked to a store where I bought six size D batteries. The Swiss gave me a puzzled look. Enjoying his bewilderment while out of the boy's hearing range, I divulged the discovery of the jumbo sexual apparatus Twila kept hidden under her bed.

"It's either these batteries or me," I said.

"What are you going to do about the boy's desire to find his father?"

"I'm not sure," I said. "I'm still working on it."

"Why don't you get Charlene to pay Kermit to look for him? It's his job. I bet the old guy gives you a price break."

I looked at him, and my heart filled with admiration. What a great idea! I hugged him. "You're one of two reasons I like Switzer-land."

"What's the other one?"

"The Swiss love to drink beer and party on Sunday mornings. They're my kind of people."

I turned to Julio and asked him to bring me any information about his father that could be used to find him.

"What kind of information do you want?"

"Personal stuff—like which village he comes from, how old he is, and I need a photograph. Also, you need to come to Huehuete-nango with us to meet a man whose job is to find missing people. You won't be able to look for your father yourself because you lost the wish, but I will let you talk to this man and see whether he will look for your father. I'm doing this because I like you. Do we have a deal?"

"Does the man-hunter do this for free?"

"No," said Ronson. "He charges a lot of money."

"But I don't even have ten *quetzales*. How can I afford this man?"

"Your dog has American money. Those ten dollars will be a big help. Borrow it. I'm sure Cacho would not object," I said. "Tell your mother that you got careless and messed up your wish. Now, you'll have to work for it, which is why you have come with us. Don't worry about the man-hunter. I will negotiate a good deal for you."

He thought about it for a minute, then smiled, shook my hand, and said he would return tomorrow with the information. When I handed him the batteries and told him they were for his mother's wish, he frowned and looked at me with suspicion.

"Why would my mother wish for these things?" he said.

"Don't worry about that, but when you give them to her, please look into her eyes and see if she is happy to get the batteries. If she is not, I will give her another wish. Please go and hurry back. Don't bring the dog, and don't forget to bring the money."

"I can't believe you're messing with the boy," said Ronson. "He's poor, Alex. Let him keep the money. If you're broke, I can loan you eighty dollars. This way, you can owe me an even hundred."

"The kid is smarter than he looks. I have been trying to get the best of him since he found me hanging from the tree. To this day, he has outwitted me at every turn."

"Why does the dog have a ten-dollar bill in his collar?"

"It's mine. The dog wished for it."

"The dog wished for a ten-dollar bill?"

"Yes, and he also wished for a collar made from my belt. That is why I have this rope holding my pants up."

"I see the boy is not the only one who has gotten the best of you. You never fail to amaze me, Alex. Your mother-in-law was correct when she said a guy like you always lands on his feet. Let me tell you just how lucky you are, Alex. Your behavior was unpardonable. We couldn't believe you had the audacity to abandon us. Most of us decided to leave you to your fate. We figured if the landing didn't kill you, you at the very least broke several bones and became food for the animals. But Junior complained. He was relentless. He wanted us to find you. Charlene comforted the boy by telling him nothing would happen to you. She said you were like a bad penny, always turning up. The boy kept on, but Kermit outright refused. He said he was paid to get you out of jail, and his job was done. Charlene had to hire him again. I work for Kermit, so he sent me after you."

"And all this time I thought you were here because you liked me."

"Oh, I like you fine, Alex, but not enough to scratch around this part of the world. You need to understand that dodging soldiers to find someone who bailed out on me when the going got tough is hard to swallow. You should have stayed with us. The Guatemalan army has to be mad as hell. We are not out of the woods yet. We need to be careful."

Since he had just arrived and we were spending the night, we walked to the *pensión* and booked two rooms. On the way there, I asked him if he knew why Charlene had hired Kermit's firm to bust me out of jail. "I thought the damn woman hated me."

"She does, but there is a new development that has forced her hand."

"What in the world could force Chucky's mother to spend her money springing me free?"

"You have a loaf in the oven," he said.

"What? What do you mean I have a 'loaf in the oven'? I'm not Swiss—I need proper enunciation. You need to speak clearly, Ronson."

"Ramona's pregnant. You're going to be a father."

I was stunned. So that's why the hyena came out of her lair. Charlene is going to be a grandmother. "Where's Ramona? Is she in Houston?" I wanted to know.

"She and the boy flew in to Guatemala City two days ago. Everyone's in Huehuetenango waiting for you."

"Who's 'everyone,' and why are they waiting on me?"

"Junior has a loaf in the oven, too. His girlfriend Rosie is pregnant, and they are going to be married by Padre Humberto. Ramona's waiting for you with your stepson, Raúl. This is going to be quite a family affair. Junior wants Raúl to be his best man. Pancho will give Rosie away."

"Where do I fit in?"

"Since things between you and Ramona went bad, Charlene wants you two to renew your vows. She thinks it's best for the new baby if you two make up and start over again. We were hired to bust you out of jail and bring you in. Charlene's planned a double wedding."

"That's just great, Ronson. I always wanted to be the groom at a shotgun wedding."

"Don't feel so bad, Alex. At least you are getting married, even if it's for the second time. I am always the best man and never the groom."

With the boy gone to get his father's photograph and the evening getting on, we found our rooms and called it a night.

The next day, Julio showed up without Cacho. He gave me an old photograph of his father, told me his name was José Calderón, and said he came from a village called Huajuapan.

"It's close to the town of Acapulco. That's in Mexico," he said. "Mamá says he's a Mexican *charro*. She says he's very good with horses. Maybe the man-hunter can look for him in a horse ranch. There must be many ranches in San Antonio. I bet he can find him there."

"I didn't know your father was a Mexican," I said.

"He was Mexican first, but now he is Guatemalan."

"Did your mother like her wish?" I asked.

"Yes, she did. You were right, Mister Angel. She was very happy to get the batteries."

We climbed into Ronson's four-wheel drive and took off. I glanced back at the town and wondered if life's idiotic twists and turns would ever send me back this way again. It would be nice to return at some point to see how Carlos Laughing Crow was getting along and if the wishes I bestowed upon Twila, Julio, and Cacho made a difference in their lives.

The burden of a traveler is to return and see whether the people he touched would welcome him with open arms or run him out of town on a rail. I was hoping Don Pedro was happy with all the money he got for his dead cow.

The ride to Huehuetenango was long. I almost lost my lunch, patience, and nerve riding with Ronson. The roads were twisting every which way, making us dizzy. He was driving like a man possessed with a death wish. We were going at speeds that would have humbled NASCAR driver, Richard Petty. Julio and I both kissed the ground when we finally made it to the hotel.

"That man is crazy," Julio said. "I will go back home on a bus."

"Listen to me, Julio, of all the people I know, Ronson is one of the most reserved. He's a Swiss. They are known for their docility. It's the Americans who are crazy, especially the female variety. In a few minutes, you will meet a number of people whom I consider to be friends and family. Compared to them, Ronson is quite sane. You need not be too judgmental. Getting behind the wheel can sometimes change a person's behavior."

No sooner had I uttered that statement than Charlene came out into the balcony of her room and saw us.

"Alex, get your ass up here. We need to discuss a few things," she said.

"Who's that lady?" asked the boy.

"That's no lady, Julio. That's my mother-in-law. She's a woman with sharp edges, so be sure to stay clear of her."

We followed Ronson into the hotel and climbed the stairs to the second floor. He walked me to a door, knocked, and left with Julio. The door opened, and there stood my odd stepson, Raúl.

"Hola, Papi, ¿cómo estás?"

"Hello, son. I'm doing fine, thanks for asking. Where's your mother?"

He shrugged his shoulders. Then Dracula's consort entered the room, "If you don't see her here, she must be in the bedroom. This is a hotel room, you idiot. Where else would she be?"

I clenched my teeth and cursed my luck. Man, I hate these family reunions. "Good to see you, too, Charlene. How's tricks?"

"You better go in there, and you better fix things up. She is still upset with you. You better do a lot of ass-kissing. I didn't come all this way and spend all this money for you two to remain cold. I want a happy grandbaby, so go in there and do what you do best. Hurry up and get on with it."

"Do you think she'll want to play Hide the Salami with me?" I said.

"I don't care if she will let you play Ride the Pony. Reach into your bag of slimy sex tricks and put a smile on her face, then come down to the bar when you are done. Please have the decency to shower after you finish weaving your magic."

Turning my back to the old wench, I knocked on the bedroom door. There was no answer. I knocked again, but still no answer. I turned the knob slowly and pushed the door open, and caution was needed. If she was mad, I might need to dodge a flying vase. To my surprise, the coast was clear. Ramona was lying face-down on the bed, buck naked. I was sure she was pretending to be asleep, for this was a familiar road. The more things change, the more they remain the same.

Whenever she was hunting for an exceptional roll in the hay, she removed all her clothes and sprawled her body strategically on the bed. She did this to kick-start my engine. Ramona knew if she touched the voyeur button, I would respond with higher than normal lovemaking intensity. Besides being a beauty, she was an intelligent woman. Ramona knew her lover well.

I checked her out, filling my eyes with admiration. Her long, wavy, dark brown hair, curvy legs, and nice round ass caught my attention. Her body was sculpted by an artist. All of a sudden, she turned around and gave me a sheepish grin. I looked at the bow tied on the monkey and smiled.

"You've been expecting me," I said, licking my lips.

"Shed your clothes and come closer," she said. "If you remove the bow, you'll find there's a big surprise inside for you."

I looked at her belly. It had a slight upward curve. Shit, she is pregnant all right. Damn the bad luck. I didn't make a move; I needed to buy a little time, for there was much to work out.

Somewhere in the inner tubes of her reproductive system was a growing son. How delicate should I be when I jump her bones? Am I going to poke something open? Should I consider shallow penetration, or is it safe to seek the bottom of the mine?

She rubbed her belly with one hand while cupping her left breast with the other. "Come kiss it," she said. "It missed you."

Ramona's body looked like a smorgasbord full of delicacies. There was stuff to eat everywhere. I didn't know where to begin, so I threw caution to the wind, removed my clothes, and zeroed in on the ribbon.

Chapter 23

Why Me, Lord?

"**W**ake up, Mister Alex," said Junior. "Today is a big day for us. We're getting married."

I opened one eye, scouted the room, and realized there were two kids in bed with me. I was sandwiched between Raúl and Julio. The bed felt wet and warm. Shit, I've been pissed on. Upset, I sat up. Junior smiled at me, sitting on the other bed. I tried to remember what transpired the night before. There is nothing like a heavy dose of tequila to wipe your mind clear of calamities.

"Why, if I'm the only adult in the room, am I sleeping with kids?" I said. "Why is it that you get to sleep in a big bed alone, Junior?"

"Because I have rules, Mister Alex, and they say men don't sleep in a bed with other men."

Julio woke up, stretched, and headed for the bathroom. I sniffed him as he passed me. Yep, he was the culprit. He went in, did not bother to close the door, and started to piss with the seat down.

"I'm surprised you have any urine left to piss out," I said. He ignored my banter.

"That was some party last night," he said. "Is it normal for people to insult each other so much? Your family and friends do not like you much, Mister Angel. Why is that?"

I ignored his inquisitiveness and told him to put the seat up next time he used the toilet. I also told him to please close the damn door. I turned my attention to Junior, who was trying to make coffee from the in-room machine.

"When is the wedding?" I asked.

"We get married at five today. It's already ten, so we need to get going. Señora Charlene promised to buy us clothes at Don Juan's clothing store. I am thinking of getting a white, double-breasted suit and black-and-white alligator skin shoes. How about you, Mister Alex? What are you getting?"

"*Buenos días,* Papi, *¿qué hora es?*" said Raúl.

"Good morning, son. It's ten in the morning. Time to get out of bed. Junior wants to go shopping."

"*No quiero comprar un saco. Quiero comprarme una guayabera.*"

"You don't have to buy a suit, son. You can get a *guayabera* shirt. They are cooler and formal enough to wear at a wedding."

We got out of bed, took turns showering, and made it down to the restaurant for a late breakfast. There, we encountered Ronson and Kermit.

"Hello, Alex," said the old sleuth. "I hope you didn't take all we said last night to heart. We had too much to drink and were just being friendly."

"Don't think anything of it, Kermit. I'm used to being mistreated by my friends and family. Did you get to meet Julio last night?"

"Yes. I met the boy who wants to find his father. His story was moving."

"Yes," I said. "It moved me, too. I told him you would help him. I also told him you would give him a good price. He is poor and lives alone with his mother and a dog."

"Is this the dog that wishes for things?" he asked.

"Yes," I replied, giving Ronson a dirty look. "The kid, his mother, and the dog found me hanging on a tree. They wouldn't cut me down unless I promised to give them each a wish."

"The dog demanded a wish?" said Kermit with a chuckle.

"The dog wished for money," said Ronson, laughing. I shot him another dirty look. I could not believe he had blabbed about my experience.

"Yes, the dog wished for a collar and burial money. The mother wished for a battery pack, and the boy wants to find out whether his father is alive or dead," I said with a serious face.

"How long has his father been gone?" asked the old sleuth.

"A long time," said Julio, interrupting. "Mamá thinks something has happened to him. I wanted to go to find him, but Mister Angel says I lost my wish because I said it out loud. Now, I have to pay you to find him for me, but I don't have any money. He took it all from me."

Kermit stopped smirking and gave me a stern look. "There's a name for a man that steals from poor children," he said, and then turned to me. "You're lucky I'm a peaceful fellow, otherwise I would be tempted to throw you out the window."

"Give me a break, Kermit. I'm expected to make wishes happen. How would you like to tackle that ordeal? The dog and mother were easy. The boy's wish required major inspiration. He's here because I care for him. I could have come alone with Ronson. How much do you charge a poor child to find his father?"

He gave me another disapproving look. "Don't play me for a sucker, Alex. You know very well there are many ways to skin a cat. This is your kill, and I don't appreciate you handing me the butcher knife."

"Mister Man-hunter," said Julio, "can you really find my father, or is this angel lying to me?"

"Angels don't lie. They are heaven-sent," said Kermit. "When Alex jumped out of the airplane I thought he was crazy, but I know better now. God was sending him to you. I will find your father, and your angel will foot the bill. It won't cost you any money."

"Hey, I don't have any money! Where do you suppose I can get my hands on some to pay your exorbitant fees?"

"You have a wealthy mother-in-law. Be resourceful."

The waiter came and took our order. Soon after, Charlene and Ramona entered the restaurant. They both had a mean on.

"I hope you all have already finished eating, because we need to go shopping. There are several things I have to attend to before the wedding, and I don't want to get a late start," growled the old grizzly.

"We haven't eaten yet," I said. "Buying clothes for men is a man's job. We certainly do not need a woman along to complicate matters. Why don't you give us some money and get lost."

"Do not speak to mother in that manner," growled the young bear. "She's the reason why we're all here. Be grateful for your freedom and new chance. I was going to file for divorce and stick you with a healthy dose of child support. Mother talked me out of it."

"That's fine, sweetie. Don't pay him any mind," said Charlene. "Every dog has her day. Mine will come soon enough. For now, I am willing to put up with his misplaced arrogance. I want a happy grandbaby, and I'm going to get one no matter what. Alex is going to be a good father if he knows what's good for him."

Why me, Lord? I looked at the sneer on my wife's face and wondered why God was being unkind to me. I began to feel Odysseus's burden. Somewhere, somehow I had managed to piss off the Earth Shaker, and Poseidon was going to make my return home painful.

"Apologize to mother!" said Ramona, slamming her fist on the table. Everyone was looking at me. A reaction to this assault was expected, but all I could do was wonder how in the hell I ever managed to get involved with a woman who had the temper of a rabid dog. Then, when she bent down to fool with the bottom of her skirt and those luscious breasts popped into view, I remembered. Hell, it's not my fault. Man cannot be expected to live by eating bread alone.

Charlene reached inside her purse and pulled out a wad of bills that opened everyone's eyes, including those of Pancho, Carmen, and Padre Humberto, who had just walked into the eatery. There had to be at least a hundred Ben Franklins in her purse. She thumbed through the bills looking for something smaller but couldn't find any, so she gave Padre Humberto three one-hundred-dollar bills. Charlene was bankrolling the wedding and buying clothes for everyone.

"Make sure everyone is dressed properly, Humberto. I don't want to see anyone wearing any *charro* outfits or peasant garb."

The women left us, and we ate our breakfast quietly. By the glimmer in the eyes of both young boys, I could tell they were excited. Julio had hired a man to find his father, and Raúl was back in his native Mexico. Junior seemed a bit nervous, but that was typical. No one gives up their bachelorhood easily. Padre Humberto and Pancho were in a tentative mood, as were Ronson and Kermit. I figured the wad of dough in Charlene's purse had caught everyone's attention. She was my mother-in-law, and that was my money. I made a mental note to keep an eye out for their greedy dispositions.

We went to Don Juan's clothing store and looked for suitable attire. Besides a nice dark suit, I picked out a pair of turtle-skin boots. Pancho, Julio, and Raúl bought black moccasin shoes, khaki pants, and *guayabera* shirts. Junior bought the double-breasted white suit he wanted with matching two-tone shoes. Padre Humberto walked out with a nice grey suit and a hat made from palm leaves.

The difference between men and women, as far as shopping is concerned is this: Men dread the beginning, finding satisfaction only after leaving the store, while women are excited starting out. It was no different in our case.

After the shopping spree, we went back to the hotel. Julio and Raúl joined the women at the pool, the Padre stayed in his room, Pancho found the bar, and Junior and I ordered room service. We had made eye contact several times at the clothing store, and I knew he wanted to talk. Getting hitched was a big step. I was sure he wanted my advice.

The food came and we ate our fill. Full stomachs aside, it was not great. It didn't take me long after arriving in Texas to become fascinated with Mexican food. Yet, to my chagrin, I found that it was not the same everywhere in the United States. What they served in Florida, California, Arizona, and New Mexico was far inferior to what we ate in Texas. The same goes for the fare served in Mexico. The food changes from south to north. By far the best Mexican food I had tasted was prepared in Texas.

We downed a couple of Carta Blanca beers and lit up a Marlboro Red. Then Junior began to fidget. When he gave me one of his serious looks, I knew the rap session was about to begin. I crushed the cigarette, crossed my arms, and started tapping my feet.

"Mister Alex, why are you marrying the same woman again? I can tell you do not like her much, and she thinks you're a *pendejo*. Why are you doing it?" he asked.

"The fact that Ramona thinks I'm an asshole has very little to do with my marriage decision. Life is way too complicated for a young man to get a good handle on it. Listen to me, Junior. We men spend all our lives trying to get to the proverbial mountaintop. It is there where we assume it's okay to make decisions based on selfish needs. But the climb is long, and we grow older. It's designed that way. Age is needed to overcome the impetuousness of youth. It's important to comprehend that selfishness is not a virtue. We have to make our decisions taking into consideration the feelings of others. We also have to learn to deal with circumstances. For example, I love Ramona but do not like her volatile temper. She is totally unsuited for a man with my take on life, yet she turns me on physically and is brewing my child in her inner vat. If the winds are favorable, a man takes a deep breath, pushes caution aside, and shoves the boat into the water. Until we reach the state where we know how to read the gauges, we navigate the boat by the seat of our pants. The boy being born will need a father to give him a name and a respectable position. Being a bastard is not socially acceptable, at least not in our culture. Americans are more freewheeling when it comes to that; kids born out of wedlock is common there. My mother would think badly of me if I didn't marry the child's mother."

"So, you are telling me it's okay to marry even if love is not in your heart?"

"Yes, of course. Love in a marriage is like gravy on mashed potatoes. It's good if you have it, but it's not necessary. Are you trying to tell me you are not in love with Rosie?"

"No, I am in love with her. Like you, there is a life growing inside her body that belongs to me. I have to be there for the boy. My problem is different than yours. I like my life. Being free is how I live. Getting married and living in the same house, going to work, and coming home every night scares me. I don't know if I can do it."

"Your problem is that you're not a man yet, and that is why this whole thing is bothering you. Men give up their freedom when necessary. It's called being an adult. I hate being one myself. Instant gratification is my thing. But, as you get older, people expect you to stop playing, and when you don't, there are all sorts of penalties thrown at you. Indulging in foolish behavior as an adult is frowned upon. It's important to remain a boy for as long as you can."

"But how can I? I'm going to be a father!"

I looked at his anguished expression. Here was someone in need of fatherly advice. Thinking it out, I laid it on him. "Listen, Junior, you need to marry Rosie and come to Texas with us. The boy will be born in the United States, there's plenty of work in the food business for Rosie, and when the time comes, you can take your leave, because fatherless families are common there. Most men end up raising somebody else's kids. If you pay child support you can pop in and out all you want. The family culture in the States is not as stifling as ours. In the United States, you don't have to pay for a lustful mistake by enduring a life sentence. They cut you a break. You're a natural entrepreneur, so making money in Texas should be an easy task. What do you say?"

"No way, Mister Alex. I am a Mexican, and we don't let anyone else raise our children. We do it ourselves. If I do go to Texas, we can't live with you and Ramona. I will be a husband and a father, and I need my own place. Besides, Rosie will be a mother, and her work is to take care of the boy and the house. If I get caught by the Migra for working without papers, they'll put me in jail, and then who will take care of Rosie and the baby?"

"You are putting the cart in front of the horse, Junior. In order to have an easy time in a foreign country, you need to know someone with connections. I am loaded with them. Remember Carlos? He gave me the keys to his apartment in Houston. It's not far from where I live, and you can rent it. You can get a job with the manhunter; he has no problem hiring people without papers. Ronson works for him; he is Swiss. I'm sure Kermit will hire you, and I'm also sure Charlene will pay a lawyer to fix the immigration problem. You can trust me when I say life in Texas will be good for both of you."

"I would like to believe you, Mister Alex, but I'm not sure I want to live there. I am Mexican, and this is my home. I like it here. People that can't have a good life here leave their friends and family to find a better one in the States. I need to try to make a good life here for us. I don't want to leave my home and sister behind. Carmen is my only family, and even though she is older, she needs me. Thank you for the advice and for the offer. I will think about it and talk to Rosie."

Junior's problem wasn't a big one. Most of us do not like to give up our carefree lifestyle, yet once we do it, we are fine with it. He would be okay. I left him to ponder his fate and headed for the shower. Tonight was my big night, and I was about to marry

Ramona for the second time. Hell, why not? I'm better off with her. My immediate agenda was to get back to Houston and find my old life again. I had had enough fun wandering around in the hinterlands of Mexico, Belize, and Guatemala. From here on out I was going to concentrate on being a good husband and father—no more harebrained escapades for me. The stint in that Guatemalan jailhouse and the subsequent parachute jump removed any and all wild hairs growing on my ass. Just like Johnny Cash, from here on, I was going to walk the line.

Chapter 24

A Priest on the Run

Junior and I walked the women down the aisle and became man and wife, me for the second time. The wedding worked out great. Carmen and Charlene hired a group of Guatemalan Indian musicians who played a rendition of "Here Comes the Bride" that will be forever imbedded in my mind. El Parque de Don Bosco, in Huehuetenango where we were married, was nice. If it wasn't for the horde of mosquitoes that came out to terrorize us at dusk, using the park as a venue for a wedding would have been a brilliant idea. After the ceremony and congratulations were over, we moved the party to the hotel bar.

In the middle of doing my rendition of the Watusi, a large *mojón* named Charlene rolled onto the dance floor and crashed my party.

"The bastard stole my money!" she said to Ramona.

"Who stole what money?" I asked.

Ramona left my arms and went to her mother who began to wail like a stuck pig. "The bastard stole my money! The bastard stole my money!"

The old woman kept on repeating the same sentence, stopping only to break into a hysterical sob. Ramona hugged her.

"Who stole the money?" I asked again.

197

Junior came over and whispered, "The bastard did it."

"Does the bastard have a name?" I asked Charlene.

"Don't get smart with me, Alex," growled the bear. "I'm in no mood to deal with your asinine sense of humor. Padre Humberto took it. My lover cleaned me out. There's nothing left. He took it all, including my credit cards and passport. I'm doomed!" she cried.

"Padre Humberto?" asked Junior in disbelief.

"Yes, he's the bastard she's talking about. It appears we have a priest on the run. Here's your chance to get employed, Junior. Tell Kermit you can find the priest. He will hire you."

"No way! The Padre is my friend. I can't believe he stole the money. There must be another priest around here."

"Maybe you are right, Junior, but right now, let's humor Charlene. It is my understanding from everything I know about the man that he has not been too successful fighting off the wanton vices of this world. Padre Humberto sets the benchmark for measuring rogue priests."

"Don't be so smug, Alex," said Ramona. "Padre Humberto has not only stolen mother's money, but he has also ripped us off. He took the money mother was going to give us for a wedding present."

"The bastard stole our money?" I asked.

"Papi," said Raúl. "*Yo sé donde está el padre.*"

I grabbed the boy and moved away from the crowd. "You really know where the priest is?" I pleaded.

"*Sí,* Papi, *yo tengo una buena idea dónde se está escondiendo.*"

"You have a good idea, or are you sure you know where he's hiding?"

"*Sí,* Papi, *yo sé dónde está el cura, pero me tienes que dar una recompensa.*"

"First we find him, then we recuperate the money, and afterwards I will give you a reward, son. No need to get ahead of the game. Don't tell anyone you know where the Padre's hiding, especially your mother. We don't want to split the money among too many."

The bar manager came over and told us to vacate the dance floor. We left the bar and gathered in the hotel lobby and formed a circle around Charlene. We understood that Padre Humberto's audacity had opened a financial opportunity for the rest of us. There was money to be made here, and we could smell it. That old saying, "Beware of a woman scorned" was true. Charlene was mad as hell, and vengeance would be hers, no matter the cost. We waited for the reward announcement.

"I'm having my bank wire me some money, and I will pay three thousand dollars to anyone who brings me the priest, credit cards, and passport. I don't care about the money. It's finder's keepers as far as I'm concerned. I'll wait here until I hear from one of you. You better go now. He can't have gone far. He stole the money while I was in the shower. He has about an hour's head start."

We all looked at each other; it was time to partner up. Kermit and Ronson tried to recruit Junior but he refused. Julio negotiated a deal and went off with them. Pancho said he wanted to work alone so he didn't want any partners. Junior said Padre Humberto was his friend, and he wasn't going to hunt him down. However, he was going to discuss it with his sister and see where she stood, and if she wanted to find Padre Humberto, Junior would go with her. Everyone scattered.

Knowing how long it takes a woman to shower, I figured Padre Humberto had at least two hours on us. I asked Ramona if she wanted to go with me and Raúl, but she declined. Her place was by her grieving mother. With the coast clear, I grabbed Raúl. "Okay, son, where can we find the priest?"

"*El cura está aquí.*"

"What do you mean the priest is here?"

"*El cura se está cogiendo a la hermana de Junior. Humberto esta en el cuarto treinta y dos.*"

"What! Are you sure?"

"*Sí, estoy seguro.*"

I looked at the little booger for a minute. I needed to digest the information he had just given me. He said the priest had not left the hotel, but that he was in room thirty-two screwing Junior's sister. If this was true, all we had to do was wait until everyone left the hotel, then confront the priest, negotiate a deal, and let him be. I wasn't buying the bullshit Charlene gave us. It may be true for everyone else, but not for me. I would never get the three-thousand-dollar reward. I was family, and my take would be, if I was lucky, half of the stolen money. She would justify my half share by giving Ramona the rest of the money as a wedding present, and my bride would give me nothing. I didn't fall off the turnip truck yesterday. I knew a stacked deck when I saw one. The plan was for Raúl and me to split the money on a seventy-thirty basis. I planned to negotiate a different deal with the wayward priest. I figured, circumstances being what they were, an eighty-twenty split would be good for him. He would have no choice but to agree. Counting my money already, I went to the hotel gift shop and purchased a colorful baseball bat and a short ceremonial machete. When engaging in financial negotiations, it is imperative that you have the upper hand.

I told Raúl to hang with his mother; we would meet after I had dealt with the rogue priest. I paid the man behind the hotel counter twenty dollars to let me borrow the key to room thirty-two for half an hour. Armed to the teeth, I broke into the room. To my chagrin, they were not screwing. I was hoping to see Carmen naked. Instead, they were sitting and talking. I noticed a bottle of tequila and three glasses on the small round table. They were certainly surprised to see me. When I raised the machete, Carmen pulled out a pistol from a pocket in her skirt, pointed it at me, and cocked it. Oh, no, I brought a knife to a gunfight. What am I going to do now?

Two hours later, a maid opened the door and found me tied to a chair and gagged. Instead of untying me, she got on the phone and called the front desk. An eternity later, the hotel manager arrived with a security guard. Charlene and Ramona were summoned to the room, and after my mother-in-law paid both men a large sum to ignore the situation, I was released.

"You're a moron, Alex. I can't believe my grandson will have your genes. Ever since I met you, you have been a source of misery, embarrassment, and expense."

"Be nice to him, mother. He was only trying to get your money back. Alex can't help it if he's an idiot."

"Thanks for the vote of confidence, sweetie," I said.

She shot me the bird. I ignored her, for I was after bigger fish, and there was something fishy in the room. I saw three glasses and one bottle of tequila on the hotel room table. Since I didn't see anyone else in the room, the third accomplice had come and gone already. Who was it? Was it Pancho, or was it Junior? My money was on Pancho. Even though the boy was an expert swindler, he would not steal everything; he would have left the credit cards and passports. There was a strong sense of loyalty in him. Charlene had been his benefactor, and Ramona was now Raúl's mother. I ruled him out. Carmen was a better bet. Her personality and lifestyle fit the mold of an unscrupulous thief. I knew where to find her, or at least where to start looking. Tía María from the brothel in Mérida should be a deep well of information, especially if we greased her palm. Padre Humberto was an accomplice to the crime, I was sure of that. Yet I didn't believe he actually stole the money. His involvement had to be limited to opening the hotel door for the bandit. Pancho was the third person missing in the room. He had been there to give Padre Humberto a donation and to grease Carmen's hand. The pistol she pointed at me looked familiar. I remembered looking at one exactly like it on Pancho's Road, when he robbed us. Padre Humberto and Carmen's job was to create a diversion. Everyone would be looking for them while Pancho got away. Anyway, that was the scenario that worked best for me. However, I could be wrong. The priest could have been a crook, and he and Carmen could have teamed up. I had to keep my eyes on them. I knew it would be nearly impossible for me to uproot the bandit. To get to him, I had to go after the priest and the whore, but in order to find them, I needed to form an alliance. Splitting the money pie into many pieces didn't set right with me, but I was a realist and knew very well that there were two trails that needed following. One was the brothel and the other was the orphanage in San Cristóbal de las Casas in Chiapas. If all three crooks remained together, finding them would be hard. But I had a feeling they would split up. I did not see a couple in the group. Pancho was a bandit. He worked alone. Padre Humberto was not going to hook up with a prostitute, and Carmen would give Junior some money and split. She'd be easy to find. A whore can only find employment in a whorehouse. If they did split up into two or more groups, then I could get lucky and find one of them in either place. At the very least I would find clues, and I needed a boatload of those if I was going to find wily Mexicans hiding in Mexico. I set my sights on Kermit and Ronson. Together we could cover more ground. Besides, Kermit was a professional investigator. After thinking things through, I decided that the best way to find those two was to let them find me.

Raúl and I said our good-byes. Ramona appeared distraught. The idea of sending the boy out on an adventure with me didn't sit well with her. She kissed and hugged him a number of times before I could get him away from her. We hopped in a taxi and stopped at a car rental place where we rented a Volkswagen Kombi.

We drove out of town in good spirits. When I passed a large Coca Cola billboard, I doubled back and hid behind it. I had an intuition, and it paid off. A few minutes later came the Land Rover. I figured they would be following me. I roared the engine and came up behind them. When I flashed the lights, they pulled over.

"Well, well," I said, as I got out of the car. "Kermit, didn't you once tell me I couldn't find my ass in a paper bag with a set of large deer horns?"

"Yes, I did. I remember the discussion very well," he said.

"Well, how do you like them apples?" I said.

"I'm not sure I understand what you are getting on about."

"I found you guys and right away, too," I said, proudly.

"Ronson and I are not lost. Besides, you're not looking for us. You're supposed to be looking for the outlaw priest. You wouldn't happen to know where he could be hiding, would you?"

I hated to get into discussions with him. He always turned things around and made it look like I was wrong and he was right. Being the determined fellow that I am, I was not going to let him off this easily.

"I knew you didn't know where to look for the priest. I knew you needed me, so I found you."

"You're correct about the first one, but incorrect about the second. I found you."

"I was waiting for you," I said, getting annoyed. "I found you."

Julio, who was part of the team, butted in. "Mister Angel, is there a problem here?"

"*No, no hay problema, todo está bien,*" said Raúl to the Guatemalan boy. "*Mi* Papi *es un pendejo.*"

"Hey! I heard that. You can't be calling me names!"

"What did he say?" asked Kermit.

"I believe the boy called Alex a dumb-ass," said Ronson.

"*Perdóname,* Papi, *pero estamos perdiendo tiempo. Tenemos que buscar al cura.*"

"What did he say?" asked Kermit

"Raúl says we're wasting time. He says we need to get going and look for the priest," Julio translated.

"The kid's right. We're wasting time, and the priest is getting away. We have to form a partnership here. We split the money on an even basis. Is everyone okay with that?" I offered.

They agreed and we told them all we knew. But to make sure the partnership worked, they gave me Julio and grabbed hold of Raúl. They felt the boys would be a good stabilizing force within the group. I was supposed to go to Mérida and scout the brothel; they were going to check the orphanage in San Cristóbal. We were to keep in touch with the women via telephone. If one of us found a clue, we would call them at the hotel and relay the information. If for some reason we ended up empty-handed, we would meet back at the Papagayo hotel in Mérida in two weeks. That being agreed, I drove to the fork in the road and turned toward the Mexican border. I had had enough of Guatemala. They followed behind us.

Thirty minutes later, I came upon a long line of cars; the road was blocked by the army. They were checking the cars and asking for identification papers. Crap, they are still looking for us. What bad luck. Pissed because my papers were in Capitán Lozardo's hands, I turned around and headed back to Huehuetenango. I knew if we could not leave the area, the Padre and his cohorts couldn't either. Humberto was still in town, probably staying under the radar holed up in a seedy hotel. His strategy was transparent. He was a Guatemalan, and he was going to stay put until we got caught, taking the heat off of him and his conspirators.

My teammates came behind me and flashed their lights. I stopped the car and waited for them to pull alongside.

"What's the next step, Alex?" asked the old sleuth.

I thought about it for a minute. "The best way to find rats is with other rats," I said. "I have a plan."

"What exactly do you mean, Alex?" questioned Kermit.

"I'm getting a job running whores," I said.

"Cut the crap, Alex. Give it to me straight," said the Norwegian, getting annoyed.

"Kermit, we can't go forward, so we go back and immerse ourselves into Guatemalan life until it's safe to leave. I'm going to get a job working in a brothel."

"I want to work in a whorehouse, too," said Ronson.

"You already have a job," said Kermit. "You're a valuable employee in my company."

We made it back to town, reoccupied our rooms, and had a conference with Ramona and Charlene. I asked them where I could find Junior and was told he had left with his sister. The decision was made to shut the operation down. Charlene and Ramona were to go back home, as was Kermit. He had a business to run. Ronson and I were to stick it out here until we unearthed the thieves. We understood the nature of our task; time and patience were required.

Before Ramona had left Texas she received papers for Raúl, thus allowing the boy the ability to travel. She took the boy home. A deal was struck between Julio and Kermit. He was to stay to help us find Padre Humberto, and Kermit would begin looking for his father in San Antonio, Texas. The price for this assignment was the boy's services plus twenty percent of whatever his share came to from the recovered money providing Padre Humberto was caught. Kermit was a tough negotiator. No one got a break—not even poor kids.

Everyone went home. Ramona didn't seem sad to leave my ass behind. Charlene, on the other hand, gave me a good-bye hug that felt genuine. While in the midst of the unnerving bear hug, she whispered. "Find that son of a bitch for me, Alex. Tie him up in a room and leave Ronson with him. Kermit is still on my payroll. You need to come home, take your place next to Ramona, and make sure my grandson comes into the world happy. I will deal with the scoundrel in my own manner. You will be rewarded handsomely."

"Sure," I said. "You can count on me."

I can't believe Charlene thinks I'm a moron. I know what's in store for me. I'll end up with her, plus a son I won't be able to raise according to my customs, her crazy daughter, and that weird Mexican kid. Some reward.

Kermit honked the Land Rover horn, and they all climbed in, waved, and took off for Guatemala City. Good riddance.

I figured they would make it to Guatemala. The profile distributed to the authorities surely wouldn't fit them. They were looking for me and the gang that broke me out of jail. Kermit, Ramona, Raúl, and Charlene did not look like criminals. I waved back and bid them adieu.

"Okay, Alex," said Ronson. "How do we get work running whores?"

"First things first," I said. "And we start by unloading the kid. You take him back to his mother, give him some money, and tell him we will get in touch with him when we find his father. Then, come back here and look for me at the Hotel Tropicana. I will do some sniffing around town while you are gone."

"The kid's not going to like it," he said. "He expects to be part of the team."

"Brothels do not hire kids, Ronson. If we are to bury ourselves in the low life of Huehuetenango, we've got to get rid of him. Be creative or be forceful, but just do it."

"How do you figure I can get past the checkpoints? I'm a foreigner. By now, the roads are probably full of them."

"The kid will be your pass. They're looking for people trying to leave the country, not tourists traveling within. You will be all right, trust me. Julio is sharper than he looks."

"What if they arrest me on the way back? And what if I come back and you have been arrested by the Guatemalans . . . what then?"

"Don't you worry about me, Ronson. I have a plan that includes calling my captors in Quetzaltenango and telling them I have escaped from my rescuers. Capitán Lozardo will protect me from the army. He will hire me to run his brothel here, and I will hire you as a bouncer. Humberto will eventually ditch Carmen and run off with the money. She will then have to find work, and she is a whore. We will advertise for Mexican whores and hopefully snag her. You need to be resourceful to get past the checkpoints on your return here. Don't get arrested."

"But if Carmen has no money, why are we interested in her? The reward is for the priest."

"Humberto is Guatemalan; my bet is he will stay here. Hell, he has no choice. He now has a bundle of money and can't be wandering around Guatemala like a homeless gypsy. And he certainly can't scour the Mexican countryside without papers. Bandits and cops will steal his newfound wealth. No, the scoundrel will probably change his identity and settle somewhere close to the coast. Those areas are populated, affording him a measure of privacy. If we catch Carmen, we will see Junior again, and he will find the

Padre for us. The young man is a bloodhound. Like I said, Ronson, first things first. Please get rid of the kid."

The following day, after my mates had departed, I grabbed the coin in my pocket, placed it in the telephone slot, and dialed the operator.

"Hello, Monsieur Capitane? It's me, Alex. I had to jump from an airplane to escape from my rescuers. I'm in a hotel in Huehuetenango. When can I start to work? I found a place we can use for the whorehouse. It's called Hotel Tropicana. It's small and perfect for us. Come with money so we can buy it, and bring Laura with you. I want to hire her to manage the women."

Capitán Lozardo was surprised to hear my voice and pleased that I was still interested in working for him. He told me to stay out of sight because the whole army was looking for me. He said he would send Sargento Moreno down the following day with some money, and he would bring Laura in a couple of days. He had some pressing police work to attend to at the moment.

Feeling good about things, I headed for the Hotel Tropicana. With any luck, I could roam the bar and find a girl for the night.

Chapter 25

Men Don't Wear Panties

"Alex, *mi amigo*, how good it is to see you," said Sargento Moreno.

"Good to see you, too, Antonio. How are things in the jailhouse?"

"Not good. Ever since you left us, things have not been the same. Everybody is mad at us for letting those people steal you. The *alcalde* is trying to get my boss fired. The *gobernador* is upset over the jailbreak, because it's election time, and this makes him look bad. Everybody's looking for you. It's going to be hard bringing you back to Quetzaltenango. The army . . . they want to lock you up in their prison."

"Why is the mayor trying to fire Capitán Lozardo? He's not responsible for the jailbreak. The people that stole me were professionals. And why is the governor upset? In the grand scheme of things, I can't be that important."

"It's the people, Alex. They are the reason for all this trouble. They liked you, and we let you get stolen. They blame the government for being stupid."

Oh, great. Now I'm in big trouble. Getting caught will surely be the death of me. "How do we fix this mess, Sargento?"

"The boss will fix it, but it will take time. Right now, you need to be out of the public eye, and we'll keep you busy working here. We will open the whorehouse. I get to work security so I will stay by your side night and day. I will protect you and the *putas.*"

Shit, this whole deal is crashing down on me. I'm in danger of never seeing Texas again. Capitán Lozardo will eventually feel the heat, and the appeal to make a deal with his brother-in-law, the mayor, will be hard to pass. I can already hear the governor say to them, "Bring me the head of Alejandro Perez, and I will reward both of you handsomely." Man, I'm dead meat.

"Okay, Antonio, I'm with you. But if we are to open the whore-house, the first thing we have to do is find some whores. How many can we hire? Did you bring any money?"

"*Sí*, I have plenty. We can hire as many as you think we need. When do you want to start looking for them?"

"How about if we go to La Plaza del Río tonight? It's a nice upscale whorehouse. Maybe we can find us several pretty young girls that are unhappy and want to work elsewhere. If we want to attract a good clientele, it's important that we have a few whores with class."

The following day, I got up early. There was a storm brewing in the horizon, and it had nothing to do with the weather. I had to flee the town but couldn't do it until my friend Ronson returned. I also needed an escort to facilitate my escape out of the country, preferably a clandestine one. Thinking things through, not everything looked ominous, and that gave me room for optimism. There were a few silver linings pushing out of the dark clouds. One of them was Sargento Moreno. Getting rid of him was going to be easy. The man trusted me, and he slept like the dead.

Our foray into the upscale brothel was an eye-opener. Two things became clear. The first was that the clientele was heavy-duty. The customers going in seemed to be either politicians, athletes, government ministers, prominent businessmen, or military officers. This was our place, and no one would expect to find a rat in a snake pit.

However, we ran into a problem from the get-go. The door-man wouldn't let us in because we were not dressed properly.

Sargento Moreno wanted to go elsewhere, complaining that if we were not dressed well enough to get in, we wouldn't be able to afford the whores. I insisted on scouting the place, reminding him that we were not going in to buy a whore, but that our mission was to talk to them.

We left the brothel and found a men's clothing store that was open late. We picked out a jacket and tie. Looking fit, I pondered the second problem facing us; the authorities were looking for several gringos. Anyone with blonde hair, blue eyes, and white skin was bound to attract unwanted attention. I wondered if I could get in unnoticed. Fortunately for me, those long days working the coffee fields paid off. I had developed a nice, dark tan. It appeared that with a bit of luck, I would be able to move under the radar.

We went back to the brothel and cursed our luck. There were a lot of police cars around, and people were being jostled by the cops. We decided to give up and try again the following evening.

I got up early, went to the restaurant, and was working on my third cup of coffee when Sargento Moreno showed up. He took the seat next to mine, ordered coffee, and with great fanfare, he opened his newspaper. The man reminded me of the American Deputy Sheriff Barney Fife from "Mayberry R.F.D." except that Sargento Moreno was taller and had more hair.

To my chagrin, there was a sketch of me on the back page of the paper. The caption underneath read, "Se busca a este hombre." Great, now I'm dead for sure.

I snatched the paper from the policeman's hands and before he could contest ownership of the paper, I showed him the back page.

"*Dios mío,*" he said, alarmed. "This is not good for us. Everyone's going to know who you are now. Going out is not safe. Eating here at the restaurant is not safe. We need to go back to the room."

"Listen, Sargento, I'm not going to be stuck inside a hotel room all day. You need to go to a women's store and buy me a wig and a brassiere. Size thirty-eight D will do just fine. I also need a dress and stockings with garters. Don't forget earrings and panties. I will shave my face and legs and dress like a woman. Everyone will think we're together."

"Why do you need panties? No one will see them. Why can't you wear men's underwear?"

"Because if I'm to play the part of a woman properly, I have to *feel* like one, and panties are important. Get me some silky, sexy ones, and bring shoes. I wear a size ten in women's. Oh, yeah, please don't forget to get makeup. I want to look good if I'm going out in public. You don't want people to think you date ugly women, do you?"

He looked at me with eyes that betrayed disgust. "Alex," he said with a voice that showed deep distrust. "How do you know about women's brassieres and shoe sizes? Men don't know about those things. You're not a *maricón*, are you? That boy that came to see you at the jail . . . he was not a *maricón*, was he?"

"Sargento Moreno, you offend me. I am as much a *maricón* as you are. Are you one?"

"I am certainly not!" he said, with bravado.

"Good, that makes two of us, so don't worry yourself sick. Go on and shop for the things that I need. I will wait for you in the room. Do not return without everything on the list, and when you buy the lipstick, look for Flamingo Red, my favorite."

Disgusted, Sargento Moreno left to run the errands. Good riddance for the man was a dumb-ass. I started to mull over a plan. I had figured a way out of the country. It was a daring plan and to pull it off we had to be audacious, especially if we were going to get past watchful police eyes. Actually, the idea was brilliant. It came to me while trying to get inside the high-brow brothel. To make our escape good, a limousine was needed, as well as whores, a chauffeur, and military uniforms. To get uniforms, I needed a disguise. I was hoping Antonio had good taste in women's clothing. Hopefully, finding a female shoe size ten in a country full of small women would take time. I needed him to be gone a long while; Ronson should be arriving any minute, and I didn't want those two to meet yet. The Swiss needed to book a room, and the one next to ours would be perfect since it had an adjoining door.

Before I left the restaurant, I secured Sargento Moreno's ominous newspaper. I walked over to the quaint terrace of the hotel, ordered a Bloody Mary, and kept an eye out for Ronson to arrive.

Even though the sketch on the back cover did not do me justice, the window for our escape was beginning to close down. The newspaper drawing signaled a stronger effort by the authorities to snag me. My plan required precision, luck, and haste. If I blew it, living in Guatemala for years to come was a good possibility.

Ronson finally showed up. I clued him in on the plan and made him get the room next to mine. I wanted him close, but as a stranger. First we were going to use the room as a drag queen's nest, then as a hostage center.

"The roads are littered with soldiers," said Ronson. "I was afraid they were going to arrest me."

"Was Julio some help?"

"Yes. He was the ticket in, but coming back was a problem."

"Why?" I wanted to know.

"On my return, some of the checkpoints were manned by different soldiers. They did not know who I was and became suspicious."

"How did you get past them?"

"I had to disarm them."

"How many soldiers did you disarm?"

"Not more than a dozen."

"Great, Ronson. Now they'll have a description of you. We are in big trouble as it is. Here, check out my photo."

I handed him the newspaper. He looked at the drawing and scratched his cheek. "It does not look like you at all. You are more handsome than that."

"Why, thank you, Ronson. I accept the compliment. You're right, I am a good-looking man. The person depicted here has a rough countenance."

Thinking things through, I made adjustments to the plan. Ronson was correct; it would be hard for someone to detect me from the newspaper sketch. He, on the other hand, would surely be noticed. Tying up a dozen guards was not smart. The humiliation heaped upon the military by the national press would certainly raise the search bar. He needed a disguise worse than I did.

Sargento Moreno showed up with bags of women's stuff. He dropped them in the room, complained about my choice of disguise, and went to book another room. Actually, this worked out well for me, for now Ronson and I could increase the hideout space by opening the adjoining door. I did my thing and turned into a woman.

The Swiss was impressed with the transformation. "Hey, you look good," he said. "Can I pinch you on the ass?"

"Only in public, Ronson. You can pinch and touch all you want, but only in public."

I took his measurements, asked whether he preferred a blonde or brunette wig, and then went out and hit the women's stores. The plan had been adjusted, and it now required two transvestites. We needed to blow out of town, and we needed to do it that very night. Tomorrow, Capitán Lozardo would arrive, and with him I suspected would come bad luck.

I bought the necessary clothes and asked Sargento Moreno to come to my room, where I introduced him to Ronson. Right after, I pointed my pistol to his side. I removed his gun and had him sit on the floor. He became incensed and called me a few names, but after the initial tantrum, he resigned himself and quieted down. I explained his place in the plan, and he refused to be included.

"You can't make me do it," he said, defiantly.

"Listen to me, friend. You and I, we have been through a lot together. Don't think of this as an act of betrayal to your boss, but as making money on the side. We are going to hire you to help us escape, and we will not only pay you well, but we will also do it at gunpoint so you can save face."

Ronson came out of the bathroom, raised his skirt, stretched his newly shaved leg, and re-connected his hose to the garters.

"I didn't do a good job with the razor," he said. "My legs are still prickly, and I already have a run on one of my hoses."

Sargento Moreno rolled his eyes and spat on the carpet. "I'm not going out in public with *maricones*," he said.

"For the last time, we're only pretending to be women. Please deal with it. Now, be a good man and cooperate. I don't want to hurt you. Please stand up and put your hands behind you."

We tied and gagged him, then left the hotel for the brothel. The plan was to snag us a military officer, hopefully one of high rank. We ordered a limousine, waited for it to arrive, gave the driver a twenty-*quetzal* note, and had him drive us to the whorehouse in style. We told the driver to wait.

The doorman stopped us. "*No pueden entrar*," he said.

"What's the deal?" whispered Ronson.

"He says we can't get in."

"Why not? Do I have too much rouge?"

"I'm not sure. Let me ask him."

"*¿Por qué no podemos entrar?*" I asked the doorman.

"*¿Porque aquí ya tenemos putas, y ustedes no trabajan aquí.*"

"He says we can't get in because we don't work here, and the whores inside do not need outside competition."

Ronson stepped in front of me, grabbed the man's hand, and forced it inside his skirt. The man's eyes popped out. He cursed and moved away from us.

"*Ustedes son unos maricones*," he said, with a gasp.

I quickly flashed him a fifty-*quetzal* note. He grabbed the dough, cursed us again, and opened the door.

"What's wrong with these Guatemalans?" asked Ronson.

"I don't think they like women impersonators," I said.

"Well, this guy sure doesn't," said the Swiss.

"Why did you stick the man's hand up your skirt? I'm trying to get us inside the brothel, and you pull a stunt like that. Have you gone mental?"

Ronson grabbed my hand and forced it inside his skirt, making me touch a huge squishy dick.

"Aaah!" I yelled. "Are you crazy? Why did you make me touch your dick?"

"It's not my dick, Alex. It's a sausage stuffed inside my panties."

"What kind of a sausage is it?" I asked.

"What difference does it make?"

"Right, it doesn't make a difference. What does need explaining is where did you get such a big one, and why did you stick it in your pants?"

"I paid the waiter at the hotel restaurant a few bucks to get it for me."

"Why?"

"Because I learned in Texas that a big dick will make you all kinds of friends, especially in queer bars."

"Oh, give me a break, Ronson."

"Believe me, it's true. I learned that trick a while back when I was on a surveillance gig in Houston. The mark I was trailing walked into a queer bar in Montrose. I followed him and noticed that the bar patrons kept shying away from me once they had felt my small dick. I didn't want to blow my cover, so the following day when the mark went back into the same bar, I stuck a bratwurst into my Jockey shorts and attracted lots of company."

"I want one," I said.

"Get your own dick, Alex. I'm not giving you mine," he said with a grin.

No sooner had we walked into the brothel and secured a table when a man came over to us. "Can I buy you two lovely American women a drink?"

We batted our eyelashes at the inebriated military man and checked the uniform lapels. The man was wearing a Major insignia. Bingo! We found our ticket out of Huehuetenango. "Why, yes," I said with my best falsetto. "You can buy us drinks, and we can buy *you* drinks."

Two hours later, we were back at the hotel. The drunken offi-cer was tied up next to the sober sergeant and pissed-off limousine driver. We went over the plan one more time: Sargento Moreno drives the limo to the coastal town of Bola del Monte, and we frol-ic in the back with the major whenever we come to a checkpoint. The town was due south, near the border with El Salvador. Surely, the Guatemalans were concentrating their vigilance toward the northern areas. If we managed to make it to the coast in one piece, we would then dispose of our companions and steal us a sturdy boat.

While we drove out of town, I kept Odysseus' problems in the forefront of my mind. I was hoping I hadn't insulted the God Poseidon because I was planning on going home by way of the sea.

Chapter 26

Escape to Texas

We drove through Guatemala without incident. I was correct in picking a route south. We only had to stop at three checkpoints. Sargento Moreno behaved. As a matter of fact, he loosened up and excelled on the role of chauffeur. The major did likewise. There is nothing like a pistol stuck in the side to make a person take a gentler approach to being kidnapped.

Twenty kilometers from our destination, we veered off the road and stopped the limo. We paid Sargento Moreno handsomely in front of the officer in order to implicate him. No need to take any chances with his loyalty. Then, we stripped the officer, leaving the naked man gagged and tied to a tree without any identification papers. We needed a good six hours to find a boat we could steal.

When we hit the town of Bola del Monte, we told the sergeant to hide his money in his underwear because we were going to tie him up and leave him in the limo's back seat. He began to howl. We tried to console him by telling him we would send back a cabbie with the keys. We advised him that if he knew what was best for him, he'd leave the limo behind, get on an express bus, and go back to Quetzaltenango, because if the officer tied to the tree saw him, he would be arrested as an accomplice. That being settled, we changed clothes, left the limo parked in front of a bar, hired a cabbie, and had him take us to where we could rent a fishing boat and crew. He took us to the Jaime Morales Yacht Club. We paid the man and gave him the key to the limo, telling him we left two full bottles of whiskey inside.

I was taken aback. Instead of the expected rundown operation, we encountered a nice, upscale facility. There were several top-of-the-line boats docked, as well as a number of them on dry dock being worked on. One of the guards at the gate asked us our business, and we told him we wanted to hire a rig and crew to go on a fishing trip. He pointed us to a yacht with the name *La Perla de Colombia*.

I thanked him but decided against hiring any boat called The Colombian Pearl. As soon as we crossed into U.S. waters, we'd be searched for sure.

Instead of taking care of business right away, we opted to quench our thirst. We were confident Sargento Moreno would get on a bus, and our officer would need time to explain who he was and why he was naked and tied to a tree.

We found the bar and walked in. No sooner had we ordered drinks when a couple of old sores appeared at our table and imbedded themselves on my ass. "Well, well," said one of them. "What do we have here?"

"I smell a dirty white rat," said the other.

"Hello, Captain Chris," I said. "Hello, Jaime. Aren't you guys a little ways off from your neck of the woods?"

Ronson sensed trouble and opened the lower part of his shirt, showing the pistol. Captain Chris did likewise. Jaime placed his hand on his huge Bowie knife and smiled. I felt left out, the only one not carrying a weapon. Still, in spite of this apparent disadvantage, I was in control of my wits, and that was enough to defend myself. After taking a quick measure of the situation, I jumped on the bull's horns. "We are looking to book passage out of here, and we are willing to pay handsomely for a boat and crew."

"What does a peckerwood mean when he says he will pay 'handsomely'?" asked Captain Chris.

"He means he will rob you," said Jaime.

"What's going on, Alex?" asked Ronson.

"These two gentlemen and I had an unpleasant commercial encounter a while back," I said.

"White man destroyed our boat and then robbed us," said Jaime.

"I'm not a white man," I said with disgust. "Ronson is, and he is taking me to jail. I'm wanted in the States. There is a big reward for me. That's why he's holding the gun."

They stared at me. I opened my jacket. "See, I'm unarmed." Captain Chris looked at my companion. "Is this peckerwood telling the truth?"

Using winged words, Ronson assured the seafaring man that I was a wanted man in the United States.

"He is wanted in Guatemala, too," said the captain. "Why don't you turn him into the authorities in Guatemala City and save yourself the trouble and travel expense. We are a long way from the States, and he is slippery."

"The Americans are paying fifty thousand dollars. The Guatemalans are offering five thousand *quetzales*. That's why."

"Fifty Gs! Are you sure? He doesn't look like a criminal. What did he do?" asked Captain Chris.

Ronson didn't answer him, and we had an uncomfortable lull in the conversation. The seafaring man began to scratch his itchy beard. I could tell by the way his eyebrows came together that he was calculating whether the European could be trusted. Jaime remained standing, with his arms crossed on his chest. I noticed for the first time that he was wet.

"Alex robbed a bank in Houston," said Ronson.

"White man puts money in bank and then comes back and robs it," said Jaime.

"Well, what do you know?" said Captain Chris. "The man is a bank robber. He looked like a harmless peckerwood to me."

"White man pretends to be stupid, then he robs you," said the Indian.

"Would you give it a rest, please?" begged Captain Chris. "You're driving me crazy with this white man crap."

Jaime smiled, showing tobacco-stained teeth. Chris turned his attention back to Ronson. "Where are you from?"

"I'm from Switzerland," he said. "How about you . . . are you an American?"

"Yes. I'm from Beaumont, Texas. My friend here is from Guatemala. He is a Mayan Indian."

"He speaks pretty good English for an Indian," said Ronson.

"Yes, he does. Jaime spent some time in Belize."

"Fuck the English," said the Indian.

"Listen, I would love to sit here and chat, but I have to take my prisoner to the States. Can we make a deal here?" asked Ronson. "Do you own a boat?"

Captain Chris kept scratching his beard. I could tell he was weighing his options. He either fought or he negotiated. I could tell he was more interested in dealing than fighting. Why not? Ronson was Swiss, and everyone knows they are trustworthy.

"Okay. I'm sure we can work out a deal," he said. "But Jaime and I, we need ten thousand plus expenses. And we need five thousand up front. We have to pay a bill we owe."

"White man makes deal, then he robs you," said the Indian.

"Quit worrying about this peckerwood, Jaime. He won't steal from us twice. Go and get the boat ready to receive paying customers."

The Indian felt his way out of the bar, walked on the narrow board walkway that led to the boats, and fell into the water.

"Your friend . . . he seems to be drunk," said Ronson. "Can we rely on his services?"

"Jaime's blind," I said. "He's also the first mate."

"Never you mind about Jaime's blindness, peckerwood. You need to worry he won't use that knife on your sorry ass. He doesn't cotton to being robbed by a white man, so he already has a problem with you as it is. You better stay off his bad side and cut him some slack. He's not too blind to cut your balls off."

Turning to Ronson, he said, "Do we have a deal or not?"

"You are my man. I can agree to the ten thousand, but can only give you two thousand upfront. It's a take-it-or-leave-it deal. What do you say?"

"You hired yourself a boat and crew. Wait till you see her. She is a beauty and can do forty knots when pushed."

We helped Jaime get back on the boardwalk and walked toward a big, shiny yacht. There were three men working on it. Ronson and I smiled.

"Nice boat," said the Swiss.

"Thank you," replied the captain. "I bought it for a song."

We looked at each other and knew there was something wrong. The yacht we were heading toward was expensive, certainly in the range of one hundred thousand dollars.

"What's your boat's name?" I asked.

"She's called *Joplin*. I named her for Janice Joplin."

The yacht we were looking at was named *Magpie*. With pessimism gripping our hearts, we sighed as we passed the nice big boat. Then, to our displeasure, we came face to face with a rundown tugboat. It had *Joplin* painted on it.

Oh, God. We're doomed. "Is this thing seaworthy?" I pondered out loud.

"She's as sturdy as a Texas mule. She worked the ship traffic in the Panama Canal for twenty-five years. I bought her in an auction here three months ago. Now she's been taking tourists on fishing trips. Jaime and I refurbished it. She can take us all the way to San Diego if necessary," said the captain.

Ronson and I looked at each other. We'd be lucky if the dilapidated vessel made it to Mexican territorial waters, but we had no choice—we were trapped. Captain Chris would become a difficult adversary if we tried to leave him behind. We had to hire him and take our chances on the high seas. To remain in terra firma was not an option. As soon as someone found the naked major, untied him, and verified his identity, we would be up to our asses in soldiers.

That wooden bucket would never outrun a Guatemalan patrol boat, so we needed a good head start.

"When do you want to go?" asked Captain Chris.

"How about right now?" suggested Ronson wisely. "Do you have provisions on board?"

"All we need. Get your gear on board, and let's push off. You'll enjoy the ride," said the captain.

With a prayer in my heart, we left the yacht club in a rickety sea vessel and chug-chugged our way out to sea.

The Swiss became upset when he realized the crew consisted only of Jaime and us. When I explained to him that not only could we not trust the captain with our lives, but the man was also a drunk, he became paranoid.

"I can't stay awake until we reach California," he said. "How are we going to handle this?"

"I'm not sure," I replied. "But it behooves us to stay involved in the operation of the boat and also to be in control of our senses. Are you a good hand?"

"Not really. I'm Swiss, and we are landlocked. I fooled around with sailboats, but that's it."

We pulled a forty-eight-hour shift, but on the third night, we were dead tired, so we left the captain alone at the wheel. Jaime was sitting by him blowing on a harmonica. I recognized the Beach Boys tune "John B. Sloop." It figured for the song was about the worst trip ever taken. I was hoping it was not an omen.

The night was bright, and the sea calm. Needing to sleep, we went below and climbed on our bunks.

The noise of the surf woke me up. It took me a few minutes to realize there was no surf in the middle of the ocean. In a panic, I went up to investigate. I found the captain was passed out on the floor, and Jaime was manning the wheel. I looked ahead and saw that we were heading straight toward a coast. There were cliffs to one side, rocks on the other, and a small entrance between them. I screamed for Ronson, grabbed a lifejacket, and started to put it on. The Swiss came up and saw me working the lifejacket belts.

"What are you doing?" he asked.

I pointed to the passed out captain, the blind man at the wheel, and then to the rocks ahead. Sleep left his eyes in a hurry.

"Why didn't you take the wheel from the blind man?" he yelled.

"The Indian has a big knife. My chances of living are better in the sea."

Without hesitation, Ronson jumped the Mayan from behind. Soon a wrestling match started. The Indian pulled the Bowie out. I managed to kick it out of his hand and picked it up. I looked at the wrestling match to see who was winning and then to the rocks ahead, which seemed to be getting closer.

"Grab the wheel and turn the boat around!" yelled Ronson. I did just that. Then, to everyone's horror, the engine sputtered and quit. "What's wrong with the motor?" screamed Ronson.

"It's probably out of gas," said Jaime.

"Where do you keep the extra gas?" demanded the Swiss.

"There is some below," said the blind man. "If you let me go, I'll go get it."

I looked at the cliffs, and they were getting closer. I looked at Ronson, and he still had Jaime in a headlock. I placed the Bowie knife in my pants and yelled, "Geronimo!" and jumped off the tug-boat.

Hours later, I woke up facedown on a rocky beach. After taking the whole scene in, I figured I had to be somewhere in Mexico. I looked for Ronson or for any sign of a shipwreck. There were none. It appeared that I was the lone survivor.

I was hungry and there were no restaurants in the vicinity. I cursed my luck and started to walk. Before long, I found a dirt road, and soon three pretty girls driving a Jeep drove by. They stopped and turned around.

"Say, fella," said the redhead. "Need a ride?"

"Only if it's free and only if I have to make love to just one of you," I said, with a wry smile. I was tired and not at all in the mood to engage voluptuous twenty-something girls in inane conversation.

"Deal," said the brunette. "Hop in the back with Orly."

The blonde smiled, adjusted her big breasts, and moved over. I climbed in, said thanks, and proceeded to tell them about the shipwreck and the death of my mates. When I finished, they seemed impressed. Obviously, they liked sailor stories.

"We can take you into town or to our villa," said the brunette. "We're spending two weeks here with our boyfriends."

"Where are they?" I asked.

"They went fishing early this morning," said the redhead. "They won't be back until evening. If you are uncomfortable meeting them, you can stay with us until dusk, and then I can drive you into town."

"Deal," I said. "I could use a shower, and it would be nice if I could get a change of threads. Your boyfriends have anything my size?"

"Orly's sweetie is about your size. There might be something in the closet that will fit you," said the redhead.

Thinking this had to be either a dream or my lucky day, I pushed the envelope further. "Where am I, anyway?"

"You're in Cabo San Lucas. Where were you trying to get to?" asked the brunette. What do you know? I'm in Baja California. Not too shabby. "Okay, girls, if you have some shrimp, rice, and a coconut in your kitchen, I can cook you all a nice lunch. Where I was going is not important now. What's important is that I am alive and well and in the company of three blessed angels. My name is Alex Perez, and after a good meal and a nap, I can probably make love to all three of you."

The girls laughed, and the Jeep roared ahead. Orly readjusted her tits and smiled at me. "You have to do me first," she said.

"I get him after you," said the redhead. "I saw him first."

"After I'm done with him, he won't have any strength left for you," said the blonde.

"Don't listen to her," I said. "I can do it twice."

"What about me?" said the dark-haired beauty, "don't I get any?"

"If you want to get any, you'll have to get in on Marcy's action," said Orly. "He won't be worth a hoot after I'm done with him."

"Alex, do you think you can make love to Julie and me at the same time?" teased Marcy with a purr in her voice.

I pinched myself to make sure this was not a dream. Then, realizing this was real life and the girls were serious, I looked up at the sky and quietly said, "Thank you, God."

We drove to a nice picturesque villa. The white iron gate opened automatically as we approached. A man that appeared to be the gardener waved at us as we passed him. I was impressed with his rosebushes.

When we arrived at the house, a woman came out to greet us. She was accompanied by a young man. The woman removed the packages, and the young man drove the Jeep away. I checked the pool with interest. My intentions must have been obvious.

"You can't get in the pool unless you shower first," said Orly.

I took a shower, shaved, and dressed with the clothes the pretty blonde had placed on the bed. Feeling good, I walked out of the bedroom and came face to face with impending doom. The boyfriends had returned and with them was Ronson. He seemed the worst for wear.

"What happened to you?" I asked. "You look terrible."

"These guys fished me out of the water."

"Where are Captain Chris and Jaime?"

"Drowned, I imagine."

Before I could say anything else, one of the guys developed a hostile disposition and dove at me. I moved to the side and he missed me.

"What's your problem?" I questioned.

"That's Orly's boyfriend," said Julie. The man got up and came at me again.

"Hey, mister, I didn't even kiss her. I don't want any trouble with you."

"You came out of my bedroom, and you're wearing my clothes," said the bodybuilder. "You're up to your ass in trouble with me."

At that moment, Orly came into the living room and decided my situation was not dire enough. "Leave him be, Tony," she ordered. "He hasn't made love to me yet."

Oh no, she's a real blonde. What bad luck. Being a quick-witted guy, I decided the best way to save myself was to point out a few things of importance to the boyfriend. Maybe he'd get confused and spare me the preposterous transformation into the Hulk.

"She's right, you know. You came home earlier than expected, so I didn't have time to touch her heavenly body, so you can't hit me."

The brute jumped me, and this time I was unable to dodge him. He grabbed me by the neck and growled at me, as he tried to squeeze the life out of me.

"You think this whole deal is funny, don't you? Let me show you what New Yorkers think is really funny."

Oh no, I'm about to get killed by a damn Yankee. I quickly scanned the brain to see if I had anything I could use on New Yorkers, especially something to soothe their sense of kindness. But in order to use the brain's output correctly, I first had to clarify the ethnic background of these New Yorkers.

"What's your last name?" I asked as Conan the Barbarian was dragging me toward an open window.

"His last name's Corleone," said another dude. "I'm Vito Martinelli, and the guy bringing the rope is Mario Tomasi."

Oh no! Mafiosos . . . I'm dead meat. My mind started to flash back to all the movies I'd seen about angry Italians. I remembered all the killing in "Goodfellas," and the horse head in "The Godfather," and I began to shudder. These transplanted wops had an ominous and limited sense of humor. I was hoping the really angry Italians came from New Jersey.

The brain sent in another wave. I picked it up and defiantly tried to arrest the hostility in the room. "Hey, my good fellows, I love the New York Yankees."

"Fuck the Yankees," said Vito.

Oh no, they are Mets fans. What bad luck. The idea that baseball could save me was ludicrous. It never had helped me before. I shot a look at Ronson as they were tying me up, hoping for some intervention. The Swiss remained unperturbed. There was no help coming from that corner. I glanced at Orly and then at Julie, and the girls seemed concerned but remained quiet. Okay, no help coming from that corner either. Where's the redhead?

Unable to fight off my attackers, I succumbed to the whims of fate. They tied me by both legs and lowered my dumb-ass out the window facedown. They fastened the rope to one of the legs of a heavy desk and let me hang there to contemplate my sins.

Normally, I would have been fine with the situation. Hell, I deserved it. I should have passed on the blonde and gone for the redhead. But what was chapping my ass was that before these damned Yankee gangsters left me hanging as a human piñata, they had a good laugh on my behalf. That pissed me off. Panamanians don't take abuse well, especially from gringos. And Texans don't like to be pushed around by people that export bad salsa. I was a Panamanian national and a Texas resident, and both sides had been insulted. I was steaming with anger and began to plot my revenge.

One of the few benefits that come with being tied upside-down is that the brain cells get a good load of blood. I took a deep breath, tightened my abdominal muscles, reached up, and grabbed the rope. During my short stint in the U.S. Army, I learned many useful things, and one was rope climbing. It didn't take me long to get up to the window ledge.

Once inside, I untied the rope and proceeded to search the area for some kind of weapon. The best I could do was a baseball bat. The idea of confronting mafiosos with a bat didn't appeal to me. I remembered the encounter in the hotel room with Carmen and the wayward priest when the bat lost to the gun hands down.

Still, that was the only weapon available. I was not going to break the Chinese vase on somebody's head; it looked like a good imitation from the Ming period.

Trying to figure out what my best options were, I stumbled onto the story about the trouble the prophet Mohammed had with the mountain. He wanted to be on the mountain, so he ordered it to come to him. When it did not, he went to the mountain. Thinking that through I decided that Muslim things are best left for Muslims. Being raised a Christian, I had to do it another way. I had to be patient. If I waited long enough, the mountain would come my way. And, even though instant gratification was my thing, today, I was loaded with religious fervor. I lay in ambush next to the door. Someone would come in sooner or later, hopefully one at a time.

My instincts were on target. The knob twisted, the door opened, and someone started to come in. I swung the bat and hit the redhead on the face. Blood sprayed the walls, and the food tray she was carrying crashed on the wooden floor. Then I heard a woman scream. "He's killed Marcy! The hitchhiker has killed Marcy!"

Shit, now I'm dead for sure. I had to think fast. There were thundering footsteps coming my way. I went to the window and lowered myself on the rope. When I reached the end, I looked down, took another deep breath, and let go. It looked like a twenty-foot drop. Hopefully, my legs could withstand the impact. They did. As I lay sprawled on the grass, one of the Italians stuck his face out and looked at me. He was holding a gun. Next to him appeared Orly holding the Chinese vase in her hands.

The brain sent in another wave. Maybe these transplanted Americans came from the north of Italy.

"Hey, mister, I have a buddy in Borgomanero and another one in Genoa. I also have relatives in Torino," I said.

"Fuck Borgomanero, Genoa, and Torino," he said as he aimed his pistol my way.

Oh great, they are Italians from the south. Damn the bad luck. I knew the bullet would find me in two seconds. My only chance was an errant shot, yet it didn't materialize. Instead of the sound of gunfire, I heard the gun-wielding mafioso yell, "Vito, the hitch-hiker jumped out the window and is down on the side patio! Grab him! I want him alive!"

Orly sent the vase my way, and it missed me. I got up and ran onto an open terrace. By sheer chance, I ran into Ronson, who was tied to a chair. They had duct-taped his mouth, hands, and feet. I untied him and ripped the tape off him. "Follow me," I said, and we took off running through a door that opened into a garden. I heard shouts coming from behind me. Someone was barking orders. I looked behind me and saw the posse. Three men with guns were coming after us. We made it out of the villa by climbing the outer wall. The Italians were fast on our heels.

"They're getting away!" one of them yelled.

"Let's get the car!" yelled another one.

"Hell with the car . . . let's shoot the bastards!" yelled another.

While they were arguing over how to bring forth our demise, Ronson and I ran down the road. Soon, a four-door sedan appeared. We asked for a ride, and the friendly men inside complied.

"*¿Qué les pasa?*" asked the man riding shot gun.

"*Nos quieren matar,*" I said. "*¿Nos pueden ayudar?*"

"*Sí, súbanse,*" said the driver. Then he checked his rearview mirror and saw a Jeep roaring behind him. "*Ahí vienen,*" said the driver to his companion. The copilot pulled out a single-shot twenty-gage shotgun. He stuck his head out the window and fired. Seconds later, we received a volley of shots in return, two of which came through the back window and went out through the front windshield.

"*¡Jesús!*" said the driver. "*Los gringos tienen revólveres automáticos. Nos van a matar.*" He pulled over and told us to get out.

Before I could explain to Ronson that our saviors were going to abandon us, he had his hand on the door handle. I quickly followed suit, and when we slowed to make the curve, we both jumped out of the car. We rolled and stayed put until the pursuing Jeep had passed us by. Then we hightailed it toward the brush and stayed hidden. We heard more gunshots, and a few minutes later we saw the three angry men drive by slowly. They did this a couple of times. If they thought they could find us without leaving the vehicle, they were going to be disappointed. We were deep in the bush.

Once we felt safe, we walked back to the road and hitchhiked a ride from a truck loaded with turnips. We climbed in the back and counted our blessings.

After a while, I said to Ronson, "What's wrong, bud? We escaped our captors. You should be happy. What's the problem?"

"You! You are the problem," he said.

"Me? Are you kidding me? I saved your ass from the mafiosos. You should be grateful. What can I have possibly done to you to make you unhappy?"

"You abandoned me while I was fighting the Indian. I came to your rescue and you bailed on me. You have done that twice. I'm trying to justify my friendship with you. I expect more from my friends."

"But I saved your ass from the mad Italians," I said.

"I was fine until they realized I was your friend. They had already saved me from the sea. I was hanging on to a piece of board when they passed by. You have been nothing but a source of problems for me, Alex."

"I'm sorry to hear that, Ronson. I have always held you in high esteem. You are bumming me out."

"Why were they so angry at you?" he asked.

"Well, that's hard to tell. Maybe it was because I was going to bang their girlfriends, or maybe it was the bat to the redhead's forehead."

"You hit a girl in the face with a baseball bat?"

"Not just any girl, Ronson. This particular one had big tits and was bringing me my lunch on a tray."

"I don't know what to think of you anymore, Alex. You stole the boat captain's money, you swindled Julio out of his wish, took his dog's money, and now you tell me you hit a woman with a bat. Are all Panamanians like you?"

"I hope so," I said. "I hate to think I'm unusual."

He looked at me with disgust, rolled over, and closed his eyes. I leaned back on the load of turnips and smiled. Yes sir, even though I was riding in the back of a turnip truck, life was good. The farmer was driving to Tijuana. Soon, I'd be heading for Texas. I could think of nothing better than sitting at Mama Ninfa's with a sizzling hot plate of fajitas and a cold Margarita on the rocks.

I looked at Ronson's face and saw a smile on his lips. The Swiss was probably dreaming of cabbage and sausages. I leaned back further and closed my eyes. Maybe with some luck, Ramona would be glad to see me. Maybe Charlene would give me some money for my effort in trying to avenge her. With that thought in mind, I fell asleep amid the turnips.

Chapter 27

After getting several rides and successfully crossing the U.S. border, we made it to San Diego. Ronson was still upset with me. He kept bringing up my transgressions, admonishing my lack of discipline and lousy upbringing. The man was relentless. I made a mental note to never argue about virtue with a Germanic man. They come from a different planet.

We called Kermit, and he wired us some money. I bought a ticket to Houston, but Ronson decided to move on to Los Angeles. He said he needed a vacation.

As we were getting ready to split up and before I offered him my hand in friendship, I told him he had to agree that a world full of Swiss Germans would lack *savoir faire*. He agreed but added that what the world really needed was less Panamanians and more Swiss Austrians. We hugged and parted ways.

The plane touched down in Houston's Hobby airport. I kissed the ground, rented a car, and with optimism in my heart, climbed on I-45 North, heading toward Ramona's house. An hour and a half later, I was finally able to get off the damn freeway. Getting to Houston on Friday at five in the evening was a big mistake. No wonder the plane was empty. No one except for me and some unsuspecting Japanese tourists were stupid enough to venture into Houston at rush hour.

I pulled into the driveway, and the only car in the open garage was the 190SL Benz. Shit, no one's home. Knowing the workings of the house, I walked to the back and pushed on the window. Crap, she locked it. Giving up on the idea of breaking into the house, I went to the front door and found a note pinned to the screen. It read, "Gone to the hospital. Call mother."

I was fixing to leave when the door cracked open. The chain was still attached to it. Inside was Raúl. "Hola, Papi, ¿cómo estás?"

"Hello, son. I'll be better if you let me in."

"Eso no es posible," he said.

"What do you mean, it's not possible? Why can't I come into my own home?"

"Ya no eres bienvenido, Papi. Lo siento, pero tengo mis órdenes."

I'm not welcome in my very own home? What a sorry state of affairs. "What's wrong with your mother, son? Is she having the baby already?"

"No, parece que lo va a perder, hay complicaciones. Está enferma."

Oh no, she's having a miscarriage. "Which hospital is she in?"

"Se fue esta mañana para el hospital Memorial."

I thanked him for the information and said good-bye. No need to linger where you are not wanted. I drove to Memorial Hospital, parked the car, inquired at the front desk, and made my way to Ramona's floor. Outside her room stood Charlene, talking to a doctor. She saw me, dismissed the man, and blocked the entrance. Her stance provided me with a sense of what was coming my way.

"Hello, Charlene," I said. "It's good to see you again. What's wrong with Ramona?"

"She's lost the baby. What are you doing here? Did you find Humberto and recover my money?"

"I'm here because Ramona is my wife, and no, I did not find the priest or your money. Sorry. What happened?"

234 | ALBERTO ARCIA

"She was moving a box and fell. She'll be all right."

"Can I go in and see her?"

"No, Alex, it'll only upset her."

"She's my wife, Charlene. I have the right to see her."

"Let me tell you what rights you have, Alex. You have the right to turn around and leave the hospital and keep on going. Now that the baby is gone, you are no longer wanted or needed. She will file for divorce as soon as she is able to do so, so get lost before I call Filipo and sick him on you."

"Your thuggish handyman does not scare me, Charlene—not anymore. I survived a raging sea and hostile Italians in Mexico. The pain that Filipo can inflict upon me cannot surpass the pain I feel right now. I have lost a son. Give me a break here."

"It was a girl. You lost a daughter. And frankly, she's better off in God's hands than in yours. I can't imagine you being an asset in her life. A person like you is better suited for a boy. Now, get lost before Filipo comes back with my coffee."

What a bitch. I didn't doubt her statement concerning Ramona's intentions. It would not be possible to scratch my way into this family without a baby. Then, it hit me. Why in thunder would I want to spend any more time with this crazy family? I had enough insults to last me a lifetime. Feeling like a boulder had just been removed from my shoulders, I smiled. "Take care of her, Charlene. I'm out of here."

Understanding very well what lay ahead for me, I began to implement a new plan, and quickly. Desperate situations bring forth desperate measures. I dropped off the rental vehicle and took a cab to Ramona's house.

Before I left Texas to free the thieving Guatemalan priest, I made a copy of the Mercedes keys and hid them outside the house. I needed money and knew where to fence a car. I paid the cabbie and opened the front gate. Unfortunately, Poppy was home and in a bad mood. When he saw me open the gate, the hairs on the back of his neck stood up, and his ears moved back. The damn dog began to growl, freezing me. What now?

The door cracked open, and there stood my obstinate son Raúl. "Papi, ¿qué quieres?"

"I want you to call in the dog, son. I need to get something from under a rock."

"El perro no me hace caso," he said.

"Listen, Raúl, quit messing with me. I'm not in the mood to play games. The dog does not listen to me either, but if you open the door, Poppy will go inside. If you let him in, I will give you twenty bucks."

"Enséñame el dinero."

What a cheeky kid. "Okay, fine. Here's the money . . . see it? I'm placing the bill on the ground. Now, please put the dog in."

Raúl opened the door, and Poppy went right in. I moved the rock, found the keys, picked up the bill I had placed on the ground, and stole the 190SL. Why not? I needed the twenty for gas and money to set myself up. Hell, it was my Mercedes anyway. I certainly earned it. Raúl should have grabbed it when he had the chance. Losers weepers.

I made a phone call, located the fence, and worked out a deal for the car. Then I headed down I-10 East to Beaumont to sell it. By the look of contentment on my face, you would think life was good. Hell, that couldn't be farther from the truth. I had lost a daughter, a wife, my home, and I was broke. Now, I was endangering my freedom by driving a stolen car. Still, a person has to show a good face, even when facing adversity.

Two miles from Anahuac, I saw a nice-looking woman standing next to her car. The hood was up, and the engine was smoking. I stopped to render assistance. She told me the car was toast, and asked me for a ride into Beaumont. I complied. Ten miles later, she stuck a gun to my side. I pulled over and watched her leave with my ride. I couldn't believe my luck. Someone had actually stolen my stolen car. Despondent over my situation, I stuck my thumb out and got a ride. A middle-aged woman was nice enough to stop.

"Where are you going?"

"I'm heading for Beaumont," I said, checking her low-cut blouse. Hey, nice puppies. This may turn out all right.

She smiled and opened the door. I climbed in, and we began making small talk. In the middle of that, we saw flashing lights up ahead. There were two Highway Patrol cars lighting up the place, and they had the 190SL cornered. The car thief had her hands on the vehicle, and she was being frisked. I smiled as the situation cleared in my mind. My stepson called his mother as soon as I took the twenty-dollar bill and snitched on me. She alerted the cops.

"Poor woman," said the woman that picked me up. "She's in for a whale of trouble."

All of a sudden, I realized I had not been abandoned by God. Instead, he had been watching over me all this time. I had a good laugh.

"Why do you find enjoyment over that woman's misfortune?"

Realizing I was about to be put back out on the highway, my countenance changed. "I'm not laughing at her," I said. "I was thinking that barely thirty minutes ago, I thought I had to be the unluckiest man in the world. My car blew the engine, leaving me stranded. The girl with the cops just made me feel there is always someone else in worse shape, that's all."

"I see," she said. "Are you from Beaumont?"

"No, I'm from Houston. My wife has filed for divorce, and the bitch kicked me out of the house. I was looking for a new life and was thinking Beaumont would be a good place to find it."

Her eyes lit up. "I lost my home and husband, too," she said. "The bastard left me for a younger woman. I'm headed for New Orleans. I have a sister there. If you don't have anyone important in Beaumont, would you like to come with me?"

"Sunshine," I said. "You and I, we seem to be kindred souls. It looks like we belong together." She grinned. I smiled and sat closer to her, placing my hand on her leg. She let out a giggle.

"I'm with you all the way, baby," I said. "Let's see what life has in store for us. I'm ready to let the good times roll."

JERRY,

MERRY CHRISTMAS bud - I HOPE YOU ENJOY MY HUMOR. ANY SIMILARITY BETWEEN ALEX & ME IS STRICTLY ACCIDENTAL.

enjoy my humor. Any similarity
Accidental.